THAILAND

LAOS

CAMBODIA

Muong May

Crossing Site

*River*

*San*

*River*

Lomphat

*Srepok River*

Kohnieh

Ban Koun

*Mekong*

• Kratie

Ban Ketang

Kantreuy
Plantation

SOUTH
VIETNAM

Phum Anchanh

PHNOM PENH •    Phum Barai

Prey Veng    Prey Komnong    Tay Ninh

Michelin
Plantation

Svay
Rieng

• SAIGON

Sihanoukville

SOUTH CHINA SEA

# The Old Man's Trail

# The Old Man's Trail

TOM CAMPBELL

Naval Institute Press
ANNAPOLIS, MARYLAND

LIBRARY OF CONGRESS CATALOGING-IN-PUBLICATION DATA

Campbell, Tom, 1938 Apr. 30–
    The Old Man's Trail / Tom Campbell.
        p.        cm.
    ISBN 1-55750-117-3 (acid-free paper)
    1. Vietnamese Conflict, 1961–1975—Fiction.    I. Title.
PS3553.A48747043    1995
813'.54—dc20                                    95-18660

Printed in the United States of America on acid-free paper ∞
02 01 00 99 98 97 96 95    9 8 7 6 5 4 3 2
First printing

*To Nancy,*
*Who has loved me and lived with my ghosts, the* bo doi, *for a long time.*

Any man who fights for his home is equal to ten men who fight for any other cause.

—Proverb

A toast to the world's finest infantryman. Aggressive in the offense. Tenacious and dogged in the defense. A master of field fortifications, cover, and concealment. Ingenious in his use of supporting arms. Without peer in the application of surprise. Brilliant in his use of terrain. Always courageous and without fear. Defeated only in death. To that miserable little bastard, the NVA and Vietcong grunt.

—*Covan My* toast, circa 1966

# Contents

# Acknowledgments

I would like to thank my family, Nancy, Kristen, and Bill, as well as my brother, Mike, for their continual interest and support. Others who have taken the time to comment or to whom I owe a debt that cannot be repaid are: Paul Atkinson; Jaffer Ajani; Polly Barnes; Mary Book-waller; Rose Colletti; Anne Collier; Colby, Linda, and Mack Denison; Dave, Pat, and Scott Griggs; Claude and Judy Hocott; Jeff Howell; Gordy Kaiser; Sara Kanter; Jeanie Lewis; Pam McGregor; Bob McInteer; John Miller; Marvin and Joyce Moos; Carl Mundy; Juanita Rodriguez; Jack Roth; Corky and Nicole Rusnak; Kelly Bolam Shea; Gerry Turley; and Ramona Van Loan.

Tom Phillpot and John McKay, two old Air Force fighter jocks, have lent considerable time and combat experience to some of the air battle sequences; Mr. Tian Chua provided insight into Buddhist beliefs and practices; and Mr. Ky Do, a former South Vietnamese Marine, provided invaluable assistance with Vietnamese words and phrases.

Special acknowledgment and thanks is given to Samuel Lipsman and Stephen Weiss for permission to use the quotation in the Historical Note from their book, *The False Peace*. Finally, my appreciation to Carol Gafford for the map artwork, and to Robin Herbst for the Magic Pen.

# Vietnamese Expressions

| PHRASE | TRANSLATION |
| --- | --- |
| *Ao dai* | Traditional dress of Vietnamese women. |
| *Attentisme* | "Fence-sitting"; "Political indecision." |
| *Bac Ho* | Endearing reference to "Uncle Ho" or Ho Chi Minh. |
| *Bo doi* | "Infantry"; "Soldiers." |
| *Chung ta ra di* | "We go . . . fast"; "Move out." |
| COSVN | Central Office for South Vietnam. |
| *Covan My* | "Trusted American Advisors." Term used by Vietnamese Marines for American Marines serving with their units. |
| *Dau tranh chinh tri* | North Vietnamese concept of political struggle. Always employed with *Dau tranh vu trang*, "armed struggle." |
| *Dau tranh vu trang* | North Vietnamese concept of armed struggle. Always employed with *Dau tranh chinh tri*, "political struggle." |
| *Di may man* | "Luck"; "Good fortune." |
| *Do cho de* or *Lo dit* | "Jerk"; "Asshole." |
| *Do khon nan* or *Do moi ro* | "Son of a bitch." |
| *Do mau* | "Yes! Spend blood!" |

| | |
|---|---|
| *Don ganh* | Carrying pole. |
| *Giet* | "Killed." |
| *I Ching* | The Chinese Book of Changes. |
| *Khoi nghia* | North Vietnamese concept of the general uprising, when people rose up and destroyed their South Vietnamese and American oppressors. |
| *Lao Dong* | The Communist party of Vietnam. |
| *Muon doc lap phai do mau* | "For freedom you have to spend your blood." |
| *My* | American. |
| *My nguy* | "American puppet." |
| *Nam Bo* | North Vietnamese name for Mekong Delta region in Cambodia and South Vietnam. |
| NLF | National Liberation Front. |
| *Nuoc mam* | Fish sauce. Basic Vietnamese condiment. |
| NVA | North Vietnamese Army. |
| *Tien Giang* | Upper Mekong River delta, southeastern Cambodia. |
| *Tien len* | "Forward." |
| *Trung Bo* | North Vietnamese name for central and coastal South Vietnam. |
| *Truong chinh* | "Long march." |
| *Vietcong* | Vietnamese Communist. |
| *Vietminh* | Customary name for Vietnamese nationalistic Communist army (1941–54). Literally, "League for the Revolution and Independence of Vietnam." |
| *Xich lo* | Motorcycle with carriage for passengers/cargo. |

# Historical Note

The Communists had made do with a maze of paths, trails, and dirt and paved roads snaking through Laos and Cambodia and known collectively as the Ho Chi Minh Trail. The steadily expanding network had served the North well, funneling a regular supply of men and arms south despite repeated American and South Vietnamese efforts at interdiction. The very primitiveness of the system had worked to the Communist advantage, making detection difficult and repairs relatively simple.

—Samuel Lipsman and Stephen Weiss, *The False Peace*

The trail network controlled and operated by the North Vietnamese was one of the most elaborate, yet primitive and unique, military logistics systems of modern times. Known to the world as the Ho Chi Minh Trail, after the enigmatic North Vietnamese leader, the Vietnamese called it the Old Man's Trail.

During the First Indochina War, the Vietminh, lacking long-range radios, and always mistrusting them anyway because of their penchant for secrecy, had developed a primitive system of pathways and trails along the Vietnamese-Laotian-Cambodian borders, where French troops seldom ventured. The system had been used mostly by communications and liaison couriers who could make a relatively rapid transit from north to south in less than three weeks on foot and bicycles, sometimes using captured jeeps and motorcycles. Following the uneasy peace of Geneva in 1954, the jungle reclaimed most of the primitive trail system.

A decision in 1959 by the North Vietnamese Central Committee, their ruling body, that all available means, both political and military, would be used to reunite the North and South and bring down the American-supported Diem government in Saigon, mandated the requirement to reopen the trail. The job of surveying and laying out the network was assigned to an old man, a South Vietnamese, who had extensive knowledge of the original network. Traveling in reverse direction from south to north, he took more than a year to mark and map the best route. The old man's name, probably in deference to his desire for anonymity, is not even remembered in legend. Thus the name the Old Man's Trail.

The North Vietnamese then moved to secure the area traversed by the newly surveyed trail, and over the next few years solidified their control of the remote and tortuous Laotian and Cambodian jungles. What developed generally along the trace of the original route was, in fact, more of a complex transportation, communications, maintenance, and logistics network than a trail. This network stretched somewhat over 650 miles on its longest north-south axis and, in some places, was twenty to thirty miles wide east to west. Task Group 559—TG559— operated the network and eventually grew to a military organization commanding around 40,000 men and women who were organized into two basic types of units. The first, the *Binh Tram* units, were similar to regimental-size logistics organizations with infantry elements for security, engineer units for road and foot trail maintenance, communications cells in charge of maintaining the hundreds of miles of communications wire strung throughout the network, as well as couriers and transportation and vehicle-maintenance companies. Later, TG559 would operate a petroleum pipeline stretching from Vinh, North Vietnam, to Loc Ninh, South Vietnam.

The second type of unit, the Guide/Billet teams, were mainly concerned with the movement of personnel. Their responsibilities included providing food, shelter, medical attention, and trail guides. Each Guide/Billet unit was composed of fifteen to twenty men and women who maintained lonely and remote way stations, most with the capacity to billet up to a hundred troops, which was the size of the largest increment ever sent onto the trail. Each way station had a food cache and cooking facilities, and some had small dispensaries that provided rudimentary medical care for those injured on the trail. Guides assigned to each station knew the trail routes only halfway to the next station in either direction. Increments would be turned over to a guide from the next station at these halfway points; in this way the North Vietnamese served their preoccupation with security.

Increments were configured into several basic types and then assigned to a suitable route through the network. There were heavy military equipment increments consisting of tanks, artillery, and antiaircraft missile batteries; bulk cargo increments that moved ammunition, food, and fuel by truck; military units infiltrating south; bicycle cargo increments; and foot cargo porter increments.

Regardless of the increment type, movement on the trail was tortuous and fraught with daily dangers. This book is about the journey of a foot cargo increment.

# The Old Man's Trail

# Prologue

## SAIGON, SOUTH VIETNAM

Every aspect of the Tet Offensive had been worked out in detail, including the announcement by the North Vietnamese foreign minister on 30 December 1967. If the Americans would unconditionally halt the bombing of the north, he said, the North Vietnamese government would—not *could*—hold peace negotiations. The announcement was carefully staged to appear that it came from a crippled opponent seeking respite. The Americans took it as a sign that the barefoot enemy was faltering, yet again, and that their side was winning.

Nothing could have been further from the truth. The North Vietnamese government, like a wounded tiger, had in fact become even more dangerous. Its leaders had searched their pragmatic political beliefs for an answer and found a clear objective. The offensive would surely drive a fatally divisive wedge between the Americans (who believed themselves omnipotent in matters relating to government and war) and their inept, corrupt, and greedy South Vietnamese allies. More important, such an attack would feed, like gasoline thrown on a fire, the growing popular opposition to the war in the United States and around the world, which would do more than any battlefield triumph to ensure an ultimate victory for Hanoi. This is exactly what the North Vietnamese achieved, but at a price.

The Americans, in their worship of the gods of technology and weapons of mass destruction, had not noticed their enemy's commitment to a new grand strategy, nor would the logic have made any sense. That sort of thinking defied quantification.

Despite the North Vietnamese government's extreme efforts at secrecy, many signals of what was about to occur were available to the Americans. There were captured operations orders; peculiar border battles with large enemy formations that served no purpose other than to draw forces away from coastal population centers; increased logistics activity in Laos and Cambodia; and Hanoi's rescheduling of the Tet celebration in the North. These and a host of other signs, if read together, would have told the story. But General Westmoreland, commander of Military Assistance Command, Vietnam, and his staff simply couldn't bring themselves to believe that General Nguyen Vo Giap would do what the signs indicated he was going to do.

The Tet attack, which took place in and around Saigon and Cholon, was carried out by thirty-five battalions of mostly Vietcong. The Vietcong were tenacious and shrewd guerrillas. They always fought outnumbered and outgunned; still, they somehow managed to keep coming back for more, inflicting as many, or more, casualties as they took. The Vietcong moved with impunity in all their operating areas among people whom they knew by name and treated with great respect. In return, people supported them by providing hiding places, supplies, and, most important, intelligence. The Vietcong always chose their fights and their fields of battle very carefully. They were disciplined, highly trained, and courageous, but many were ruthless and vicious killers. They rarely took prisoners.

Four thousand Vietcong troops attacked Saigon on the second night of the offensive, 31 January 1968. Among them was Brother Nguyen Thanh Loc, the political, executive, and operations officer of the 267th Independent Vietcong Battalion, a Saigon Military District local force unit. Had there been a rank structure in the Vietcong, he would have been a major.

Brother Loc had been heavily involved in the planning and preparations for the offensive, which was the boldest Communist initiative of the Second Indochina War. Much effort had gone into preparing political cadres like himself. Loc's job was to motivate the South Vietnamese people to shift sides and join the Communists in the *khoi nghia,* which would be the final, victorious clash of wills with the American imperialists, represented by the 492,000 U.S. troops in Vietnam and their South Vietnamese puppets.

It was up to Loc, and hundreds like him, to implement Ho Chi Minh's thrilling attack order. Plans were developed and rehearsed to perfection; they had to be executed aggressively for the offensive to succeed. No detail would be overlooked. Unforeseen obstacles must be anticipated and prevented; no one would be allowed to stand in the way. Victory was at hand.

Armed with these orders and his strong personal belief in the cause, Loc set about his tasks with customary intensity. The 267th Battalion had successfully operated for years around Phuoc Binh, several miles southwest of the southern tip of Cholon, the Chinese suburb of Saigon. The battalion was versatile, as all Vietcong units were.

On short notice the 267th could conduct a wide range of operations: day or night attacks; large or small ambushes; rapid emplacement of lethal booby traps and minefields; inner-city bombings; assassinations; sniper attacks; and a score of other military and political actions. The 267th had pulled off terrorist bombing attacks on the Brinks Bachelor Officers Quarters and the popular Saigon Floating Restaurant, both of which had inflicted heavy casualties on the Americans. Much of the battalion's success lay in Loc's ability to plan. He was known as a hard-core cadre, and all of his capacities would come into play on 31 January 1968.

The battalion's mission was to seize and hold the An Quang Pagoda and three square blocks surrounding the Buddhist shrine. Once in control of their objective, the battalion would politically indoctrinate the South Vietnamese residents of the district, enlisting them into the ranks of the National Liberation Front with the aid of the An Quang monks. The monks were sympathetic to any attempt to overthrow the South Vietnamese government, which had viciously persecuted them for years. The NLF's intelligence analysis indicated a strong desire on the part of the people to join the Communists, but suggested they were being held back and imprisoned by the American imperialists and their South Vietnamese lackeys.

On this score the NLF's intelligence was dead wrong. The average South Vietnamese was perfectly willing to let both sides beat each other into semi-consciousness and then join up with the winner. It didn't matter who won as long as he and his family were protected from the fray. Loc was familiar with this attitude, called *attentisme,* and with characteristic care he had developed a plan to deal with just such an obstinate and unpatriotic attitude, should it arise. Loc was determined to make the *khoi nghia* a reality in his objective area. It was his duty to the Lao Dong party, and he always fulfilled his duty.

His first major challenge was to bring the battalion's 250 troops into the city covertly and position them. In this task he was inspired by Mao Tse-tung, the Chinese Communist leader, who taught that the people were the water and the guerrillas were the fish moving through the water.

Beginning in September 1967, Loc, dressed as a peasant farmer and carrying the ancient oriental *don ganh,* or carrying pole, laden with vegetables swaying rhythmically from either end, began making daily trips into the city. There he set up his stand on various street corners near the An Quang Pagoda. Since he had tuberculosis and carried forged South Vietnamese government papers declaring him unfit for military service, after several weeks he was quickly recognized and waved through the government roadblocks. Sometimes he gave the guards choice pieces of produce and fruit, ensuring his safe passage.

From his corner stand, he was able to establish close contact with the An Quang monks, and soon all the necessary details for occupying the pagoda by 30 January had been worked out. The monks provided Loc with a list of contacts in the neighborhood who could hide some of his troops before the attack and assist him as block captains after the battalion had established control. Loc narrowed his list down to five of the poorest families in the neighborhood, which was, by Saigon standards, upper-middle-class. Those selected were servants of the more well-to-do families and so were badly mistreated, in keeping with the ancient class structure of Vietnamese society.

The people on Loc's list had not been servants for long, but had come from the masses of refugees uprooted by the heavy-handed government efforts to deny the enemy access to people in the provinces. These former farmers and merchants and their families suddenly had found themselves on the Saigon streets with no homes or jobs. Bitter over their government's treatment of them, they played well into Loc's hands.

Loc had developed a clever plan to position the battalion's weapons, uniforms, and ammunition. In October 1967, he began staging a series of funeral processions that culminated at the An Quang Pagoda. The mock funerals—ostensibly for South Vietnamese soldiers killed in action—were staged as processions on foot or with "mourners" riding behind the caskets in a hodgepodge of vehicles.

With their heads shaved, and wearing the traditional saffron robes of Buddhist monks, the battalion and company commanders established a routine rapport with the guards at roadblocks along the way. Inside the coffins, hidden under the bodies of freshly killed South Vietnamese soldiers, were rifles, RPG-7 and B-40 grenade launchers, machine guns, communications gear, and other necessary equipment for the attack.

The mourners from the 267th followed, carrying as much as a hundred rounds of ammunition or half a dozen grenades strapped to their bodies under their traditional loose-fitting peasant garb. Once inside the pagoda, the disguised soldiers stored their gear in a large cellar that also served as a bomb shelter.

In November the 267th began leaving four or five men at the pagoda after each bogus funeral. They were assigned to set up communica-

tions gear, to maintain weapons, to plant booby traps and preset demolitions charges, and to handle reconnaissance duties and reinforce
key strong points within the pagoda for the forthcoming battle.

Loc prevented these men from succumbing to the capitalist temp-
tations of Saigon—rich food, freedom, and beautiful Vietnamese
women in flowing *ao dai*—by assigning Pham Van Duan, the First
Company commander, to the Saigon detachment. Duan, a highly regarded, much-decorated Vietcong cadre, was the best company commander in the battalion. He and Loc had met as members of the Vietminh fighting the French and were veterans of the battles at Tu Le and
Dien Bien Phu. In 1959, at the start of the Second Indochina War, they
had made the arduous journey together down the Old Man's Trail,
known in the west as the Ho Chi Minh Trail. They had been among the
ten surviving members of their company, and after their convalescence,
which had taken three months, they had been assigned to the Ninth
Vietcong Division. Loc had eventually been promoted and assigned to
the 267th Vietcong Battalion, and in February 1967, Duan had been assigned as a replacement cadre to the 267th, following the loss of key
leaders at a battle near Long Dinh.

Loc and Duan had never seen eye to eye. Loc was a longtime member of the Lao Dong party and moved easily between the complex in-
tellectual realm of party politics and the field of armed conflict. A fear-
less soldier, he was avidly political and a zealous Communist. Duan had
little interest in party politics. He was a courageous and charismatic
combat leader, and as an ardent nationalist, he harbored a deep hatred
for foreigners in his people's land. For generations his family had
fought the colonialists who had come to Tonkin, Annam, and Cochin
China—the Chinese, the French, the Japanese, the Chinese National-
ists, the French again, and now the Americans and the separatist government in Saigon. Nationalism for Duan had been a calling, an hon-
orable profession, a way of life.

Farming, fishing, and shop-keeping were professions for the meek.
Strong men used power, and a rifle was power. Duan had never encountered anything more powerful, with the exception of airplanes,

which were a power of great and fearsome magnitude. Since he would never have an airplane, he trusted in his rifle.

Duan was not a member of the Lao Dong party, even though he had served its Revolution all his adult life. He met the criteria for membership, but he had always declined, feeling that better-qualified men should take up party leadership. Duan was more comfortable with the *dau tranh vu trang*—armed struggle—side of the political equation that governed the party's strategy for unification of Vietnam. His superiors had always agreed with him.

But Duan was adamant in his opposition to Loc's heavy-handed approach to the business of the Revolution. His experience was that education and persuasion were far superior to coercion and intimidation in gaining support of the people. Loc knew this. By putting Duan out of the way in Saigon, Loc figured he would save himself a confrontation that would interfere with his preparations. His plan for a general uprising of the people in his objective area would fail unless the people immediately accepted his call for volunteers. He knew this was unlikely, and he intended to force compliance with a bloodbath. Loc knew that Duan would oppose this method and wanted him out of the way while he completed his planning.

The 267th Battalion began to move into Saigon on the morning of 25 January, and the entire battalion was in by early afternoon of 30 January. Only three men and two women were detained by South Vietnamese security forces and all were released, based on the perfectly forged identity documents they carried.

As the sun set on the holiday atmosphere of Saigon on the eve of Tet, the 267th Battalion prepared to fight what it hoped would be their last battle. Most of them were billeted in the pagoda bomb shelter, which Duan had organized into a crowded but comfortable barracks. Some troops entering the city, disguised as husbands and wives coming home for the holidays, were billeted with the five sympathizing families in their unsuspecting employers' homes. The troops ensured their welcome by providing their hosts with generous gifts of American whiskey and cigarettes, bought with funds from the battalion's treasury.

On the eve of 30 January the city came alive in celebration. Families strolled through the brightly lit streets, dodging vehicles of every description on their way to parties all over the capital. At around 8:00 P.M., the fireworks started. Such a display could only be duplicated in a war zone. There were firecrackers and bursting Chinese rockets—along with a dazzling display of artillery and mortar illumination rounds, pop-up flares, and thousands of tracers fired into the air from every type of small-arms weapon imaginable. The sky over the city glowed from the pyrotechnics, and in some sections of the city revelers had to shout to be heard over the noise.

While most of Saigon celebrated, the 267th troopers were suiting up for another battle in brand-new North Vietnamese Army—NVA—dark green uniforms, made especially for the occasion by Uncle Ho and their brothers and sisters in the North. The uniforms would initially deceive the enemy as to the type of units they were facing. The troopers wore bright red arm bands, web gear, and traditional Vietcong floppy bush hats. They were rotated in groups of four through the pagoda courtyard, each firing a five-round test burst from their AK-47s and other assorted weapons. The armorers had done their work well, and there was only one malfunction. The weapons fire from the pagoda caught no one's attention—it blended in with the mad commotion happening all over town. At 10:00 P.M., Loc briefed the unit leaders one last time on the plan, which by then everyone, down to the lowest *bo doi*, had committed to memory. The battalion commander gave a last-minute motivational speech, and everyone turned in for several hours of sleep.

Three A.M. on 31 January 1968 was their H-Hour. The 267th moved quietly through the still-noisy neighborhood to their assigned positions. Most people had gone up to the flat roofs of the neighborhood buildings. Some families, sitting on balconies, noticed the armed men and quickly moved inside and shuttered their windows. Designated troops moved to the rooftops and ordered everyone into their apartments or homes. Shocked and scared, the people did as they were told. Rooftop sentries signaled clear to unit leaders in the streets. Precisely at 3:05 A.M., in a flurry of gunfire, Duan's company killed six National Police walking beats in the district and twelve drunk Regional Force militia troops stationed at three sandbagged street-corner strong points.

The neighborhood became quiet as death. Then Loc began speaking over a secretly installed loudspeaker system, at first in a conciliatory tone: "To all the people of South Vietnam, I bring you Tet greetings from your brothers and sisters throughout both North and South Vietnam. Your government leaders in this great city of the people are nothing more than puppets on a string doing the bidding of the fascist imperialists and baby rapers of Wall Street. We have come to make this Tet celebration truly memorable by freeing you from the yoke of oppression, which has hung so heavily around your necks all these years. Throughout the South, this night, powerful forces of the National Liberation Front and our brothers from North Vietnam are moving to destroy the Thieu-Ky regime and their American masters in their drunken sleep. By morning they will be nothing more than bloody bodies fit only for dogs. Join us now. Help us to overthrow these corrupt and despicable oppressors of the people. Join the winning side!"

Sounds of battle could be heard coming from all around the city, mounting in intensity as thousands of troops on both sides closed in mortal combat. For the moment, at least, the 267th had time to carry out their plan. As political cadre officers moved to each block of buildings, troops went in and herded residents into the streets.

Two blocks from the pagoda, in a narrow side street, two American officers lived with their Vietnamese mistresses. They had been taken prisoner at the outset of the operation. Now, in front of three hundred terrified people the two Americans were brought out, hands tied behind their backs. Loc strode confidently into the middle of the street. A murmur ran through the crowd as the people recognized the former street vendor, now a Vietcong officer. He said, "This is how the NLF deals with enemies of the people." Then he calmly walked over to the two shaking Americans and, with a look of intense hatred on his face, shot each of them in the forehead.

The crowd drew a deep collective breath. Some women and children began to cry. Loc called for quiet. He assured everyone that what they had just witnessed only happened to proven enemies of the people, but this did little to calm their fears. Then he shouted for South Vietnamese Army Lieutenant Colonel Binh, who was led out with his wife and three small children. Loc asked Binh if he was ready to renounce his allegiance to his American masters and join the people in their struggle against the United States. Binh meekly responded that he did not serve the Americans but the South Vietnamese government. Loc seemed understanding of this statement and announced that only a little indoctrination would be required to reeducate Binh and his family to the real facts. They were led to the pagoda.

Loc now called out the name of one of the local collaborators, who came out in the street. Loc announced that this man had provided a great service to the people by helping plan the great popular uprising. A trooper brought out a uniform and helped the collaborator put it on. Loc administered the oath to him and placed a rifle in his hands, making him a member of the 267th. The rifle had a jammed action and no ammunition, but no one knew that. The troops led the applause and prodded the crowd to join in.

The people were beginning to settle down, after the shock of seeing the Americans executed.

Loc turned to his newly sworn-in soldier and asked loudly, "Do you know of anyone in the neighborhood who has been involved in illegal activities that stole from the people?"

The former servant answered dutifully as a Vietcong soldier: "Yes sir, I do know of vile capitalistic corruption in the neighborhood." A hush fell over the crowd; everyone had been involved in corrupt schemes of one kind or another. It was the way things were done in Saigon. But they had another reason to be nervous: virtually everyone present had done something mean to this small, toothless man and his family, who belonged to the lowest servant class.

Loc asked for names and charges, which the man recited, implicating the well-to-do-family of four that employed him. This family was called forward: a distinguished-looking gray-haired man, a middle-aged woman, and two teenage boys. Soldiers tied their hands.

The former servant began to recite a list of transgressions that the family supposedly had committed. When he had finished, Loc regarded the accused family solemnly and said, "Guilty of crimes against the people." With an almost wistful smile on his face, he shot all four of them, beginning with the youngest boy. Each had a long moment to look into the emotionless, snakelike eyes of their executioner.

Again the crowd recoiled in horror. Weeping and sobbing broke out. Loc called for quiet, and the crowd obeyed. He told them to return to their homes and remain there unless they were summoned by the NLF. The street emptied immediately.

Loc began working through his meticulously prepared lists, which categorized each family in the district. Those on the enemies list were brought to Loc, who first accused them of their crimes, then shot them on the spot. By 4:00 A.M., forty-eight bodies littered the once placid and peaceful streets. The criteria for the death sentence were accumulated wealth and success under the South Vietnamese system. Husbands, wives, and children were executed together, as if to stamp out their corrupt genes. The bodies were left where they fell as reminders to those who would oppose the Revolution. All over Saigon and throughout the country, similar scenes of horror were being played out, directed by the invisible hand of Hanoi.

The Buddhist monks, who had come to trust Duan during his two-week stay in the pagoda, asked him if they could dignify the bodies by removing them from the street and preparing them for burial. Duan consented, and the bodies were moved into an alley, neatly lined up and covered with blankets and ponchos. Loc overlooked this violation of his instructions, to avoid a confrontation with Duan and the monks, who were becoming increasingly uncooperative.

As dawn broke on 31 January, the 267th braced for the attack they knew was coming. In the morning they occupied themselves by shooting up any vehicle or person seen on the street. At one point a South

Vietnamese Army staff car strayed down one of the streets and was stopped by a squad. Three officers and a driver were taken prisoner and escorted into the pagoda. The young enlisted driver quickly joined the 267th, but the three officers weren't given the chance. After an hour of brutal interrogation they were taken into a side street where a crowd had been assembled. Loc made another impassioned speech about the consequences faced by enemies and exploiters of the people, while a demolitions platoon trooper wrapped several loops of American-manufactured detonating cord around the necks of the officers.

The cord was primed with a blasting cap and then hooked up to an electrical detonation box. While the three officers waited to die, Loc harangued the crowd with more political rhetoric. He concluded his remarks with a quotation from Ho Chi Minh, then turned to the South Vietnamese driver who had just been drafted into the cause. He praised the terrified young man for seeing the light of the Revolution and turning his back on the South Vietnamese American puppets, then gave him the electrical detonation box and said, "Strike a blow for the people, and destroy our enemies."

The boy looked blankly at Loc and then at the officers with their necks looped in the cord running to the box in his hand. Tears ran down his face, and he protested that he couldn't do this because the man in the middle was his father.

Loc was enraged by this news; he saw that his whole motivational program for the morning was in danger of falling flat. He pulled his pistol and shot the boy in the face. Then he turned on the crowd, shrieking and cursing them all for their sick capitalistic attitudes. He picked up the detonation box and, searching the crowd, found a frightened small girl clinging to her mother's leg. He spoke soothingly to her in the gentle, singsong Vietnamese voice reserved for children. Reaching in his pocket, he produced a stick of American chewing gum, unwrapped it and slowly fed it into her mouth while she hesitantly chewed. Then he reached for her hand and placed it on the detonator handle. Covering her hand with his, he gave the handle a sudden turn, sending an electrical charge to the detonation cap, which instantly blew up the explosive cord.

There was a loud explosion. The three victims' bodies were jerked upward and then flopped like rag dolls onto the pavement. A second's pause, and their perfectly severed heads thudded to the ground and bounced like cantaloupes. The child began to cry hysterically. Loc patted her on the head and walked to the front of the crowd, somewhat calmer now, but still angry. He knew he was failing in his mission of raising a revolution among the people. They were all whimpering cowards and American lackeys accustomed to luxury and decadence. If they weren't for the Revolution, then they were its enemies and must be destroyed. Uncle Ho was always right, he reasoned. Now is the time to get tough.

He ordered the platoon guarding the crowd to pick out all men over the age of seventeen and under forty and line them up in the street. Quickly a single line of sixty men was formed, while the crowd of women and children began to wail. Loc faced the first man and asked him if he wanted to join the Revolution. The man was petrified. When he opened his mouth to speak he couldn't form words, he just stood there, eyes pleading, jaw moving. Loc watched a moment, smiled, and shot him in the mouth.

The next man eagerly expressed his desire to join the cause and was told to stand over to the side. Loc worked his way down the line. It became a game. A game of chance. The remaining fifty-eight men, when asked, all volunteered for the Revolution. Loc shot fifteen of them indiscriminately. There was no pattern to his choices. The random deaths were meant to demonstrate the godlike power of the Revolution.

When Loc was halfway down the line a dozen monks emerged, single file, from the pagoda and lined up with the remaining men. The oldest monk began, in a loud chanting monotone, to disavow any complicity with the atrocities being committed. He confessed his sin of not recognizing that Loc was a hungry ghost—a devil—who had disguised his murderous intent. Loc casually reloaded his pistol and shot all twelve monks in the forehead. The monks showed no fear and prayed up until the moment of death.

From their rooftop observation post, Duan and his second-in-command watched the insane butchery in the street below. Both were veteran soldiers accustomed to extreme hardship and death, but neither was accustomed to Loc's kind of killing.

Duan's face was grim. "I have never understood Loc. I didn't understand him when we first met, years ago. It was impossible to tell what he was thinking. We always knew he was a killer, even when he was a young *bo doi.*" He shook his head. "Loc never took prisoners, even when we were ordered to. The man is a butcher. These people will never join us after watching this."

Duan turned away and began to inspect the organization of his position. As he went from one strong point or firing position to another, the impossibility of the mission became increasingly clear. With only 250 troops, they were holding a three-block enclave in the midst of the enemy's capital city. They were out of range of any significant supporting arms, which were committed to attacks on Long Binh, Bien Hoa, Cu Chi, and other outlying areas. The key to the mission's success lay in a spontaneous uprising of the people, which clearly was not going to occur. The enemy would retaliate with a vengence and push them out of their objective area. Duan knew that if the 267th didn't withdraw they would be trapped and forced to pay the price for Loc's carnage.

He watched the battle intensify from the rooftop. Smoke filled the air; the incessant rattle of small-arms fire mingled with the crunch of artillery and mortars. Airplanes were like a swarm of locusts over the city.

He considered their open and exposed position, and cringed. Never leave the jungle, he had counseled at planning sessions. Don't stand and fight. It was fruitless against American airpower and artillery. Move quietly and strike suddenly. Gain the all-important element of surprise.

But no one had listened. The people will rise up and help us, they had said. Now the message was clear: There was to be no uprising and no way out. They must fight an open, conventional battle against vastly superior forces and hope for a timely order to withdraw. Duan realized that the timely order would not come. They would be expected to hold at all costs, which would probably mean at the cost of their lives.

Meanwhile, behind a screen of buildings and smoke, a flight of twenty U.S. Army CH-47 Chinook helicopters, each carrying eighty Vietnamese Marines from the Marine Task Force, landed on the parade field of the old French Headquarters for Indochina, now occupied by the Joint General Staff. Bodies littered the landing zone. A Ranger Battalion mopped up the remains of a Vietcong sapper company that had attacked the complex the previous night.

The two battalions of the Marine Task Force had moved to the fence and tree line surrounding the parade ground. Four trucks were parked under a tree, issuing ammunition and supplies. The task force commander, the battalion commanders, and the American Marine advisors—*covan my*—were holding a meeting by the trucks. The task force operations officer issued the attack order. They were to jump off in one hour, at 3:00 P.M. The mission: clear the An Quang Pagoda district of enemy resistance.

At precisely 3:00 P.M., the Marines moved southwest out of the JGS compound, two battalions abreast. They cautiously leapfrogged through familiar streets, now deserted and littered with demolished cars, bodies, and burning buildings. Six blocks from the JGS compound the Marines slowed their advance and cautiously entered the boulevards leading into the objective area. The 267th outposts reported the Marines' approach to their battalion command post under the pagoda. The battalion commander issued the final defensive order, since they now knew from which direction the attack would come. Troops burrowed into their positions in anticipation of a hard fight. Duan issued orders to his strong points to release the hostages that Loc had spitefully placed in the line of fire. The terrified hostages ran for several blocks and passed unharmed into the protective ranks of the advancing Marines. Duan had reminded his men that soldiers of the Revolution did not hide behind bound women and unarmed men. The troops, who admired and trusted Duan as much as they mistrusted Loc, had unanimously agreed to the order.

From his protected observation post on the balcony of a third-floor corner apartment, Duan watched the lead Marine units enter the first of his kill zones. On command, his company opened fire across the broad, flat esplanades and boulevards. The Marine units reacted swiftly, after sustaining their first casualties. They sought covered positions and continued to advance in short, small unit rushes under a heavy base of fire that inflicted casualties on Duan's men and drove his troops to seek more substantial cover.

At first the wide streets gave the 267th an advantage. Gradually, however, the Marines worked artillery and mortar smoke rounds into position and managed, with heavy casualties, to clear and seize the first buildings in the district. Intense fighting gave them access to the roofs of the corner buildings, and now they hauled up machine guns, 57-mm recoilless rifles, and grenade launchers and began clearing the roofs of buildings adjacent to the 267th's strong points.

At the An Quang Pagoda, Loc tracked the course of the battle with growing concern. All companies had reported that they were under attack by South Vietnamese Marines, and in less than an hour of fighting the enemy held the rooftops of the three northeast buildings. Loc knew that if they couldn't knock the Marines off the rooftops, it was only a matter of time before they would be defeated.

The battalion commander ordered the demolitions platoon to blow the explosive charges set inside the buildings held by the Marines. He left for the roof of the pagoda, leaving Loc in charge of the command center. Moments later, Duan reported that the battalion commander had been killed in a machine-gun burst. Loc was now in command.

Communications were cut off to the demolition platoon, so Loc went to find them. Emerging through the small trap door to the roof, he saw the true shape of the battle. Casualties from the 267th littered neighboring rooftop positions. A withering volume of fire raked the roofs, making any movement, except a low crawl, suicidal. He crawled over to the next building and slipped through another trap door, emerging in the block of buildings behind the pagoda. He found the entire demolition platoon dead at their post, killed by a 57-mm recoilless rifle round fired through the shuttered window. He hooked up the wires leading to the charges in the northeast buildings and plunged the detonator a dozen times, with no effect. The wires had been cut. He moved back to his command post in the pagoda.

The Marines controlled the roofs, and by nightfall they held a little less than half of the district.

Loc had reported the battalion's situation to his division commander. His orders were to hold their position at all costs, which to that point had been well over half the battalion killed or wounded. Only a hundred effective troops remained. With few tactical options open, Loc ordered his troops to strengthen the remaining positions and reestablish rooftop strong points after nightfall, which was approaching.

After dark, however, Loc was stunned to see that the Marines were continuing to attack under illumination. He had never before seen a South Vietnamese unit attack at night. They fought all night, and it went badly for the 267th. By sunrise Duan's company was the only effective unit remaining. It held about half of the block surrounding the pagoda. Loc ordered Duan to continue fighting with his twenty-five men and pulled the remnants of the other units back into the pagoda, along with a hundred or so hostages. Only thirty troops joined him, and half of them were wounded.

Again Loc reported his situation to higher headquarters. He was ordered to break out as best he could and return to base camp. Loc sat for a few moments and let the reality of his mission's failure sink into his exhausted mind. He was not accustomed to defeat, and he wouldn't take it lightly. The enemy must pay.

Heavy small-arms fire continued outside. Loc ordered his troops to change into civilian clothes that had been stored in the bomb shelter and prepare to withdraw from the city. Under the NLF's plan, all units committed to Saigon were to wear either plaid or checkered shirts when they withdrew, so that units on the outskirts of the city could recognize them. Loc donned an old plaid shirt and black shorts, the clothes he had worn as the neighborhood vegetable vendor.

He intentionally did not issue breakout orders to Duan and his beleaguered company. In view of the disastrous outcome of his plan, he wanted to ensure that only one version of events—his—would be told in the inquiries that would surely follow.

The battalion positions were now completely surrounded by the Marine Task Force, but Loc had another plan. He ordered Lieutenant Colonel Binh, who had been selected from the crowd for reeducation two nights earlier, and his family to be taken out by the narrow gate entrance to the pagoda grounds. Hiding behind the wall next to the gate, Loc and two troopers roped the Binh family together. He ordered the two soldiers to douse them with gasoline. The soldiers balked and refused. Loc cursed them, vowing to deal with them later, and poured a five-gallon can of gas over the Binh family. He shoved them into the street. The Marines ceased fire. Loc screamed, "Death to the enemies of the people," and fired a single shot from his pistol into the pool of gas surrounding the family's feet. The spark from the bullet on the pavement ignited the gas, and it exploded in pale orange and blue flames, engulfing the man, his wife, and three small girls.

Duan heard the Binhs' pathetic screams and crawled out on the second-story balcony to investigate. He hissed Loc's name. Loc alone was capable of such an atrocity. To hell with him, he thought. I must save as many of my men as I can. That is my only concern now. The battle is lost.

The Marines across the street watched in horror as the people slowly burned, their pathetic screams gradually subsiding. Some wept, others shouted obscenities, beating their fists bloody on the masonry walls. Some looked away. The bodies burned for three or four minutes and then collapsed in a rank, smoldering pile.

The advisor was the first to speak. "God have mercy on those poor people! God forgive the son of a bitch who did this, because I can't," he said, wiping tears from his dirty face.

The task force commander stood expressionless, looking across the street. Finally, his voice cracking, he said, "Attack the pagoda." There was a pause, a rattle of equipment, and 200 Marines charged across the street, their weapons blazing.

The Binh family's cremation had achieved Loc's aim. It had given him a five-minute lull in the fighting. He and his remaining troops mingled with the hostages and herded them out the back gate of the pagoda. The Marines across the street saw the civilians and held their fire. The hostages were screaming in terror. Loc feigned supplication, hands together as if in prayer, and bowed and mumbled about the horrors he had seen. His act worked; the Marines paid no attention to him. As they untied the women and children, he drifted off from the crowd. But one woman noticed him staggering away and shrieked after him. Three Marines grabbed and held Loc at gunpoint, searched him, and found the pistol tucked in his belt.

The hostages, now free, encircled Loc. Women beat him with their fists. One old man hit him hard across the mouth with a board, drawing blood. They spat on him, shouted, and cursed, and would have torn him apart with their hands had not the Marines intervened.

The Marines tied Loc's hands behind his back and a sergeant shoved him before the task force commander. Loc bowed his head, presenting a helpless and innocent figure. The commander calmed the shouting crowd and began asking them questions. They identified the five charred corpses across the street as the Binhs. They recited the names of the civilians Loc had killed, then the names of the executed Americans. They told the whole story, reserving no detail. Loc stood, head bowed, contriving an expression of confusion.

Several jeeps pulled up and a Vietnamese army colonel got out. The commander went to meet him. They talked for a few moments and the task force commander pointed to the Binhs, whose bodies still smoldered. The colonel's face turned ashen. Then he faced the crowd and told them to go home. He spoke with authority, and they began to move off. He motioned to the two Marines to bring Loc over to him.

He turned toward the captive, who instantly recognized the murderous intent in his eyes. The colonel stepped toward his enemy just as a knife appeared in a flash from the crowd, slipping easily into Loc's exposed stomach and penetrating straight to his heart. He was dead before he hit the ground, a look of bewilderment on his contorted face.

The colonel stood over him, then turned to the commander, forcing himself not to look at the pile of smoldering bodies. His voice quivering in anger and grief, he said, "Would you pick up the bodies of my daughter and her family for me? I will send a truck later."

The commander nodded, his hand on the colonel's shoulder.

Meanwhile, Duan had ordered his ten remaining men to change into their checkered and plaid shirt escape outfits and stood watching the scene below. As he saw Loc crumple to the ground he murmured, "Bastard, you got what you deserved."

He crawled to his men at the back of the apartment. They had carefully arranged twenty-one wounded men in the living room. They would be left behind without their weapons to face certain captivity and, hopefully, medical care. Duan knew the Vietnamese Marines would not harm them, as they always admired courageous enemies, and his company had indeed fought courageously.

Duan's men slipped into an empty alley and barely passed behind several Marine units. Using carrying poles loaded with fruits and vegetables as a disguise, they split into groups and began walking toward their base camp southwest of the city.

Duan, his second-in-command, and a radioman made it successfully through two lines of Vietnamese army units, using their forged papers. But on the outskirts of the city, only four miles from their destination, an American helicopter attacked them on an open section of road. They had identified the checkered and plaid shirts as a Vietcong recognition sign. The helicopter's first pass killed the radioman, and in the second, Duan took two 7.62-mm rounds through his left arm and chest. His second-in-command picked him up and carried him the rest of the way.

Of the 250 troops from the 267th Independent Vietcong Battalion attacking Saigon, only 27 made it back to the base camp. Ten of those were seriously wounded.

Within hours the Marines were given another mission and moved out of the An Quang Pagoda district with its litter of bodies and rubble. The people were left with the job of rebuilding their shattered homes and lives. For hours they wandered the streets aimlessly, consoling one another or sitting and looking blankly at the shambles that had been their homes. Like a bad dream, Loc and the terror of the past few days would slowly be erased from their minds.

In the late afternoon, an old man with a scraggly goatee hobbled across the deserted street with an adolescent boy to examine Loc's spread-eagled body. No one noticed them. They stood silently for a few moments and looked down at Loc, grotesque in death. The old man spat on the body and kicked hard into the groin. He spat on Loc again, still holding the boy's hand. Then he motioned to the boy, who uncapped a can of kerosene and poured it over Loc. They stepped back. The old man struck a match and handed it to the boy, who dropped it in the kerosene. They moved back further to avoid the heat and stench. The old man said, with a toothless smile, "Burn in hell, you miserable son of a whore." They turned and walked slowly across the street. Between the two of them they had lost two sons, a father, and an uncle to Loc's butchery.

# ONE

# Send-Off

## VAN XA HAMLET, NORTH VIETNAM, 1969

"Uncle Ho and the glorious Lao Dong party wisely have foreseen that this is the year of victory and liberation for our oppressed brothers and sisters in the South—liberation from the tyranny of the American pirates Johnson and Nixon, who have sent their bandits to rape, murder, and starve us in the name of their corrupt colonial capitalism. You and I will further this struggle by supplying our courageous soldiers with the weapons and ammunition to make the jungles run red with American blood. You, Ky, how will you help?"

The young boy named Ky looked up, startled. He hadn't been listening to Lieutenant Ba, the political cadre assigned to his porter platoon. Like most fifteen-year-old boys he was easily distracted, and at this moment his friend Trang had been engaging him in a game of Vietnamese tic-tac-toe. They were playing it in the dirt between them as they squatted on their haunches in a logistics training area south of Vinh, North Vietnam. Ky was on the verge of another win when he heard his name called.

That was all he had caught of Brother Ba's political indoctrination speech for the past ten minutes; it was the second such speech that day. Ky and Trang unwisely had decided that Brother Ba wasn't very smart or worth listening to; but that did little to help Ky out of his present fix.

He knew he was in trouble because he had jerked his head up when he'd heard his name, which was a sure giveaway of an inattentive Young Brother, as the porters in his platoon were called. Unlike some of the other young rice-farm and fishing-village boys who made up his porter platoon, Ky was a quick thinker, especially in tight situations, a trait he partly owed to being the youngest of six brothers. Instinctively he raised his right arm above his shoulder, palm flat and fingers joined, as he had been taught to when called upon by an officer of the Revolution. Then he stood up. A whisper from behind him prompted, "What will you do?"

"I will use all my strength to help supply our brothers and sisters in the South so they can kill the American colonialists, Brother Ba," he shouted. It was always the same question. His response was always the accepted answer. All day, every day. Ky stood at attention, looking straight at Brother Ba, who returned his stare with a scowl.

Ba looked deceptively academic in his round, dark-framed plastic glasses, an appearance that belied a second-generation Communist and ardent nationalist. In 1944 Ba's father, the son of a fisherman, had seen his parents and two sisters publicly beheaded by the Japanese in a mass reprisal execution for what was termed "subversive Vietnamese guerrilla activity" in the Haiphong area. That same day he had joined the Vietminh, the nationalist resistance organization fighting the Japanese occupation. By 1945 Ba's father had proved himself a dogged fighter and loyal Communist and had been inducted into the Indo-Chinese Communist party, later to be the Lao Dong party, headed by the zealous anticolonialist Ho Chi Minh. After the Japanese surrendered, Ho and the party aggressively moved to form a nationalist Vietnamese state from the former French colonies of Tonkin, Annam, and Cochin China. The French, determined not to lose their lucrative control of Indochina, decided to settle the diplomatic quagmire by force. In 1946 they shelled Haiphong, killing Ba's father and 6,000 other Vietnamese soldiers and civilians. After his death, Ba's father was accorded the honor of Hero of the Revolution.

Following the Vietminh victory over France in 1954, Ba, a somewhat hesitant, scholarly boy, and his mother were given certain privileges, thanks to his father's status. Selected on the basis of competitive exams to study at the University of Hanoi, Ba decided to become a teacher. A university education meant prestige and an almost certain escape from farming or fishing, the lots of most young men. Ba became active in Communist groups at the university and finally was admitted to the lower ranks of the Lao Dong party during his second year at school. University enrollment usually meant a student draft deferment, but during his third year he had been ordered into military service before graduating because of the shortage of political cadres. Many had either proved themselves unreliable in upholding the unrelenting party dicta concerning the conduct of the war or were being killed and wounded at an alarming rate. After only a two-week basic military training period and an intense three-month political indoctrination at the Son Tay Indoctrination Center west of Hanoi, Ba had been ordered south as a political cadre with this porter platoon.

Ky's response had the right effect. Ba's menacing scowl faded into a smile. "Very good, very good, Young Brother Ky. Wonderful! Come join me here, my courageous Young Brother," he said, extending his arm.

Ky ran to Ba's side and stood at attention. Ba wrapped his arm around Ky's shoulders and turned him to face his comrades, the sixty young, expressionless boys, squatting before him in neat military ranks. Ba began to clap, which prompted the boys to break into smiles and applause. Ky stood rigidly at attention, face impassive, but his mind raced. The boys stopped clapping and smiling the instant Ba stopped and assumed his usual dour countenance.

With a jerk, Ba turned to Ky and shouted, "Tell your Young Brothers why you were masturbating this morning in the woods outside the village!"

Ky had known when he was called forward that he was in a precarious position. Seldom did a Young Brother stand before the group and not receive some kind of punishment.

With a steady gaze he shouted back, "Brother Ba, I was not masturbating," even though he had been. Among a group of sixty fifteen-year-old boys, masturbation was rampant.

"Then maybe you can explain why I saw you behind the tree like this," said Ba, hunching his shoulders and pushing his pelvis forward, hands in front of his crotch, and assuming a comically dazed expression. Discipline broke and the boys began laughing, slapping each other on the back and pointing at Ky. Unfazed, Ky held a straight face.

"Enough! Stop!" Ba shouted. "As I have told you repeatedly, masturbation is a serious problem for the Revolution. You will need all your strength where we are going. You cannot cast your manhood on the jungle floor and hope to survive the *truong chinh*—long march—we are about to undertake. Masturbation takes away your strength. Isn't that right, Ky?"

"Masturbation is evil and more suited to capitalists, colonialists, and American bandits like Johnson and Nixon than to us in the struggle of freedom, Brother Ba," Ky said staunchly.

"Then, Ky, tell us what you were doing behind the tree before the sun rose," said Ba, in a mocking singsong voice. This time the other boys didn't laugh.

"Brother Ba, I had a tick on my penis and was removing it before it could make me sick and prevent me from serving *Bac Ho* and my brothers and sisters fighting the imperialists in the South," Ky said in an even voice.

"A tick! A tick! Ky, are you saying that I didn't see what I know I saw?" Ba said, shoulders thrown back, fists on hips, and shoving his face close to Ky's.

"Brother Ba, I can show you the mark of the tick if you don't believe me."

"Yes, yes, I would like very much to see that, Young Brother," said Ba, his voice betraying that he knew he was losing face to this impertinent little son of a rice farmer.

Ky modestly turned his back to the platoon and for the first time in the whole incident showed hesitation and concern.

Ba shouted, "Well, show me, Ky. Show me the tick bite. Now!"

Ky slowly untied the drawstring of his black cotton trousers and shyly reached inside to expose a small section of red skin with a black center for Ba's inspection. Ba examined the exposed skin with a dramatically turned-down mouth, the traditional Vietnamese expression of disgust reserved for death or filth. Ky endured this invasion of privacy with a poker face, thankful that he had indeed discovered and removed the tick while masturbating.

Ba patted Ky on the shoulder and told him to return to his place in the squatting ranks. The platoon stared ahead impassively, hiding their pleasure in watching Ky embarrass Ba, who had been annoying them for the past six weeks.

For a few moments Ba stood silently and wiped his glasses with his black cotton shirttail. He put them back on and said evenly, "I apologize to Young Brother Ky for wrongly accusing him of masturbation. The Revolution is good and just, not unfair and corrupt. But it needs every man's full strength, and masturbation drains away that strength. Isn't that correct, my Young Brothers."

"Yes, Brother Ba," they responded in unison. Throwing a last glowering look their way, Ba motioned to a man standing at the rear of the platoon.

Pham Van Duan, formerly of the 267th Independent Vietcong Battalion, now recovered from his wounds, walked to the front of the formation. The boys shouted attention in unison and faced their commander. With an infectious smile, Duan waved them back down into their squatting ranks.

Duan was in his early thirties but looked older. He wore the NVA rank of sergeant major and was assigned as the military commander for this porter platoon. Although Lieutenant Ba outranked Duan, under the dual military-political command system Duan had complete authority over the platoon's movement south and all military matters. Ba was charged with the boys' political orientation and indoctrination. But Ba's seniority and party membership gave him several measures of clout that Duan did not possess as a nonparty member.

Duan was a greatly admired father figure among the boys. Soft-spoken and encouraging, a brilliant and demanding teacher, Duan was a stern disciplinarian. He was the leader the boys trusted as he took them through the rigorous endurance training in preparation for their long march down the Old Man's Trail. Even though Duan and Ba treated each other respectfully, everyone knew there was no real friendship between the two.

Duan sometimes wondered what he would do if the Revolution succeeded and there was no more need for his skills. He would never become a paper shuffler like Ba. He supposed he could go west. There were other good Communist armies in Laos and Burma. He had seen them. There was always a job for a good soldier in Indochina. Maybe in the poppy fields high in the cool Burmese mountains. He had been there once with a battalion transporting opium to finance the Revolution, and had met a pretty girl.

Duan quickly pulled himself from his thoughts, back to the task at hand. He thanked Brother Ba for his efforts to indoctrinate the next generation of freedom fighters. He said nothing about masturbation because he knew it wasn't a real problem, and even if it were, he doubted anyone could stop the behavior in fifteen-year-old boys. He paused to look at their young faces, thinking with a twinge of guilt that he would be the one to lead them through the terrible trials that lay ahead. It gave him solace to remember that he had been their age when he had joined the Vietminh in 1952. He knew that strong young bodies and hearts were the lifeblood of the Revolution. He had grown up carrying a rifle, and so would they.

His problem now was how to get sixty fifteen-year-old boys through 650 miles of jungle carrying 2,500 pounds of weapons and ammunition. The obstacles seemed almost overwhelming. He knew them well. Raging rivers and swollen streams, steep mountain passes, narrow muddy paths, food shortages, incessant rain, ambushes and bombings, disease and the lesser problems of snakes and tigers. The *truong chinh* was good, though. It tested a man. But it also marked him. The hardships had worn Duan down in his youth, and the same would happen to these boys.

That was the way of Vietnam, the natural course of events. "The fire in the lake," it was called. A phrase that captured the *I Ching*'s message of eternal change. The first step for these boys on their lifelong journey would be to change from boys into men. Duan would be the one to push them through this second birth and, like coming into life for the first time, some would survive and others would perish.

"My Young Brothers, tonight we have a great meal to fortify us," Duan said, smiling. "As much as you can eat, and beer, and some special sweet cakes made by our Young Sisters. And a special show by the Revolutionary Dance Troupe." Food and dancing were always pleasers with troops and kids. This porter platoon was both. The young faces beamed back at him. "Young Brother Ky will lead us to the village where our banquet awaits us," he added, trying to humiliate Ba about his political talks, which were the worst Duan had ever heard. Besides, political rhetoric had never gotten anybody over the Truong Son Mountains and the Bolovens Plateau. Guts, rice, and leadership were the only answer. Every *bo doi* veteran of the Old Man's Trail knew that.

Ky was a smart boy who showed promise. He had courage. The rest of the boys didn't know how to stand up to Ba. Ky reminded Duan of himself when he had joined the Vietminh. And Ba had never been down the Old Man's Trail. He speculated how long Ba would last. Maybe to the Kong River in southern Laos. No farther. Schoolteachers didn't do well in the jungle. Of course General Giap, chief of the North Vietnamese war effort, had started out as a history teacher. It had, in truth, been Giap's understanding of the jungle that had allowed him to position more than 50,000 Vietminh troops in a siege ring around the 15,000 French troops at Dien Bien Phu in 1954, a tactical coup that had led to victory. Giap was a tough and smart old bastard for a schoolteacher, he thought. But he was an exception.

"Tomorrow we will begin our march to the South," Duan said. "At a special place we will pick up our cargo for the Revolution in the South.

We leave at 6:00 A.M., carrying our training loads. Eat well, Young Brothers."

The platoon fell in quickly. With Young Brother Ky in the lead, carrying their red banner on a bamboo pole, they marched off to the small hamlet of Van Xa, where they had been billeted for the past six weeks. The villagers of Van Xa heard the boys singing as they approached and, with no prodding from the hamlet chief, a man named Hung and his assistants went out and lined the main path leading through the village.

The people were loyal to Brother Hung. He was a veteran of the victorious Vietminh and a voting member of the Provincial Communist party. He had used his political position to help the villagers, who in turn felt deeply grateful. A sign of his skill as a negotiator was the fact that the nearest antiaircraft battery lay almost two miles away, which was why Van Xa was one of the few remaining unmolested hamlets in the area.

Hung had recognized as early as 1963 that soon the airplanes would come and begin to drop bombs. From his experience in the 45th Artillery Regiment in the Red River delta and, later, at Dien Bien Phu, he had learned a simple and bitter lesson: airplanes attacked things they could see, and guns were their favorite targets. So when members of the Home Defense Bureau came to Nghe An Province, Hung masterfully convinced them that the best firing positions for the antiaircraft guns were to be found far from his hamlet. He considered the other village chiefs naive and stupid for arguing to get the biggest guns around their villages, thinking this would protect them. What fools, he thought. There is no protection from a screaming airplane. Bombs and fire rain from the sky, and no gun on the ground can stop them.

Of course, by mid-1967 the few village chiefs who had survived the almost daily air attacks knew what Hung had known all along. While they were trying to get the cursed guns moved from their hamlets, Hung had already established Van Xa as a billet and training site for the constant stream of porter platoons staging for the march down the Old Man's Trail. Since his villagers were required to cook for the platoons, this meant extra rations for everyone at a time when food was scarce. The North Vietnamese rationing system gave more than three times as much food to a trainee preparing for the march south as it allocated to the regular soldiers. Through careful planning and bargaining, a little innovative bookkeeping, and Hung's close relationship with the military cadres of the platoons, he had managed to keep his secret underground bunker well stocked with whiskey, vodka, beer, rice wine, rare canned goods, and medicine from all over the Communist world.

Since he loved strong drink and disliked drinking alone, Hung had, over the years, gained a reputation as a generous host. Only once had he experienced trouble, when a political cadre with a porter platoon accused him of being a war profiteer, the worst capital charge. But his vast network of allies and informers had given him two days' warning, and he had easily hidden his cache.

When the pompous Political Bureau sons of whores, as he called them, had arrived to arrest him, Hung had met them wearing his Vietminh dress uniform, replete with seventeen decorations for wounds and heroism. Hung was in the midst of delivering a patriotic harangue. The looks on their faces told him that he had won again. How could they arrest a hero of the Vietnamese people, whose "secret cache" turned out to be stocked with bandages, condensed milk, and baby food? Granted, the amount was more than was allowed a hamlet chief—but when an elder from a neighboring village arrived on cue to ask Hung to hide some bandages and baby food so the airplanes wouldn't destroy his precious store, he got off without so much as a pious lecture. When the Political Bureau men left Van Xa that afternoon, drunk and laughing, they didn't realize that their promise to send more porter platoons to his village was not an imposition but rather another means for the old man to manipulate the rationing system for the prosperity of his people.

Hung preferred having young porters around to the antiaircraft gun crews, who always caused problems with the daughters of the village. The boys in the porter platoons flirted shamelessly, but they seldom went any further. That kept the village mothers happy. A village chief's worst nightmare, next to airplanes, was the irate mother of a pregnant girl.

The families lined the path waving red handkerchiefs and clapping as the porter platoon, with Ky proudly in the lead, marched to the tables set up under six coconut trees, heaped with a bountiful feast. The women had been cooking since dawn. Platters of grilled and spiced pork, deep-fried rabbit, broiled chicken, glazed sweet ducks, tender fish, and red sausage; heaping bowls of steaming rice and noodles; plates of lettuce, cilantro, onions, and hot peppers; small bowls of *nuoc mam* fish sauce; and oversize bottles of beer and smaller ones of Vietnamese root beer crowded each table. Each place was set with a rice bowl, tin plate, soup spoon, chopsticks, and a big glass holding a chunk of rare ice. The village women and children smiled and stood off to the side, ready to serve the porters.

Hung, the three hamlet elders, and the ten men remaining in the hamlet sat down at the head table. Brother Ba was given the seat of honor to Hung's right and Duan sat on his left. Hung would have preferred to have Duan on his right. Hung liked Duan because he was a true soldier and had grasped immediately the importance of manipulating ration statements. Hung and Duan wore their military decorations on their black cotton shirts as did the rest of the village men, who had all seen military service. Brother Ba's shirt was conspicuously free of such recognition from the People's Revolution, a fact that escaped no one, including him.

Hung began the banquet with a speech wishing the platoon a trouble-free and swift journey south, a rapid victory, and an equally swift return, even though he knew none of those things would occur. The expensive send-offs for these platoons always conveyed genuine heart and concern from the people, and Hung's words reflected this. The boys were so young, and only a few were ever seen again, so the villagers threw themselves into these banquets. On each table were portions of food that represented a sacrifice for some family. Everyone would have a good time.

The people filled their glasses and gave a rousing toast to *Bac Ho* before draining them. The boys ate hungrily; Hung and Duan began to drink thirstily. Ba declined a second glass of beer and ate little, in silence. Then the village mandolin player came out and performed folk songs to applause and laughter.

Hung's favorite wife (he had six) appeared as if on cue and placed a bottle of Thai whiskey before her husband. She shyly poured Brother Ba a small glass and helped raise it to his lips, then poured it into his mouth, laughing pleasantly through betel nut–stained teeth. By coaxing Ba to drink the illegal whiskey, they prevented him from turning them in. It turned out that although beer upset his stomach, Ba was very fond of whiskey. Soon he was as drunk as Hung and Duan. Ba turned out to be much more likeable drunk than sober, even if he was a little silly.

The ringing of the water buffalo bells off in the distance was their first warning. As the primitive air-raid signal grew more insistent, the hum of huge jet engines rose to drown it out. Planes were approaching from the east. Conversation stopped and everyone gazed skyward. Each face betrayed fear. Hung stood up and squinted toward the low-flying aircraft, which were coming fast. He studied them, then smiled and raised his glass of whiskey, shouting, "To hell with the shit-eating Americans," and drank it down. "Don't worry," he added. "They will not bother us. They are after the missiles at Phan Thon."

But the noise grew deafening as the jets flew straight for the village. Hung laughed and yelled, "See the bombs! Carrot-shaped fuses with wings. They always drop those on missile sites." To everyone's astonishment the planes passed right over the village with a roar that made the children cry and hold their ears. Then the planes banked sharply to attack the missile site north of the hamlet, just as Hung had predicted. He casually refilled his glass and resumed his conversation with Duan.

"How long has it been since they bombed your village?" Duan asked nervously. Airplanes scared him. They were among the few things he had encountered that were more powerful than his rifle, a fact that disturbed him deeply.

"A year ago they hit a convoy of trucks out there on the road," Hung said, pointing across the rice paddy to the elevated roadbed of Route 8 that the platoon would follow south in the morning. "I told them to move before sunrise, but the stupid political officer held up the convoy commander for some propaganda pictures. We only lost one woman when several bombs fell on those houses over there." He waved his hand toward them. "Stupid bastards lost all ten trucks and twenty-five men. I wonder how we can win this war, with such idiots for political officers," he said, loud enough for Ba to hear. Ba sipped his whiskey and pretended not to notice the insult.

The mandolin played on and several boys, enlivened by the beer, began dancing. Soon they were joined by several village girls.

The main event now unfolded as the Revolutionary Dance Troupe performed songs and folk ballads. Then they enacted a dance drama in which a young man, his face painted white and with an exaggerated long nose, attempted to persuade one of the women to desert the Revolution with enticements of luxuries, while the rest of the dancers touted the virtues of the party's struggle for freedom. In the finale, the white-faced one attempted to rape the girl and was killed by her brothers and sisters. The show concluded to exuberant applause.

Finally, a procession of women and girls carried out plates of small sweet cakes, a cordial sign that the party was over. Then the tables were cleared and the villagers said farewell to the boys, who reluctantly headed off to bed under Ba's drunken glare.

Hung and Duan were engrossed in telling war stories and singing old Vietminh marching songs. Hung's usually watchful eye missed his pretty daughter slip off from the village with Ky, who would find with her pleasure much more fulfilling than his frequent masturbation habit. Vietnamese fathers couldn't let their guards down, even for an evening. There was a war going on, and people did things they would not do in normal times—and times had not been normal in Vietnam for well over a hundred years.

The night passed punctuated by the distant sound of American airplanes over the North Vietnamese panhandle and sporadic small-arms fire from villages and hamlets, as hundreds of people fired rifles, shot-guns, and ancient muzzle-loading muskets at the aircraft noises passing overhead in the night. Seldom was an airplane hit, which was not the real purpose of the random fire. It served mostly to make the people feel they were fighting back and to remind the pilots—as if they need-ed reminding—that this land was a hostile place.

The next morning Duan awoke promptly at 4:30 and reeled out-side his billet to vomit. Damn that Thai whiskey! I knew better, he thought. It did it to him every time, which, in his line of work, was in-frequently. Duan had been hung over before, and he knew it would take until the next morning for him to feel normal again. He swallowed two strong Russian aspirin, cleverly hoarded for just such a moment, and drained his canteen, which made him dizzy. He still felt horrible. Nev-er again, he vowed, thought for a moment and then laughed to himself. Nights like that were rare events for a *bo doi*. Of course he'd do it again. Great guy, Hung. He would have to give the old bandit something to get out of debt to him, though. He reached into his pack and fished to the bottom where he had hidden a prized American survival knife. He had taken it off a dead door-gunner on a downed Vietnamese helicopter. He moved silently to Hung's hammock where he was snoring loudly and slipped it into a fold of the blanket, next to his hip. "That evens the score with you, old man," he said softly. No Vietnamese could afford to stay in debt to another for very long, since the debtor was required by custom to return a favor whenever asked. Duan figured he had better settle with Hung. Hung was North Vietnamese, which meant he bore closer watching than the southern village chiefs with whom Duan was used to dealing. The northerners were always very clever. Duan knew, because he was one of them.

He neatly folded his gear and made up his pack, an old and much-mended French rucksack, and ordered the boy on watch to wake the platoon. A dozen women were busy preparing *pho*, the Vietnamese ver-sion of the traditional oriental noodle soup, and rice balls for the day's ration. Duan went through two black-out curtains into the village cook house and was received jovially. His hangover showed on his face, so they gave him a steaming bowl of soup and some motherly advice. He ate slowly and watched the cooks skillfully form the sticky hot rice into balls the size of a grapefruit and wrap them in parachute fabric or cotton cloth, to be eaten cold later that day.

Outside in the dark, the porter platoon quickly went through its morning routine. Each boy had a small canvas pack containing a hammock, mosquito netting, a vinyl poncho, a blanket, an extra uniform of black pajamas, a small towel, and a Chinese toothbrush, toothpaste, and comb. On a rope slung over one shoulder, each carried a two-quart canteen. They wore loose-fitting black cotton uniforms, sandals made from the rubber of old automobile tires, and floppy green bush hats. Only Duan and Ba carried weapons. The boys, disciplined by the last six weeks of training, filed into the cook house and were each given a bowl of soup, two warm rice balls, and two cans of pasty prepared meat made in China, their protein allotment for two days. All this went into their packs along with leftovers from the banquet.

The women smiled and teased them, invoking folk prayers for their journey and providing admonishment, just as they hoped some woman would do for their own sons someday. Although new platoons passed through their village nearly every six weeks, the Van Xa women never resented the inconvenience. The villagers had come to regard the porter platoons as good omens. *Di may man*—good luck—or "josh," was important, and the porters were a part of that mysterious spiritual equation that everyone believed in but no one understood. There were no Communist slogans spoken, there was no encouragement to be brave for the Revolution or to kill the despised Americans. The Van Xa women saw this as a purely human event.

Young Brother Ky tarried in the line, confidently and affectionately holding Hung's daughter's hand on top of the narrow counter. She gave him a bigger package of leftovers than most of the boys got and a letter containing a poem she had composed. For good luck, she told him not to read it until the following morning. Her mother noted the event with mixed emotions. Her daughter was young, but then she herself had been only fourteen when she had first lain with Hung. And Ky

was a handsome and smart boy. Everyone had heard how he had best-
ed Ba the day before. Still, the likelihood of Ky's ever returning was remote, and she hoped she would not have to deal with another baby in
the house in these uncertain times. But whatever had occurred could
not be changed now. Although open affection between unbetrothed
men and women was taboo, out of respect and friendship for the village chief's number-four wife, the other women pretended not to notice the scene.

Suddenly Duan's order came for the porters to fall in at the designated assembly area, which sent the boys scurrying. Duan graciously
thanked the women for their exceptional hospitality and fine cooking.

In the village banquet area the boys lined up in two ranks of thirty
and stood at attention. Between the front and rear ranks sat the despised training loads they had been carrying every day for the past
forty-five days. Each load was a sturdy, rectangular wooden box, four
feet long, two and a half feet deep and wide. Two strands of one-inch
manila rope crossed under each box and passed through four strong
metal grommets on each corner, and a three-inch-thick, eight-foot-
long bamboo pole lay on top. The boxes contained rocks and sand,
weighing precisely 150 pounds.

The training program they had undergone with these unyielding
loads had been simple and effective. Six weeks ago they had struggled
just to lift each end of the carrying poles off the ground. For a week they
had stood in the dark to avoid the ever-present airplanes, lifting the
loads onto their shoulders and moving off for half-mile treks on the
side roads and rice paddy dikes surrounding Van Xa. Each team of two
boys used the traditional oriental short choppy step that, when done
properly, caused the bamboo pole to bend and straighten repeatedly
under the shifting pressure of the weight. This centuries-old technique
allowed the body to bear the total load only half of the time. Each time
the pole straightened, the inertia created by the porters' synchronized
bouncing steps carried almost the entire weight for a full step. On the
second step the weight came down on the bearers' shoulders, then recoiled again with the naturally straightening pole. Since the average

weight of the porters was only about 140 pounds, if they mastered this technique they could carry a load somewhat over 50 percent of their combined body weight for eight to ten hours a day.

At first the short treks were designed to force the porters to work together. Those who couldn't get their strides coordinated were punished mercilessly by the awkward and heavy burdens. Gradually the training marches were extended and were always run at night. Terrain was carefully selected for its similarity to that of the Old Man's Trail. They carried their loads on rice paddy dikes, narrow jungle trails, and in the small hills dotting the area, even though Duan knew there was nothing around Vinh, or for that matter in the rest of the world, as tough as the road that lay ahead.

The boys had successfully carried their training loads for six straight days for a distance of fifteen miles in a little over eight hours, with only a few stragglers. These Duan handled brutally but effectively; sometimes he did not arrive back at the village until after sunrise, pushing the recalcitrant boys who were always near physical collapse. Generally, only a few additional training sessions with Duan were required to persuade them to keep pace. Their black eyes and bruises gave grim testimony that you did not disappoint the sergeant major. Only a boy's best was acceptable, and the alternative was dramatically more painful than the burden of the training loads.

Not everyone who had arrived at Van Xa six weeks earlier stood there this morning. The original platoon had consisted of seventy-five boys. Fifteen had been weeded out for various reasons. A lack of proper motivation was not included among the rules governing discharge. There had been broken legs, crushed feet, dislocated shoulders, and several cases of disqualifying illnesses, including tuberculosis and rickets. One boy had died on a training march from heart failure induced by extreme physical exertion and sickle-cell anemia. The ones remaining were tough young men who, through rigorous training, had proved to be in good health. According to the North Vietnamese system of induction, unforgiving training was the best way to discover physical infirmities.

Ba now made his first appearance of the morning. He looked ill, and the boys were thankful he did not launch into one of his political speeches. He took his place beside Duan, who stood easily in front of the formation in spite of the heavy pack on his back. Duan's AK-47 glistened in the early light. "Pick up your loads," he ordered. "Ky and Trang, take the lead. Follow me." They strode off at a slow, even pace and began to move east toward the raised roadbed of Route 8, a mile away.

Two battered civilian buses pulled up to the crossroads just as the platoon arrived. Duan and Ba walked over to the first one and exchanged salutes and handshakes with two men who were waiting. The porter platoon watched carefully. They knew only that they were headed for the Old Man's Trail. The rest of their schedule had been left deliberately vague for security reasons. After five minutes of conversation, the two men yelled for everyone to disembark and fall into formation opposite the porter platoon.

In the early morning light, young boys dressed as porters stepped down from the buses in confusion and wandered to the other side of the road while being harangued by the two men. Ky and Trang squatted on their haunches, smiling derisively at the dazed expressions of the other group.

Then Duan shouted, "On the buses and leave your loads where they are. Now! How are your spirits today?" Obediently the boys shouted, "*Tien-len,*" or "Forward," and leapt aboard. They left their training loads where they lay by the side of the road. As they drove south down Route 8, the boys watched the new Van Xa porter platoon struggling to get the training loads off the ground under loud threats and shouting by their handlers.

The single act of leaving the loads behind constituted an even more significant rite of passage than last night's banquet. This was their true graduation ceremony, their parade. Their reward, likewise, lay within themselves. They had become much tougher, but they were still boys and yearned for home. Still, on this morning they were less homesick than they had been six weeks before. There was pride in their new physical strength and they had a sense of belonging, both to their platoon and to their load mates. Most important, while they recognized the uncertainty and the unknown hardships that lay ahead, they had an unshakable confidence in Sergeant Major Duan. To them he was ten feet tall, even as he snored, in hung-over sleep, on the front seat of the bus.

# TWO

# The Old Man's Trail

## ROUTE 8, SOUTH OF VINH, NORTH VIETNAM

The sky was clear and bright, promising a hot day ahead. The boys were in a holiday mood, talking and pointing excitedly at everything they saw. A bus ride was a rare event for them and that in itself made for the excitement.

Route 8 was a two-lane main artery that branched off Route 1 near Vinh. At one time it had been completely paved with asphalt, for which the Communists took credit; the fact that the French had originally laid the road years earlier got lost in the rhetoric. Now, however, the hard surface stretched for no more than half a mile, with countless dirt and gravel bypasses that were erected by thousands of men, women, and children drawn from villages and towns along the way and employed by the National Militia as road-repair crews. The roadside was littered with piles of rock, dirt, sand, and gravel, which handily provided the material for their extensive work. Between the piles of surfacing material were small stacks of military equipment and supplies. Three boxes of small-arms ammunition here, crates of gun barrels there, boxes of grenades in yet another pile farther down the road. To the unpracticed eye these appeared to be caches of abandoned equipment. In fact, they represented the North Vietnamese supply storage system, which was based on dispersion to deprive the airplanes of a single, lucrative target.

Route 8 was targeted for air strikes almost daily, and it showed the devastating effects of road-cut bombing. Despite these obstacles and detours, the buses made good time. Only bicycles, motorcycles, cars, and buses used the road by day, easily negotiating the crude repair work. Heavily loaded military trucks came out at night, testing the limits of these makeshift bypasses.

The roofs of the buses were painted with red crosses on white backgrounds. Duan had told the platoon that there was no danger of being bombed today, and he proved his lack of concern by snoring loudly from his seat at the front of the bus. American planes did not attack buses and other apparently civilian traffic, and from their position on the ground, the porters could see many "civilian" buses and small vehicles moving military gear and troops along the road.

They encountered their first obstacle where Route 8 crossed the La Giang River. Once a bridge had spanned the river. Now only a rusted skeleton of the structure protruded from the water. An inadequate pontoon ferry provided a slow crossing, while a growing line of vehicles patiently awaited their turn. Road crews were busy digging two trucks out of the roadside ditch, where they had been forced by attacking jets several nights before. The salvageable cargo had been off-loaded immediately and was long since headed to South Vietnam. Both vehicles had been badly burned; it was hard to imagine that within a month both would be repaired and back at work for the Revolution. The road crews chanted their motto: "The enemy destroys, we repair." A hundred yards to the east and west of the ferry landing, on the north and south banks, were antiaircraft gun batteries. This morning they were fully manned, the muzzles of their guns searching the sky for targets.

After an hour's wait the porters, who had not been allowed off the bus lest they sneak off for home, were again startled by the faint sound of clanging water-buffalo bells and sirens far to the east. Watchtowers along the coast had spotted in-bound aircraft. Panic gripped the crowd waiting to be ferried across the river, and they scurried into the two dozen small bomb shelters dug into the old bridge culvert and along the roadside ditches. Duan shouted to the boys on both buses, "Stay where you are. Get under your seats." His apparent calm masked the surge of fear he felt as the growl of the engines grew louder. His strict orders were to keep the platoon on the bus in the event of an air attack. This contradicted his instinct and everything he had learned from fighting in the South, which screamed to him to get down flat on the ground.

The four American planes bore in low, following the river. Their big engines gradually swelled into an overpowering roar. Fire from anti-aircraft batteries farther east along the river could be heard. Antiaircraft guns at the ferry site began to fire only when they saw the planes clear a tree line a half mile away; by then it was too late. The planes darted straight for each of the four gun emplacements, two on either side of the river. The gun batteries got off only a few rounds before the planes released their bombs almost simultaneously. A deafening roar sounded and three emplacements erupted in balls of fire. The planes streaked west and pulled up, climbing for altitude, their shrieking afterburners glowing bright orange. The remaining antiaircraft battery fired at them defiantly. Moments later, to the west, huge plumes of dust and streaks of white smoke could be seen as half a dozen missiles launched skyward after the aircraft.

People began to emerge from the ditches and shelters, talking excitedly with the exhilaration that accompanies facing death and surviving. There were no casualties in the vicinity of the ferry, but bells rang frantically as an ambulance made its way over a bumpy path toward one of the gun battery positions. Smoke billowed from the three positions that had been hit and their gun barrels drooped, indicating they had taken severe damage. No troops moved around the gun positions. There was only devastation.

Duan checked the boys on his bus and called for a report from the other vehicle. It was slow in coming. The bus was sitting lopsided with a blown tire. At last Ba yelled for Duan to come quickly. One boy was dead and another had a serious head wound. In violation of their orders, they had been watching the attack from their window when several large bomb fragments hit them. Duan quickly dragged the wounded boy off into the shade of the bus. Feverishly he tried to stop the bleeding and calm the boy's thrashing. As two soldiers with a stretcher arrived the boy grabbed Duan in a death grip, gasped, and stopped breathing. They could not revive him.

Duan stood up slowly and spoke quietly to Ba. "Your job is to ensure that your men do as they are ordered. You did not do your duty because you were scared shitless on the floor of the bus, like an old blind woman. Don't ever let this happen again. Do you understand me?" He glared.

"Brother Duan," Ba blurted in protest.

"Don't call me Brother," Duan snapped. "It's Sergeant Major. I'm a soldier, not some damn witless political idiot like you, who drones meaningless slogans. To survive what's ahead you need to acquire some soldierly virtues. You'll soon learn the true meaning of sacrifice for the Revolution. It requires much more than words." He turned on his heel and Ba flinched, thinking Duan was going to hit him.

In a louder voice, Duan said, "Young Brother Ky and Trang, over here. Assist Brother Ba in gathering the personal effects of these two dead soldiers and preparing the bodies for transportation to their homes."

Death was a common experience in the small farming and fishing villages where the boys had grown up. Each had seen bodies prepared for burial, but they had never done it themselves. They gritted their teeth and began to clean out the pockets of the two dead boys, dropping the meager possessions into the cotton toothbrush bags taken from their packs. They placed the bags on the boys' chests and folded their hands around the bags. They straightened out the feet and legs, so that when rigor mortis set in after forty-five minutes or so, they would freeze in this peaceful pose instead of the contorted positions in which they had died. But the bodies still looked grotesque, with their awful head wounds and the plastic-looking gray pallor of their skin.

Ba sluggishly filled out the standard body identification chit that would be attached to the remains. The chit gave the name, hometown, and family information, along with the cause of death, which was always listed as, "In action against the Americans," which this time happened to be true. The certificate was left undated. The bodies and their chits would go to the boys' provinces and village chiefs. They would decide when and if to inform the parents. Sometimes a family wouldn't be notified for years, depending on the current level of morale and degree of popular support for the war effort. The bodies were carefully wrapped in the boys' ponchos. The remaining contents of their packs were distributed among the platoon.

Duan returned from talking to the ferry officer and called the platoon to gather near the bodies. He said a short Buddhist prayer. Ba stood by looking dazed. Duan paused, scanned the faces of the porters, and then broke into a screaming tirade.

"When I say get down, you get down," he shrieked. He grabbed a boy and threw him down in the dirt next to the bodies.

"Now, when I say down, I mean all the way down." He pushed the boy's face into the dirt with his foot.

"Now, down!" he roared. Most of the boys looked at him blankly. They were still in shock. But when Duan waded into them with his fists, they dropped flat to the road.

He shouted, "Down!" and they responded with, "Down!" Over and over. Anyone who was not lying as flat on the ground as possible was assisted by a foot on the neck, back, or legs. When Duan finally shouted, "Back on the buses!" it was a melee of struggling boys trying to evade Duan's swinging fists. When they were on the bus he screamed, "Down!" again, and this time the faces disappeared in a split second behind the rows of seats.

A crew from the ferry platoon fixed the flat tire, and the buses were motioned forward by the guards, who told them to pull around the other traffic. They were the first to board the ferry when it reached the north bank. Duan's style, more than his rank, commanded most people's attention.

An hour later the buses were bouncing down Route 8 south of the La Giang River. They appeared empty as the porters made themselves as comfortable as possible on the filthy, rusted metal floor. Duan slept soundly in the front seat of the lead bus, but his dreams were disturbing. In one he was naked, running as fast as he could over terrible open ground, trying to reach the thick green lushness of the jungle. Finally he crashed into the rain forest and dove behind a huge banyan tree just as an airplane dropped its bombs barely out of range. Thanks be to the Immortals for the jungle and something substantial like a tree to hide behind, he thought. Then he awoke with a start and automatically shouted, "Down!" to the miserable boys on the floor.

By late afternoon the buses were headed west on Route 8, entering rough, uphill terrain, toward their nighttime stop. They were now the only traffic on the deserted highway.

The buses pulled off the main road and drove several miles to the small fortified and camouflaged village of Da Mong. Their journey had taken them thirty-five miles that day. The military commander, a wounded but cheerful NVA veteran officer with one leg, moving slowly on a crutch, led them to the entrance of an underground bunker where they would sleep. Duan hurried them into the tunnel and followed them in, ignoring Ba, who still seemed to be in shock. After crawling twenty feet they came to a large bunker chamber reinforced with coconut logs. Duan lit the wick of a small oil lamp and ordered everyone to squat facing him with their packs in front of them.

He talked softly now, in a fatherly tone, explaining the events of the day, talking about the danger of airplanes, the need for teamwork, the rough terrain ahead, and his firm belief that they would win the war eventually, even though sometimes he had his doubts, which he kept to himself. He quietly asked Lieutenant Ba to add anything he thought appropriate. For the first time, Ba spoke like a man and not a political recording. He confessed his shortcomings in not supervising his bus better and blamed himself for the deaths of the two boys. He looked and spoke humbly; no one could remember seeing him show such human traits before.

Duan thanked him and shouted, "Down!" The response was instant. Duan smiled and thought, That should be the last damn time I lose a man for not obeying orders.

"Now it's time to get acquainted with your new loads—the ones you will carry south to our brothers and sisters fighting the Americans," he said.

The village military commander limped into the faint light and said, "We have your loads all bundled and ready to move in the morning. Under the operational control and protection of Transportation Group 559, you will be transporting a complete battery of six type-53 82-mm mortars, plus 165 rounds of ammunition. Each load is in the two-man carrying pole arrangement that you have become familiar with over the past six weeks. There are six loads consisting of one complete mortar each, in five pieces." He pulled out his manifest and began to read. "Tube, inner and outer base plate rings, bipod, and sight. Weight, 120 pounds. There are fifteen loads of eleven 82-mm rounds for a total weight of 120 pounds." He smiled cheerfully. "The lieutenant and sergeant major will inspect the loads and sign for them."

Duan took the manifest and led the platoon through another tunnel into a similar but larger log-reinforced chamber. The flickering light revealed twenty-one neatly wrapped loads in heavy oilcloth, bound tightly with manila rope, which looped over a bamboo pole. After the attack that morning the platoon was down to fifty-eight effective porters, which left eight two-man teams with no load. The loads would be rotated when they passed through the difficult areas of the trail. But there was another reason for the extra porters. The platoon would experience a minimum of 20 to 30 percent casualties on their journey, and the extra porter teams would ensure the mortars and ammunition would make it to their destination. Each team of two boys was told to unwrap the loads carefully. Duan and Ba moved from load to load, inventorying contents. They were numbered from one to twenty-one with a stencil on the bamboo pole.

Ky and Trang knelt by their load, a brand-new mortar. All five pieces gleamed with fresh blueing and oil. Everything was in order. The serial number was checked against the manifest and the load was ready to reassemble. Two flat boards lay inside the oilcloth. On top were the inner and outer rings of the base plate. A piece of oilcloth lay on top and the mortar tube came next. Then another layer of oilcloth, and on top of that the bipod, with the small sight box nestled between its closed legs. Each layer of oilcloth was folded over neatly until finally the outer cloth was wrapped around with its corners tucked in. The ropes were then looped around the oilcloth package and tied off tightly in a no-slip knot. The ends of the rope were tied and looped over the bamboo pole at two places, about three and a half feet apart. Ky and Trang smiled broadly as they lifted their load for the first time. It was thirty pounds lighter than their training loads and felt light as a feather.

Promptly at 4:30 A.M. the platoon was awakened and quickly assembled their gear. In groups of four they shared two cold rice balls and one can of the meat paste. By 5:15 the loads had all been maneuvered through the narrow tunnels to the village square, where the boys performed their morning clean-up. Duan inspected them using a small oil lamp. They filled their canteens with boiled tea and boarded the two buses, arranging their new loads carefully along the center aisle.

The boys watched Duan alertly, anticipating his command to get down, as the buses, headlights off, bumped down the dirt road toward Route 8. They crawled slowly onto the hard surface of the highway as the sky lightened to a gray dawn. The drivers eased their buses into low gear and began the slow 4,000-foot ascent to Nape Pass, which would lead them into Laos and the beginning of their great journey south.

The day was overcast, which suited Duan better than the bright sunshine of the previous day. His hangover was gone, which also helped his attitude. After years of soldiering for the Revolution he had developed a markedly different point of view from most people. His spirits rose on dark, rainy days and sank when the sun was bright. On a clear day he was always looking up over his shoulder, listening for sounds of airplane engines or rotor blades. Low clouds, rain, and fog all had become his closest allies. He believed the Immortals of the spirit world sent these natural things to confound the Americans and their damned airplanes and spying machines. He had learned to treasure the bone-chilling cold he felt on rainy nights as proof that he was still alive. He clung to feelings of discomfort, even pain, and judged them to be vastly superior to the nothingness of death and therefore something to enjoy. He was a survivor and had proven it in countless battles. Now he must make these boys survivors, if he could.

He glanced at his charges, who sat soberly looking out the windows at the devastation repeated bombings had brought to the once-beautiful mountain forest stretching on either side of the steeply climbing road. Most of them had never been at a higher altitude than a lowland rice paddy, and none had seen such extensive bomb damage. The area was saturated with craters, evidence of the Americans' frenzied efforts to interdict the Old Man's Trail. Duan glanced to the back of the bus, flashed his infectious smile at Ky and Trang, and said in a conversational tone, "Down!"

Half the boys were out of sight and on the floor before he came out of his seat and moved with catlike grace down the aisle, slapping and punching the slow and recalcitrant boys. He noted with pleasure that even they took only several seconds to disappear under the seats. Six of them had been particularly slow, and he remembered that they had been sluggish at everything since they started training six weeks ago. They would continue to need his special attention, even though he knew it probably wouldn't save them.

Some boys were just slow to learn and slow to react. They usually paid for it. But Duan would try. That was his job, and besides, the way they had been loaded out didn't give much margin for losses. With eight spare porter teams, he figured that he and Ba wouldn't have to start carrying a load until they reached a point just south of the Srepok River in Cambodia. If Ba survived the trek.

But Ba's whole attitude had changed significantly in the past twenty-four hours. Duan had seen it happen before to political cadres. The realities of war dissolved the political rhetoric. Fear, survival, and rooting out the foreigners were the real motivators. Not political abstractions. He looked back at Ba's bus and noted with a smile that no heads were visible; Ba had followed his lead and was running a drill for his boys.

After two hours of tedious movement the road leveled somewhat, and the drivers were able to pick up a little speed as they approached the Nape Pass, one of three major gateways to the Old Man's Trail. As they approached the crest of the mountain, they passed into the clouds and began the downhill run to the big depot area at Nape, Laos. The bases at the beginning and the end of the trail, depending on the direction of travel, were terminal facilities, and they teemed with activity.

Their buses were directed off the road and passed under the forest canopy into an immense city that never saw sunlight. Among the many buildings made of bamboo, thatch, and corrugated tin were marked paths, half-mile-long sections of hard-surface roads and open storage areas with vehicles of every description. On one section of paved road, under an elaborate overhead camouflage net, were fifteen brand-new Soviet trucks towing as many immense and gleaming 130-mm guns. Neatly lined up beside the guns were twelve trucks with SA-2 antiaircraft missile trailers, each with a camouflaged missile perched in its cradle. Ten PT-76 tanks sat nearby with their engines idling.

The base teemed with people moving briskly about their tasks. Troop formations numbering between sixty and a hundred soldiers dressed in the standard black pajama uniform, bush hat, and rucksack, marched out the southern end of the base. Through bitter experience, the NVA had learned the dangers of putting too many people and too much equipment in one place. Staging areas were nothing more than targets to the Americans, and targets were made to be destroyed. The Nape base existed only to control the flow of men and materiel on their way south, and each increment that passed through was formed up and dispatched in a matter of hours. No one was allowed to tarry long.

The buses that had brought the porter platoon were already being loaded with seriously wounded evacuated from the south. Now they were headed for hospitals near Hanoi and Haiphong. Duan looked on soberly, remembering his similar passage north more than a year before.

It was 10:00 A.M. The commander of Transportation Group 559 (TG559), which controlled the whole trail apparatus, had just issued orders that all troop units, supply, and vehicle increments would make a rare daylight transit to the next way station on their route. Hanoi had radioed that weather was foul over the coast and the Vietnamese pan-handle. The Pathet Lao headquarters near Lak Sao, Laos, had provided a similar report for eastern Thailand and most of western Laos. At the headquarters of TG559 in Tchepone, Laos, there was jubilation. It appeared that the monsoon had set in several weeks early, which meant six weeks to two months of minimum interference from U.S. and Royal Laotian government air strikes. The fact that much of the trail would turn into a quagmire of mud and rain-swollen, rushing rivers and streams posed much less of a problem for the TG559 staff than for the people struggling on the trail. The terrain and weather were viewed by the staff as everyday hardships, easily overcome with extra effort and a little more time. The Revolution expected no less from its soldiers. Of course, the fact that the high-level staff themselves were dry, comfortable, and well-fed added to their zeal and enthusiasm for the onset of bad weather.

The porters were hurried off the buses and led several hundred yards to a hut on stilts with a hand-painted sign that read Porter Supply Increment Route Office. Like most administrative offices in North Vietnam, TG559 was staffed predominantly by wounded veterans and women. The major in charge looked sickly but was cordial in deference to Duan, whom he recognized as a veteran. But he made it clear that his orders were to get everything moving south as soon as possible. He ignored Ba, who appeared dazed and awed by the level and intensity of the activity in the base.

"You will pick up your guide in front of the hut, Sergeant Major," the major said. "She will take you and your platoon to your first overnight station. Your platoon increment number is 1008, and here is your route card. You know the procedure." He handed Duan a clear plastic bag containing a card with alphanumeric codes neatly typed down the left-hand column. Duan counted the codes quickly, noting that there were sixty-five, which meant he had sixty-five days to arrive at the platoon's last station in Tay Ninh Forest, 650 miles south. Other columns on the card were for the dates of arrival and departure from the stations indicated, the cargo inventory, and the number of porters assigned. Duan thought the schedule was tight, but he was relieved to see that they didn't expect a speed run, probably in view of the onset of the monsoon. He figured they would have to travel around ten miles per day. He had hoped for something in this category, and accordingly had trained the boys to walk distances of around fifteen miles.

The major looked at Duan, his face briefly betraying his sympathy in view of what he knew would be a terrible journey. The ones in monsoon season always were. Monsoon increments suffered almost twice as many casualties as dry-season increments. Duan understood the look. His first trip down the Old Man's Trail had been the worst experience of his life. He had blocked it out for a long time, but now it would not leave his mind. He was worried about what lay ahead but did not allow his face to betray his feelings.

For the first time the major addressed Ba. "Lieutenant!"

Ba's head jerked toward the major, his face still betraying his confusion. "Yes sir," he responded in an almost-even voice.

"Listen to your orders," snapped the major. He began to read from a typed sheet of paper. "Your porter-platoon increment, number 1008, consisting of fifty-eight porters, six complete 82-mm mortars, and 165 rounds of ammunition, is hereby assigned to the operational control of TG559. You will proceed as directed by competent authority of TG559 subordinate commanders and guides and deliver your cargo to the Ninth Vietcong Division. You have sixty-five days to accomplish this order. Upon arrival all members of Increment 1008 will be inducted into that division as replacements. In transit you are subject to all orders issued to you by TG559."

The major handed Duan the order and a U.S. government-issue ballpoint pen. Duan said to Ba, "Sir, it's all in order. I am signing it. We've got a long way to go before night and only half the day to get there. We need to get started."

The major gave Duan the original and kept a single copy. Duan folded his neatly and put it in the plastic bag with the route card. The major shook his hand and confided, "Watch the south side of the Truong Son Mountains. Very bad in the monsoon."

Duan smiled. "Yes sir. I've been there twice, both times in the monsoon." His eyes betrayed no fear, even though he was scared.

Ba managed a brave smile as he shook the major's hand. "Power to our brothers and sisters in the South. May each of your mortars account for a thousand American imperialists," the major intoned like a prayer.

Ba nodded and said firmly, "Yes, sir."

Outside, under the supervision of Ky and Trang, the boys were finishing the last of the rice balls and cans of meat paste they had been given at Van Xa. They watched excitedly as the vehicle convoys lumbered out of the base. Duan quietly issued orders, which sent the platoon scurrying. They rinsed the parachute and cotton wrappers that had held the rice balls, using water from a barrel by the hut, and hung them from their packs to dry. They collected the meat tins and put them in a bucket marked Metal in front of the transit office. Later the tins would be melted down and made into something useful for the Revolution. Finally the boys waited by their loads.

The trail guide watched these preparations in silence. She wore a straw cone hat and black pajamas like everyone else and carried an AK-47 with two thirty-round magazines taped together, one inserted in the receiver. She said quietly to Ba, with no deference to his rank, "We go now." It was an order. She turned and strode off at a quick pace. Most of the boys would notice today that she had a very nice walk.

The platoon filed off in two parallel columns, easily handling their loads. Duan brought up the rear. For a mile or so they passed through the hidden base. People were moving about their jobs, working on the overhead camouflage, loading cargo boxes on trucks, laboriously fueling vehicles using hand-crank pumps fitted to fifty-five-gallon drums of fuel that were staged in clusters of two to three hundred. The people waved to the platoon and some yelled encouragement. Everyone saw they were young and hoped they made it through what faced them. As they passed from under the jungle canopy into the open, they picked up a wide footpath that paralleled Route 8. As the last of the vehicle convoys pulled away, hundreds of women, children, and old men pulled huge camouflage mats over the roadbed to cover the vehicle tracks.

The sky was low and the clouds were moving fast to the east. It hadn't started raining yet, and they made good time on the flat, even ground. The temperature was cool. Boys with no assigned loads rotated in at thirty-minute intervals. The guide called a ten-minute break at each rest stop, all of which were meticulously marked and located off the trail well under the jungle canopy. Each rest place took about an hour and a half to reach and was spaced at a distance of about two miles from the last one.

After they had passed three stations, they entered what resembled a wasteland. Bomb craters, some still smoldering, pockmarked the jungle and roadbed. They passed through an abandoned base that had been repeatedly hit with air strikes. It was similar in size to the one they had just left, and Duan recognized it as the base he had passed through on a stretcher the year before. Bombed-out huts sat askew on broken stilts; blackened, scorched ground marked where there had been intense fires, and charred trees littered the path. A work crew was busily arranging overhead camouflage panels made from bamboo and natural foliage. Two PT76 tanks and three old trucks drove in various patterns under the camouflage leaving deep track and tire prints, after which they drove for distances of a mile east and west along Route 8. A battery of 37-mm antiaircraft guns and a dozen 12.7-mm antiaircraft machine guns were being emplaced in hidden positions high up along the sides of the valley.

For several months TG559 had deceived the Americans as to the Nape base's actual location. Through a complex plan involving dummy radio traffic and high levels of vehicle activity timed to coincide with overhead passes of American reconnaissance satellites and aircraft, TG559 had drawn attention away from the Nape logistics base and tricked the American pilots into dropping hundreds of tons of bombs on this abandoned site. The last strike had occurred only the day before. Now the plan called for older, less serviceable vehicles to simulate a high level of activity while antiaircraft guns were emplaced to shoot down the airplanes that would surely come in response to this bait at the first break in the weather. The monsoon would enable the three crucial vehicle convoys to put distance between themselves and Nape. Should the weather break unexpectedly, the decoy base activity would draw the Americans' fire away from the convoys.

The guide increased her pace to keep the unit moving through this area. Had there been another route available, she would have used it. No one was allowed knowledge they didn't need. The porters saw the feverish activity but did not recognize its significance. Duan, however, understood. Clever, he thought to himself, but as always, hard, dangerous work for a lot of people. He knew through long experience that people were the strength of the Revolution. The mortars and ammunition, the tanks, artillery, and missiles that they had seen this morning would help, but ultimately, in the eventual *khoi nghia,* it was people who would make the difference. The Revolution had always been richer in people than in equipment.

The trail stayed flat and slightly downhill, so they picked up speed through the gloomy jungle, which teemed with life. Through breaks in the canopy they could glimpse mountains towering above the mist, and clouds on either side of the winding valley. Their path crossed several streams, which were only knee-deep in water. The guide moved at a steady pace, knowing the route well. She led them along side paths that provided a smoother, flatter ground than other routes that represented a shorter distance but would pose difficulties for the boys with their loads. Part of her job was to evaluate the porters on their stamina and on their understanding of the standard arm and hand signals used by all units under TG559 operational control. During a break, after six hours and twelve miles on the trail, she walked over to Duan and smiled for the first time.

"The platoon is in first-class condition. One of the best I have ever seen. Usually they struggle on this first leg. They are well trained on the signals. I will include these things in my report tonight." She whispered, holding his eyes a moment longer than necessary.

Duan looked at her and smiled his slow smile. "Thank you, Sister. Sister what? What is your name?" he whispered. All verbal communications on the Old Man's Trail were whispered.

"I am Su, Sergeant Major Duan," she replied, flattering him that she knew his name and extending her hand. He held her small hand a moment longer than called for. She turned, went over to Ba and gave him the same report, but without the smile. He formally thanked her.

The break over, Su moved to the head of the column and signaled to pick up the loads. Looking down the column she held up two fingers and the sign for "miles to go," followed by the signs for overnight stop and dinner. The boys beamed at her when she signaled food, and she smiled back, some of her sternness gone. They would cover fourteen miles this first day, with no casualties or stragglers.

The last leg departed the flat ground of the valley floor and took a steep path through the light and shadows of the jungle up the side of the western ridge paralleling the trail. After an hour of hard climbing they came to a shelf at the entrance of a vast natural cave. Su led them inside, amid the aromas of rice cooking and two small deer roasting on a spit. She reported to the older man in charge of 601ZA, TG559's number for this way station. Twelve people were assigned to the station, and they all knew precisely what their jobs were. The man in charge shook hands with Duan and Ba and welcomed them in the name of the Revolution, offering them tea and seats at one of the three tables set around the cook fires. Another man led the boys to a section marked off by neatly piled rocks where they lined up their loads, numbers one to twenty-one. Another man led the platoon deeper into the cave, where a series of bamboo poles was driven in the ground and braced against the walls with rope and old strands of communications wire. Each boy strung his hammock and stowed his pack in it. Then they were led to a stone well where, working in teams of two, they stripped to their shorts in the cool air and drew buckets of water, pouring them over each other's shivering bodies. Then they filed through the kitchen and filled their canteens with water boiled with a little tea and went back to their hammocks. There they dried themselves off with the washcloth-size towel issued to them, changed into dry shorts, and put on the clean trousers and shirts from their pack. These rituals completed, they squatted on their haunches and quietly awaited the next event, which they fervently hoped would be dinner.

Three armed men in black uniforms entered the cave thirty minutes after the platoon had arrived. They reported all clear; no one had followed the platoon. Duan was the only one who had noticed them on the climb up the hill. Two women followed them carrying bundles of wood, which they piled by the fires. Two men and a woman stirred the twenty-gallon pots of rice and cabbage, while a young one-armed man tended the roasting spit.

Squatting silently in the shadows were two Hmong tribesmen, with their beautifully crafted and ornately carved bows and arrows leaning against the wall next to them and old American M-1 carbines cradled in their laps. Duan knew the Hmong were equally skilled with either weapon, but he also knew that hunting with rifles was not permitted on the trail network. Now he understood where the fresh deer had come from. Very clever of this way station commander to work out an arrangement with the Hmong for fresh meat, and a nice way to pad a ration statement, thought Duan. He walked over to the tribesmen and impressed everyone by conversing with them in their language.

The man leading the cook team began to work with a flourish, darting from one pot to another, talking in a low sing-song voice, which was the traditional Vietnamese cook's way of indicating that a meal was almost ready. Finally, with great deliberation, confident that all eyes were upon him, he cut a piece from the flank of the deer with an American K-Bar knife. Blowing to cool it, he then popped the morsel in his mouth and began chewing slowly and with relish, eyes raised dramatically heavenward. After a moment he looked sternly at the inquiring faces and with a sudden smile quietly pronounced his creation perfect, to everyone's amusement.

The boys lined up while the cooks filled their tin bowls with rice and cabbage and the chief cook slapped a generous hunk of venison on top. Ba and Duan were served next, followed by the station team. The last person to be served was the commander of the way station. The reverse seniority in the food line was a long-standing NVA and Vietcong tradition. It ensured that the officers and leaders provided enough food for the troops, who did the real work of the Revolution. If there wasn't enough, the leader went hungry, thereby ensuring that the person with enough clout to solve the problem was personally interested in finding a solution.

There was enough food for everyone to pass through the line a second time, and the porters heaped praises on the cook. Bowls were washed and the cook and his crew began making rice balls for the next day's ration, lining them up neatly on a stone shelf next to the fire. Duan and Ba inventoried their loads, which the way station commander verified. He placed his special code in the column next to his station number on the increment route card.

Duan gathered the boys in a semicircle for their daily political indoctrination session. Lieutenant Ba began speaking in a sincere and confident tone, with no trace of his shrill rhetoric. He spoke of the daily bombings of their people, of the cruelty of the murderous Americans, and of the sacrifices the people would have to make to defeat these dangerous and ruthless imperialists. He criticized himself once more for not taking better care of the two boys killed at the river crossing. When he had finished, everyone in the cave stood and clapped. The gesture seemed to clear the air and give Ba a fresh start. Everyone felt better.

Then, with his black eyes flashing in the firelight, Duan began to hypnotize those in the cave with stories of the old Ninth Vietcong Division in the Tay Ninh Forest, Binh Gia, and the Tet Offensive. Su sat outside the circle and never took her eyes off him.

After the indoctrination session, as the platoon readied to bed down, Duan approached Ba's hammock. "Sir, where we're going there will be a lot of losses, deaths, and injuries. Quit worrying about the boys at the ferry," he said softly. "I will need your help down the trail. Things will be hard. You need to step in and help lead. I will help you." He reached out and took Ba's hand and shook it.

By 8:30 P.M. the boys were sound asleep in their hammocks. Half an hour later the station commander posted his guard and the cave became dark. At midnight Duan felt a soft hand slip under his blanket and inside his shorts. At first he thought he was dreaming and then, as he slightly turned his head, he felt the warm, hard nipple of Su's breast at his lips. She grabbed his hand and pulled him quietly from his hammock, leading him deeper into the cave to a straw mat that she had laid out behind several cribs holding sacks of rice. There she passionately directed him through a remarkable night for them both, which involved brief snatches of sleep. The only words whispered were her repeated commands, "We go now," which always brought a response from Duan. When she finally signaled with her small, expressive hands, he reluctantly stole back to his hammock in time to see the cook light the morning fire.

Fraternization was like masturbation to the Revolution: something to be stamped out and controlled. Not because it was immoral, but because of the age-old dread of overpopulation, which in Asia spells famine. So Duan and Su knew they had to be careful.

# THREE

# Monsoon Strategy

## TG559 HEADQUARTERS, TCHEPONE, LAOS

A coded six-word message was flashed to the three principal North Vietnamese commanders conducting the war in the south. The news had a different effect on each of them. The message stated that TG559, with the approval of the Central Unification Department in Hanoi, had shifted to the daytime movement of men and materiel due to the onset of monsoon weather.

The Tri-Thien-Hue zone commander, 300 feet underground in a cave on the western side of Tien Cong Mountain, thirty miles west of Hue, South Vietnam, instructed his staff to prepare to execute the monsoon offensive that he had been planning for six months. His command was always well supplied with troops and equipment because they were at the northern end of the supply line and therefore closest to the source of the lifeline that was the Old Man's Trail. The monsoon would aid his operations by inhibiting American air strikes.

The Military Region 5 and B-3 Front commander, in a well-camouflaged headquarters and logistics complex west of the American Special Forces camp at Dak To, cursed quietly to himself when he received the message. The monsoon affected his operations much as it affected the trail network. Operating in dense, triple-canopy forested

60

jungles in the vast, forbidding terrain that was the Central Highlands, he depended on the adequate stockpiling of supply caches throughout the area to sustain attacks against widely dispersed enemy strongholds. This task had been seriously hindered by enemy operations during the recent dry season. The news meant that new supplies would arrive at a slower rate and that, with the monsoon, he would be bogged down in moving them to forward areas. He also knew that his superiors in Hanoi weren't interested in his problems concerning time, distance, and terrain—they simply demanded action.

The commander of the Central Office for South Vietnam, or COSVN, received the message deep in the underground headquarters bunker that had been built into the sturdy root system of neatly rowed rubber trees in the old French Kantreuy Plantation, on the Cambodian side of the South Vietnamese border in what was called the Fishhook. He lay in his hammock and read the message several times. After a few moments he handed it back to his cook and valet, who patiently awaited instructions. The commander wiped the sweat from his face and neck and pulled his blanket closer. He was shivering from an attack of malaria. He finally responded in a weak whisper, issuing orders for the Ninth Vietcong Division to be ready to move back to Tay Ninh in South Vietnam at the end of the monsoon. He also instructed that priority of men and supplies went to the Ninth Vietcong.

As he drifted into a fitful sleep, his cook passed the instructions to the operations officer, who had already anticipated the response of his commander. Several handwritten coded messages made the plan official.

# FOUR

# The Treacherous Maze

## WAY STATION 601ZA, THE OLD MAN'S TRAIL

The platoon was awakened at 5:00 A.M. and quickly went through their morning routine, lining up their loads next to the cave entrance. The cook served them cabbage soup with onions, garlic, rice, and soy, and each boy was given a cold rice ball for the day's journey. In the center of each ball was a small piece of venison. At 6:00 A.M. the station guards signaled all clear, and Su led them back down the trail to the valley and turned south on a narrow, densely forested path. After an hour it began to rain. The canopy was so thick that at first not much rain reached the jungle floor. Then it began to deluge. Traction became difficult, and the porters began to slip. Two hours after leaving the way station, they found themselves struggling slowly through a sticky mountain bog nearly a mile wide. Their path was only a raised dike across the flat area, and it was narrow and made slick by the wet clay soil.

The porters now were unable to use the rhythm of their walk to shift the weight of their loads, which forced each team to struggle constantly with the full swaying weight. They slipped often from the dike into the knee-deep swamp. One of the teams lost its balance and the load came down on a boy's leg, snapping his femur bone with a sickening crack.

The boy, Anh, cried out in anguish, and Su stopped the column.

With the help of several porters Duan laid Anh on the dike and tried to calm his thrashing and screaming. Despite the torrential rain he saw this as an opportunity to teach a lesson, so he gathered the platoon around while he showed them how to splint and immobilize a broken leg using two of the wooden boards from the loads. He put two Chinese aspirin under the boy's tongue and washed them down with a splash of tea from his canteen. When he gave the leg a sudden push to align the bones, Anh passed out from the pain. He then quickly applied the splint, rigged the boy's hammock under a carrying pole, and carefully laid him down in it. The teams were reassigned to handle the additional load. Two mortars were rigged under a single pole, and Ky and Trang were assigned to carry it.

In ten minutes he told Su they were ready to move again. She watched him admiringly, as though congratulating herself on her ability to pick a man. He smiled slowly as rivulets of water ran down his face. He said, "Sister Su, we go now." It had the tone of an order. To Duan and Su it had a very private meaning. She smiled and led out.

A mile south of the swamp, the guide from the next way station materialized like a ghost out of the rain and jungle onto the trail. He exchanged a few words with Su and signaled the column to follow him. The platoon followed him past Su, who said goodbye with a smile and words of encouragement. Duan hung back as they rounded a bend in the trail. When the last team was out of sight he reached out and touched her lovely, stoic face.

"Su, I will miss you. There will not be a night I won't think of you. I will see you again."

She held his gaze for a moment with her big, sad eyes. "I hope so Duan, but I don't think I will ever see you again." She stroked his cheek and raised her face to kiss him lightly, then turned and disappeared into the rain. Duan watched her go. She never looked back.

The distance to the next way station was a mile and a half shorter than the first day's march. It had been laid out for dry weather, though.

By 2:00 P.M., when they finally stopped to eat, they had covered only seven miles. The guide told Duan and Ba he was worried about making it in before nightfall. The trail was more difficult up ahead, he said. They had to cross two mountain ridges and two deep valleys and there was a tricky river crossing.

Duan explained the situation to the drenched porters, who responded well, considering the miserable circumstances. The injured boy was relatively comfortable and quiet now, thanks to Duan's expert splint job. His friends offered to share their rice with him, but he had no appetite.

The guide set out again and the porters struggled to keep up with his pace. The rain had subsided somewhat, but the trail was still slick and muddy. Duan rotated his best boys every fifteen minutes on the double load, which was especially awkward in the slippery mud. The guide did not stop for the hourly break until they had cleared the first mountain ridge and reached the river. Normally the crossing at this spot would have been a series of large dry rocks. The rocks now formed a rapid. The way station team had strung a rope head-high and tied it off to trees on each bank, but even using the rope for balance and support, it was obvious the crossing would be treacherous. The water seemed to gain force every minute.

Duan sent two boys across without loads. Their job was to hold and steady the rope on the far bank. He now ordered the boys to rig the loads tight against the poles to stop them from swaying. Four boys carrying the casualty were sent across first. Then each of them reentered the rapids and stationed themselves along the rope to steady it and assist the other teams across. Next came the double load, which with four porters made the crossing easily. The rest of the platoon followed.

With everyone on the far side, Duan and the guide called for a break and inspected the loads, which were all intact. They left them tightly trussed to their poles. Ba, Duan, and the guide then talked. They only had two miles to go, but it was over another steep ridge and into a deep valley. It was now 5:00 P.M., and in another hour and a half it would be dark. Duan warned the porters that if they didn't move fast, they would have to cross this terrain at night. This stiffened their resolve, which had been weakened by the abominable conditions.

At the whispered "*Tien len,*" the boys shouldered their loads and followed the guide up a steep trail leading to a mountaintop lost in the clouds.

Their descent was far worse than the climb. The trail had been skillfully engineered and cut for men bearing heavy loads. It crisscrossed the mountainside to ensure a gradual descent. Three-inch-thick logs formed steps in the steepest places. The difficulty was the sheer drop-off to the downhill side of the trail. The rain was coming down in torrents, making traction with the rubber-soled sandals difficult. A hundred yards down from the mountain crest one of the slower-witted porters, a boy named Diem, lost his footing and dragged the load and his teammate down forty feet, where they were stopped abruptly by a rocky outcropping. Neither boy moved.

The guide led the platoon to a spot about fifty yards below the two motionless porters. Duan and Ba climbed up to them. Diem was dead, his face and skull crushed by a rock. The second boy, Sai, was unconscious. The load of mortar rounds had split open, and the metal containers were strewn back up the hillside. Ba and Duan looked at each other and decided they had to act fast. Ba took charge of the casualties and Duan's group began collecting the scattered ammunition containers.

Once back on the path, Ba and Duan worked together for the first time. They ordered the platoon to rig two hammocks on carrying poles, one for the body and one for the still-unconscious Sai. The broken load was rewrapped and two additional loads were doubled. The platoon moved through these tasks looking gloomy and afraid. One boy, a friend of Diem's, began to sob. Duan consoled him and spoke to the platoon. "Diem was slow," he said. "All of us know that. His mind wandered. He didn't think about his duties but of home, food, and comfort. He is with the Immortals now. We must think of ourselves. Help each other to concentrate. The Old Man's Trail is long and dangerous." He scanned the boys' faces, then said to the guide, who also appeared shaken, "*Chung ta ra di.*"

The platoon made it to the haven of way station 601UC after dark. The station was a dozen or so thatched huts on stilts, built in a small box canyon against the side of a mountain. In the center was a large open kitchen under a thatch shelter. The way station commander, a woman who looked sixty but was only in her mid-thirties, was obviously relieved to see the increment arrive. Had they not made it in, it would have been her station team's responsibility to go find them, a terrible task on such a night. She launched into a harangue, berating the guide in a shrill, sarcastic voice. Ba pushed his way to the head of the column and commanded, "Sister, we have casualties, and I need to get my men out of the rain before they all become casualties, useless to the Revolution." She glared at him but did not retort. She set the way station team into action.

The porters placed their loads in a special hut along with Diem's body. The two casualties were taken to a hut where a competent field medic stripped the shivering Anh and got him comfortable on an elevated board under three blankets, then gave him a shot of liquid vitamins. He examined the unconscious boy and could find nothing broken. Sai moaned softly but remained unconscious. The medic cranked up an old Chinese-made battery-powered telephone and talked with the doctor assigned to this section of way stations. He was authorized to start the boy on an intravenous glucose bag—one of six he had on hand—and to inject him with a double shot of liquid vitamins. The medic administered four aspirin, stripped the boy, and left him uncovered in hopes the cold would bring him around. With the exception of an old surgical scalpel, two probes, and three clamps, he had used every medical remedy available to him on the two porters.

Duan and Ba supervised the platoon in changing into dry clothes. Bloody feet and ankles were washed clean of dirt and mud. The wet clothes were placed on sticks close to the cooking fires to dry. Dinner was good—rice, chicken, cabbage soup, and strong hot tea, which the station commander had grown herself in a clearing farther up the mountain. Ba said, as he was finishing his ration, "She might be a bitch, but she sure can cook." Duan agreed, wondering when such support would disappear. This trip, so far, had been nothing like his first.

After inventorying, oiling, and rewrapping all their loads, Duan assembled the platoon around a grave dug for Diem outside the camp. Ba began. "We started out less than three days ago with sixty men and twenty-one loads." Until that moment he had always referred to them as Little Brothers. The change was intentional. He and Duan had agreed to it during dinner. "We have already lost three, which leaves us with fifty-seven. Of those, two are injured and questionable for the rest of our long march. With only fifty-seven men and sixty-three days to go, we must be careful. We will deliver our twenty-one loads to the Ninth Vietcong Division regardless of the hardships," he said emphatically.

He stood for a moment, looking at them. Most were downcast. Their exuberance had faded, and they were unsure and afraid of what lay ahead. So far their long march had been a long nightmare.

From the shadows at the rear of the platoon, Duan spoke quietly. "The monsoon is not our enemy. It is our greatest ally against the damned Americans and their airplanes and artillery. They cannot kill us unless they can see us, and no one can see in the rain. We must learn how to live with our great friend the monsoon. Soon you will learn to fear sunlight. It brings death. Cling to the rain and the night. It makes you wet, but it hides you. It should not hurt us as it has Diem, Sai, and Anh. We trained in dry weather, but you are strong. Lieutenant Ba and I agree that you are conditioned for this. All we need is concentration and teamwork. Do not let your minds wander. We must whisper and encourage each other. We must be a team." Still their eyes were unsure.

Duan moved up next to Ba and continued. "We have seven or eight more days before we reach Tchepone. After that, another twenty days before we are out of the Truong Son Mountains. The trails on the downside of the mountains are always the most treacherous, as you saw today. The load should always be carried toward the downside of the trail. It you feel yourself slipping, drop the load to the ground and balance yourself. We will no longer have to double our loads. The station commander will give us five extra carrying poles and rope when we depart tomorrow."

His eyes scanned the station crew until he saw the station commander glaring at him in the faint light. He held her gaze for a long time until she turned to say something to one of her men. Then he said a prayer over Diem's body, and they buried him in a shallow grave in the station burial ground.

"It's late. Now we will sleep, and tomorrow we march south. *Tien len*." The porters responded with a weak "*Tien len*" and moved silently to their assigned huts. Duan prodded them with a barked order to move out, and they jumped.

The way station grew quiet, but the silence was punctuated with continuous coughs. Throughout the night there were cries of anguish as boys woke up with cramps in their feet and legs, from continuous exposure to the cold and damp. But some of the outcries belonged to boys in the throes of nightmares. Before dawn, when the guards went to awaken Duan and Ba, they found their hammocks empty. They had spent the night moving from porter to porter, encouraging them, calming their fears. Two had been caught trying to desert. Duan handled them roughly and put them back in their hammocks. Ba was learning fast that only leadership, guts, and rice got you down the Old Man's Trail.

The cook started her fires at 4:00 A.M. and the camp came to life. Ba filled out a death certificate for Diem; cause of death was listed as "In action against the Americans." The station chief would meticulously note the spot where Diem had been buried so that he could be exhumed at the end of the war and returned home for burial in the family plot.

The field medic pronounced Sai fit to travel, even though he was still dazed. Anh, because of his fractured leg, would remain behind, over the station commander's strident protests. She pleaded with Duan and Ba to take Anh with them, insisting he would get better care at the next station. Duan took her aside and quoted the regulation number that gave full responsibility for casualties sustained by porter increments to TG559.

"Damn you," she said, and spit on the ground. Ba said heatedly, "I intend to make a full report of the poor treatment received from your way station at Tchepone." She spit again.

Both Duan and Ba knew she had access to a communications system that would allow her to get her side of the story to TG559 before they could. It was a chance they would have to take. As they were getting ready to leave, Duan suddenly ordered the men to rig Anh's hammock under a carrying pole. The station commander came over and began bowing to Duan, hands together in the prayer position, thanking him profusely for taking her problem with him. Duan eyed her coldly and announced, "I wouldn't leave a wounded American with a bitch like you." He turned and walked away.

The next few days were tough. The northern section of the Old Man's Trail covered some of the most forbidding terrain on earth. The trails assigned to Increment 1008 were called heavy-cargo porter routes. The route schedulers made every effort to give as even a trail as possible, which was a relative term when it came to the Truong Son section of the Annamite Mountains. There was no easy terrain, but some routes were better than others. So wherever possible the trails generally followed valleys, in an attempt to avoid steep uphill and downhill movement. Still, virtually every day's march required negotiating at least two major mountain ridges, some of which rose as high as 5,000 feet, and their treacherous downhill backslopes.

The rain subsided somewhat on their third day and by mid-afternoon had become a light drizzle. The jungle glistened with moisture that muted its brilliant shades of green, brown, and yellow. They made good time. But at the way station that night, Sai came down with a high fever. There was no medic available, and he went into convulsions and died in the night. At first light Duan led the platoon into the jungle and conducted the Buddhist funeral service, asking the Immortals and the man's ancestors to receive him into their spirit world. Ba prayed that his soul not be tormented in an endless cycle of birth and rebirth. The platoon muttered in agreement when he said, "To live is to suffer," a basic tenet of Buddhism and one in which they found an increasingly deeper meaning. Religion was strongly encouraged by the Lao Dong party, and virtually every Vietnamese clung to some sort of spiritual belief, usually of a Buddhist or Taoist persuasion.

Duan and Ba had decided that they had to carry Anh to the next medical facility, if for no other reason than to convince the porters that they would not be left behind on the trail in similar circumstances. Morale was low, and they needed to be reassured. Duan explained to them the NVA and Vietcong tradition of never leaving behind dead or wounded, and this seemed to improve their spirits.

On the fourth day the rain subsided but the clouds remained. To that point the trail had seldom left the sanctuary of the forest jungle, but now it broke into the open and they made fast time across several miles of rice paddy dikes. Above the clouds they could hear the roar of jet engines, but no planes dropped below the overcast. That night Duan told them that they would reach the major hub at Tchepone, Laos, in six days. "As we get closer to the larger base areas, the threat of air attacks will increase," he said. He recited his favorite Vietcong adage: "To struggle and fall in the jungle is better than to be caught by planes in the open." They seemed to understand but would not really understand until later. All Vietnamese had developed a healthy fear and loathing of the screaming airplanes. To serve in the NVA or Vietcong, a soldier developed a much more extreme sensitivity to these hazards.

On the seventh day they lost a man to a water snake while crossing a river. The snake caught him neck-deep in the water and struck his jugular vein. He died before they could get him to the bank. The death certificate listed the obligatory "Killed in action against the Americans" and the precise location of the grave. The platoon buried him in a shallow grave beside the trail. Their strength and their numbers were waning.

By the time they reached the vicinity of Tchepone, they had been on the trail eleven days. Five men had died, and they still carried Anh with his broken leg. When they dropped him off at the big underground hospital complex at Tchepone, that left fifty-four porters. The casualty rate to this point was about average for porter increments.

None of the TG559 officers expressed any concern, nor were they interested in replacing members of the platoon. These were the transportation bureaucrats, and their ratio of supplies to movement means was always high on the supply side. If it had not been for TG559's strict increment structure rules, which always allowed for spare porters, they would have loaded down the twelve extra men with some of the tons of supplies that required movement south.

Duan knew a tricky and dangerous situation when he saw it and quickly hustled the platoon through the base, which resembled the one at Nape. His reason was simple. Places like Tchepone, though well-camouflaged, had a way of attracting American bombs. Southwest of the base they crossed the Hieng River on a pontoon ferry camouflaged to resemble the riverbank.

They were now in Zone 604, directly west of the DMZ between North and South Vietnam. The trail had gradually moved eastward and they were no more than fifteen miles west of the South Vietnamese border. As they moved south they could count on two things: first, the trail gradually drifted closer to the enemy border, increasing the risk of enemy interdiction attacks. Second, and most significant, the supply line was lengthening from its northern source, and food began to grow scarce.

The Vietcong and NVA insurgency in South Vietnam had struggled for years to topple the South Vietnamese government, expel the Americans, and unify the country. A consistent objective had been the political and economic control of the peasant rice farmers and their fields. The sheer size and power of the combined U.S. and South Vietnamese efforts to control the same segments of the south had caused the loss of thousands of acres of rice fields, which, in fact, represented the bottom line to both sides. Food in Indochina had always been the bottom line. Vietnam, and in particular the Red River delta in the north and the Mekong delta in the south, had been the rice bowl of Indochina for centuries. The war, with its draw on manpower and its sheer destructiveness, had upset that balance. The American and South Vietnamese strategy of relocating people from the agricultural areas that they could not control further tilted that delicate balance, in addition to creating countless refugees. The food problem on the trail was intensified by the fact that the 40,000 TG559 troops had to eat, in addition to all the people making the journey.

The jungle in this section of the trail did a remarkable job of concealing the struggles of masses of people, vehicles, and animals. Miles of improved road, much of it hard surface, passed through tunnel-like passages skillfully cut through the dense foliage. The technique used to make these highways left intact a hundred or more feet of forest and jungle canopy to conceal the trail from enemy reconnaissance planes. So thick was the canopy that bombs dropped on it exploded harmlessly above their intended targets. When a section of jungle withered under American defoliation operations, the trail network was quickly shifted to unaffected areas. The hard-surface roads were more difficult to reconstruct due to shortage of material and the difficulty of the terrain, but thousands of people labored around the clock to accomplish the almost impossible task. On the Old Man's Trail, full acceptance of the *I Ching*'s doctrine of constant change was required for survival.

South of Tchepone, the platoon sat on a side trail and watched in amazement as an increment of thirty Thai elephants loaded with tons of rice and ammunition moved east toward a forward supply base in enemy territory. None of the porters had ever seen an elephant except in pictures. And twice they shared the trail with heavily loaded pack trains of small but sturdy Laotian ponies.

The route that Increment 1008 took south of Tchepone resembled the earlier dense jungle terrain, but here the rivers and streams were even more swollen by the heavy rains. The trail would barely cover a mile before they were confronted with another water obstacle. It was always the same: they would climb a back-breaking ridge on a mud-slick trail, tediously negotiate the downhill side and make a stream crossing. Then repeat the cycle. All the major rivers had either ferries or makeshift bridges. It was the smaller streams that posed the greatest threat.

Guides now began to appear in groups of three and four, all *bo doi*, heavily armed infantry—and all business. Flanks of the porter column were secured out to twenty-five yards, partly to protect against ambush, but mostly to search for unmanned American ground sensors, which had been heavily seeded in this section for several years. The guide teams were friendly with the porters and particularly with Duan. They never hesitated to help manhandle a load over a tough spot, were well-disciplined, and were oriented totally to their mission of moving the porters and their materiel south.

Due to the monsoon they continued to move during the day. At night they were pestered by fleas and mosquitoes, which attacked in black swarms. Even though TG559 policy was for food to be given first to porter increments, their diet gradually dwindled to rice, small portions of chicken or pork, occasional canned meat or fish, and edible roots. But their loads never dwindled, so the men began to lose weight rapidly, and with it their strength.

On their third day out of Tchepone one of the porters collapsed with a sudden high fever. It was malaria. The first attack of the disease is the worst, and the fact that he collapsed halfway between way stations made it even worse. Despite a dose of precious quinine that the guide gave him, his fever rose until his skin turned crimson. In less than an hour he went into convulsions, vomited violently, and died as the platoon watched. They buried the porter under some rocks off the trail. They had little strength to dig a proper grave.

Several hours later they faced another swollen stream. Half the platoon had made it across, using a rope the guides had strung earlier in the day. Then, as two porters carrying mortar rounds inched across, suddenly a thirty-foot fallen tree careened around a bend in the rushing water and swept over them.

After two hours of searching and diving, everyone agreed it was useless to try to recover the bodies or the ammunition. They probably had become entangled in the branches of the floating tree and been swept miles downstream.

A demoralized platoon finally staggered into way station 604DE, the usual series of open bamboo, log, and thatch huts under the jungle canopy. The station crew got the platoon and gear situated and passed around hot tea with sugarcane sweetener, which did little to raise their spirits or to stop the shivering that set in each night after they had ceased the exertion of carrying their loads. The uniforms in their packs were as wet as the ones they had on, and it took several hours for the fire to dry out their soaked clothing, which was becoming tattered and torn from the hazards of the trail.

The meal consisted of captured American rice, which the Vietnamese didn't care for because it was too refined and not as nutritious as the Southeast Asian variety. The only other food was boiled manioc roots. They were too tired and dejected to complain. The solicitous station commander bowed repeatedly and apologized for not having more food, while lamenting the hardships of running a station on this section of the trail.

After dinner Duan ordered the platoon to assemble in the cook hut. He cuffed the slow movers behind the ears to speed them up. His tone of voice told them this would not be the usual nightly political discussion. "I was your age when I joined the Vietminh," he began. "After the battle at Tu Le, I was transferred south and made that journey by boat. After fighting for two years, I came back north in early 1954 to fight at Dien Bien Phu. I stayed in the army after the war and finally, in 1959, my unit was ordered down the Old Man's Trail. We trained the way Lieutenant Ba and I trained you, with heavy loads, marching all day, carrying boxes of ammunition in our packs. Since we had to carry all our food, in addition to our weapons and ammunition, we marched every day for three months carrying sixty to seventy-five pounds. We chanted 'Sweat more in peace—bleed less in war.'" He paused to read the effect of his words in their eyes. "There was nothing we could have done that would have prepared us for what we faced. There were no way stations, only wide places in the trail. There were only a few guides, and most of them were sick and not able to help us. We started with seventy men, all healthy, conditioned soldiers. We began in the monsoon like we have. Food and the jungle were our enemies. We could only carry so much, and there were only three resupply points. When we reached the first one it was abandoned. In this whole area, south of Tchepone, the trail was easy to follow. The hammocks with the sick, dead, and dying were strung all along it. There was nothing we could do for them but try to save ourselves. Sometimes we would not move for two or three days while we tried to gather enough roots and leaves to regain our strength. We threw away our grenades fishing, sometimes eating the fish raw because we couldn't start a fire in the monsoon. Men began to come down with the trail fever, the fever you have seen take one of our number so far. If a man became sick we couldn't wait for him to get better, because of the food shortage. We would put him in his hammock and string a poncho over it and leave him a few scraps of food and some water. Sometimes he would find us in a week or two. Most of the time we never saw him again. I was put in my hammock and lay there delirious for three days. I was lucky. A Pathet Lao platoon found me and gave me enough food to get back on my feet and find my unit. My company was surprised and glad to see me. They thought I was dead like the rest. My company commander did not even punish me when I produced ten kilos of rice that I had traded for my AK-47 rifle. When we reached Tay Ninh there were only ten of us left. We were all so sick it took us four months of rest to regain enough strength to join our division."

He waited. For the first time in a week, the platoon looked alert. He had saved the story for precisely this moment. He went on. He told them that he was afraid when they ordered him to begin training a porter platoon and rejoin his division in the south. "I asked myself, who were these bureaucratic louts to order a man down the trail a second time. No one should be able to order someone onto the Old Man's Trail until he has made the trip himself. The nightmares haunted me for months. I tossed and turned at night. My first trip was the worst experience of my life. I dreaded this, but after seeing the work that *Bac Ho* and the party have done, I say it is much better than before. We lost hundreds of good men and women before to starvation and disease. The

party has changed all that. It is well-organized now. It is hard marching, but we have food and shelter at the end of each day. The guides are
good soldiers. We are not yet attacked by the enemy, but we will be, the
closer we get to our objective." He waited for his words to sink in, then
went on.

"So I am angry when I see you with your heads down. This is not
like the old trail, and I will not babysit you to see you do your duty. We
will remain united and bear the good and the bad. We will help each
other. We will stick together. We will not falter. Each man will help carry his load or we will leave him and he will not be allowed in the way
station with us. You will, as of now, quit acting like a gang of blind old
women. *Tien len!*"

The platoon responded with a crisp *"Tien len."* He ordered them to
their hammocks, and they moved quickly.

"Ky and Trang, over here," ordered Duan. He motioned them over.
"Here is what you will do tomorrow. You are the strongest and bright-
est among this group of weak, slow-witted thatch farmers." He smiled
at their eager faces. "You will take the lead, and you will stay on the
guide's ass as close as you can get. Lieutenant Ba and I will be at the end
of the column, and we will march fast. I am tired of dragging into these way stations after dark. We must make distance before the
monsoon leaves us open to the damn Americans and their airplanes,
or everybody will start getting sick. Understand?" They quickly responded that they did. He tapped them on the cheek with a mock slap
and told them to get in their hammocks.

Ba, Duan, and the guide conferred with the station commander.
The ammunition lost during the stream crossing had to be accounted
for somehow. The station commander was reluctant to sign the route
card, which would declare the missing gear an unavoidable loss. He was
holding out for a bribe in return for his cooperation.

After fifteen minutes of haggling Duan walked over to the cook
fires and with his toe flicked a camouflaged mat away from the top of
a nearby hole full of Russian canned sardines and herring, condensed
milk, and large sacks of Vietnamese rice. He looked the station com-

mander in the eye and said, "You are a war profiteer, and I will sign the capital allegation, as will Lieutenant Ba. I was going to let you short-ration us until you started squeezing. Sign the route slip for the un-avoidable loss of eleven 82-mm mortar rounds, you *do khon nan*—son of a bitch—and we will take sixty cans of sardines and herring and twenty cans of condensed milk with us in the morning." Duan glared at the station commander as he dejectedly initialed the card.

He spoke quietly to the guide. "Does this change anything?"

The guide smiled and said, "No, Sergeant Major."

"How did you know about the sardines?" asked Ba as they walked to their hammocks.

"I smelled them on his breath while he was apologizing for the terrible food that he fed us at dinner," said Duan.

"How do you know we can trust the guide?"

"Because he didn't have sardines on his breath." Duan smiled. "The station commander is nothing now. Don't worry about him."

The night was still, except for the sounds of bombing to the south and east and the long, moaning sound of Gatling guns firing on convoys from the big four-engine American gunships called Thugs. The porters were too exhausted to worry much about it.

They rose in the darkness, footsore and weary but in better spirits. Ky and Trang talked quietly to them as they put their gear together. The message was simple: Everyone must keep up, regardless of how bad it hurt. Most had accepted the reality of their dire situation. Either they got tough and worked together or they would not survive. Duan would get them through, but it would take every ounce of strength they possessed.

The porters were given bigger-than-usual American rice balls the station commander was trying to get rid of, and prized cans of sardines and herring. Duan ordered them to share two cans of fish among four boys to go with their watery cabbage and root soup. They added several cans of condensed milk to the sweetened tea, which was the only palatable thing the station's kitchen produced. As they lined up to leave, Duan took a dozen cans of sardines from the hidden cache and gave four cans to each of the guides. He didn't look back as they moved quickly down the trail.

The rain had lightened to a fine mist and the sky was brighter than it had been in a week. They made good time on a relatively flat trail and around noon scrambled up a steep trail that crested on a hill. The new team of guides waited for them there. Looking west, they could see a section of Route 23 several miles away, where black smoke billowed from a dozen burning trucks that had been hit during an attack the night before. Artillery pieces were overturned behind the vehicles. Duan thought it was the convoy they had seen two weeks before at Nape.

The sound came slowly, rising in volume, until it was a reverberating roar. Six American jets appeared below the clouds and began circling over the burning artillery convoy like great vultures. Instinctively the platoon crouched low, nervously looking up to see if they were hidden by the jungle. The guides assured them they were.

A small spotter plane circled under the jets and fired a marking rocket into one of the trucks. A plane then pulled out of the circle, climbed, and went into a steep dive toward the burning vehicles. Four black tubes slowly tumbled from under the plane's wings and fell lazily, bursting into an immense fireball and engulfing three of the trucks in flames. Everyone gasped. The artillery shells in the vehicles exploded in a spectacular show of fireworks.

The first plane was followed by a second and third, each dropping fire bombs. The remaining planes then dove and dropped high-explosive bombs that echoed cracking explosions across the small valley. After that the planes circled over their blazing target. One plane pulled out of the pattern and went into a flat dive, strafing the convoy with machine guns from one end to the other. The other planes did the same.

The last one dove toward the ground just as a steady stream of green tracers from four sites slowly arched to meet it. The aircraft lurched and belched white and black smoke as its dive entered the tracer streams, and it flipped over uncontrollably as a wing erupted in yellow and red flames. The whole event happened in seconds. The plane crashed into the fiery convoy, victim of an NVA antiaircraft ambush.

After an astonished pause the platoon began to clap and cheer, slapping each other on the back. It had been a magnificent show. Only Duan and one of the guides had ever witnessed an American airplane being shot down. Elated, they stood talking for a few minutes, then watched the other planes circle, apparently out of ammunition, and fly off to the west. The antiaircraft guns did not fire again.

Duan pulled everyone back to the job at hand. "They will not take losing one of their planes lightly. The sky will be black with them in a short time. Be thankful you are not with the antiaircraft gunners down there. *Chung ta ra di*—pick a well-covered route east!"

As they moved due east on an overgrown trail, they heard a frightful battle developing on the road behind them, just as Duan had predicted. The guides stuck to auxiliary trails for the rest of the day. As they entered their way station that night they could still hear the battle, which now sounded like distant thunder. It raged all night, as the Americans took a terrible vengeance for the loss of one of their own.

The next day was dark and rainy and they picked up a main road as called for by their route card. For the first time they were traveling with other foot and bicycle cargo increments on a wide open road that also handled vehicle traffic. Duan knew an American target when he saw it, and they moved as fast as their loads allowed.

When they reached Zone 611 Headquarters at Ban Kadap, Laos, Duan and Ba tried to get a change of route, back to the more difficult but safer jungle routes. The answer was a flat no from irritated bureaucrats who rankled at the number of decisions already required of them.

The way stations in the Ban Kadap depot area sometimes handled up to two hundred porters and troops apiece, and there were several large camouflaged vehicle parks. Billet areas were in cramped, wet underground bunkers. But the food was good and plentiful, and they gorged themselves on fresh bread made in a depot bakery. Using Ba's rank as an officer of the Revolution and a few liberated trinkets, Duan managed to scrounge up fifty new sets of black uniforms, which improved the platoon's appearance to match the fresh haircuts they had received from a toothless old man who claimed he had been cutting hair at this way station for ten years. The porters were gaunt, and the new uniforms hung loosely on them. Duan also picked up three old but serviceable AK-47s. He gave one to Ba and hid the other two in the loads. Ammunition was harder to find than rifles, and he could only find one magazine and ten rounds per weapon.

Two porters came down with malaria and were dropped off at a dispensary that provided only a place to string a hammock off the trail to sweat out fever and chills. Quinine and chloroquine, used to counter the disease, were in short supply. A man's survival usually came down to his will to live. Later they heard that one of the porters had died. He had been one of the slow learners.

The porters noticed that Duan became more irritable and agitated the farther south they traveled. Like all great military leaders, he was a skilled actor. He could shift characters almost instantly, becoming a consoling friend or a tyrant. Tyrant was the role he had chosen most often since they had reached Zone 611. He had taken to shouting the "down" command at the most inopportune times, sometimes fifteen to twenty times a day. He would then critique their positions and show them how to use the terrain or their loads for cover from the unseen whistling death of the battlefield. The drills he ran during meals, in the middle of the night, or while the men were relieving themselves early in the morning, had a humorous aspect to them that never seemed to affect Duan. A man lying motionless, face down on the wet ground with his trousers around his ankles, was criticized on his position as if nothing were out of the ordinary.

The morning they left Ban Kadap, Duan moved down the line shoving cans of herring and meat paste into each porter's pack. He stood at the head of the column in the faint light and held up a big bottle of *nuoc mam* and a plastic bag full of red peppers, neither of which they had seen since the fare-well party at Van Xa. He smiled at their pleased faces and whispered, "Down!" The response was instantaneous. He stepped along the row of prostrated bodies and adjusted their positions, taking time to vigorously kick several of them.

# FIVE

# Opium Trails

## BAN KADAP, LAOS

Only one guide had been assigned for the day's march. He led them to an area just off the main road where two truck convoys were staged in preparation for the journey south. The first consisted of five trucks loaded with a hundred young *bo doi* who carried, in addition to their rifles and packs, thirty-five long, bulky tubes wrapped tight in vinyl waterproofing. The company commander was berating his men to get them loaded quickly. He didn't want them talking to the depot troops, who curiously eyed the peculiar weapons concealed in the protective wrapping.

"Increment 1008 will board these trucks for transportation as far as Ban Mun Lan junction," the guide announced. "There you will meet guides who will take you by foot to station 613DS. You will pass four way stations in one day," he added proudly.

"This is ridiculous, *trung si*," Duan said, addressing the guide by his rank of sergeant. "These whoring trucks are easy prey for the Americans, and my men will not be fuel for the fire that will occur when they are spotted—and they will be spotted. The Americans are very clever, not stupid men." He glanced around anxiously, receiving some consolation from the low black clouds and drizzling rain.

The guide looked puzzled. Most increments were eager to rest their tired feet and backs aboard trucks. Ba jerked the card from the guide's hand and studied it. "Duan, I think we must accept this decision," he said, handing him the card.

Duan scanned it quickly and said through clenched teeth, "A pile of bureaucratic shit. The last time I came down the trail there wasn't all this magnificent efficiency. You either made it or you didn't. It was much simpler. A soldier had a say in his own death. With a little josh and good comrades, he could survive. Now we have damned paperwork assigning us to the Immortals in heaven—all in order, stamped, proper, official." He spat toward the guide, who stepped back.

"Sergeant Major, you should not be so upset," said the young sergeant. "You are safe! Traveling with you today is one of the new antiaircraft companies that will blast the Americans from the sky with their new Soviet missiles." He beamed. Duan glared at the man.

Ba grabbed the sergeant by the shoulder and spun him around, chastising him for disregarding the Revolution's security. However, both he and Duan were glad to know what the strange-looking weapons were that had been carried by the unit now sitting quietly in the truck beds to their front. The Vietnamese love of gossip was a problem never overcome by the rigid discipline of the Revolution.

The confused sergeant anxiously looked around to see if anyone had overheard Ba's accusation of a security violation. Duan turned on his heel and vented his anger on the platoon, shoving them up on top of the ammunition loads in the truck beds.

Ba and Duan declined offers to ride in the drivers' cabs and positioned themselves on top of the ammunition in the first and last of the three trucks in their convoy. While they waited for word to start, Duan ran four dismount drills to show the platoon how to get off quickly, with all their gear, in the event of an air strike. His mood was sour as they began bumping down the exposed road. For the rest of the day he sat on a box of 130-mm ammunition uttering the foulest curses many of the porters had ever heard, interspersed with fervent prayers that the Immortals would confound the Americans and their shit-eating spying machines.

They followed a loose-surface graded road paralleling the rushing Kong River, which lay to the east of the roadbed. Road-repair crews were everywhere working on rain and bomb damage. At one detour they saw ten American prisoners working on a road gang that was repairing a culvert. They were guarded by a Pathet Lao squad and appeared not to notice the convoy as it drove by slowly. They towered over the Vietnamese and Laotian workers with them. The platoon gawked. These were the first Americans any of them had ever seen. Emaciated and shivering like everyone else in the cold and rain, they didn't look like the devils the porters had been raised to expect. One American looked up at the passing trucks and smiled, raising his hand with the middle finger extended. He withdrew it quickly when one of the guards yelled at him. Several of the porters innocently waved back and smiled. Duan quietly told them to stop.

At 4:00 P.M. they arrived at Ban Mun Lan having covered fifty-two miles, which would have taken them more than four days to walk. The houses and huts of the village were abandoned. A large refueling depot had been constructed under three layers of overhead canopy in the jungle north of the road. The trucks carrying the antiaircraft company continued south on the road that now disappeared into a tunnel cut in the mass of vegetation.

Three armed guides emerged from the jungle and strolled down the hillside toward the stopped trucks. Duan shouted for everyone to get off and form up. He walked the several hundred yards to the guides and motioned the platoon to follow. The men were stiff from sitting all day in the rain and they hobbled over to Duan, struggling with their loads. Ba brought up the rear, kicking the stragglers. The guides stood casually smoking cigarettes, apparently in no hurry to begin moving, more intent on watching the activity around the fuel depot.

"*Chung ta ra di!*" Duan ordered, in a tone that usually left no room for argument.

The senior guide laughed arrogantly and said, "We go when I am ready." He was used to foot increments who were desperate and disoriented by this point in their journey, helpless without his assistance.

Duan glared at him, turned, and motioned the platoon to follow as he strode off quickly up the steep trail. The guide yelled after him, "We don't go that way, old man. Our trail is in another direction," and the guides laughed, still smoking out on the open hillside. Duan ignored the insult and pushed ahead deliberately, seeking the protection of deep jungle.

It began as a faint whisper, unidentifiable to the untrained ear, and rose in a matter of seconds to a loud, oscillating, unearthly rushing noise. There was no sound like it. It hypnotized most people. The sensation was particularly mysterious in the rain. Five-hundred-pound bombs dropping from an A-6 aircraft at 10,000 feet made a splashing noise, like rocks dropping in a stream. The noise was not continuous; it was a series of increasingly loud splashes that finally became sharp cracks, like from a whip, as the bombs crashed through the thick canopy. Then came the sickening thud as the bombs hit the soft mud, which tripped their delayed-impact fuses and sent whistling shards of steel, rock, and debris in all directions.

Even though the aircraft crews could not see their target, the bombs fell with pinpoint accuracy made possible by an intricate system of radar beacons and navigation and target acquisition equipment that gave the precise location of the planes in relation to the target. A ballistic computer released the bombs. Each of the three A-6s dropped twenty-eight 500-pound bombs from a tight triangular flight formation, creating a similar but larger pattern on the ground.

The A-6s were Marine Corps aircraft that had been targeted on this mission by Task Force Alpha, a U.S. Air Force staff that controlled a large and expensive high-tech system specifically designed to interdict Communist logistic traffic on the Old Man's Trail. In keeping with the American penchant for innocuous names, the program had evolved over a number of years and was eventually dubbed Igloo White.

Duan's keen ears caught the first deadly whisper. His mind took only a second to translate it into extreme danger. "Down!" he shouted. Their training paid off. No one paused to question the command. They instantly dropped their loads and hugged the muddy trail, squirming for the safest positions. Duan caught himself instinctively moving down the column to correct positions. Realizing his error, he flung himself down between two porters and yelled for Ba to do the same. This was for real. Ba hesitated and then, with a startled look of understanding, dove flat to the welcome protection of the cold, wet mud.

The Igloo White network comprised thousands of people, facilities, and aircraft, all targeted against the 650 miles of the Old Man's Trail tracing through Laos and Cambodia. Task Force Alpha integrated countless ground and airborne sensor readouts from its air-conditioned Surveillance Center, housed in what was proudly heralded as the largest free-standing structure in Indochina, at Nakhon Phanom, Thailand. Incoming target information was processed by colossal IBM 360-65 computers, which continuously printed out data on reams of paper that were then analyzed and stored in the cavernous facility.

The doomed fuel depot's location had been pinpointed just before the monsoon hit by high-resolution aerial photographs taken by one of the reconnaissance aircraft that continuously crisscrossed the Laotian panhandle. A small mistake by the depot crew caused their destruction this day. The cameras had caught two men rolling a fifty-five-gallon drum of fuel in the open. Until then the aerial photography interpreters had been fooled by the camouflage.

The bombs hit a hundred yards north of the target and walked directly through the center of the closely stored fuel drums and ended two hundred yards to the south.

The sound of impact was paralyzing. Bombs exploded in rapid succession followed by a roaring fireball as hundreds of gallons of fuel ignited. The depot and the hundred or so people who manned it were consumed in less than ten seconds. Two of the big bombs hit ten yards from the ammunition trucks that had delivered the platoon to the road junction. The drivers and their young guide for the day were instantly killed. There was a pause, and fuel tanks and ammunition began to explode.

With heads buried under their arms, the platoon was bounced and shaken off the ground, engulfed in the high-pitched, roaring noise. The jungle was alive with the whispering whistle and sharp thuds of shrapnel and debris hitting trees. Duan felt a violent tug that pulled him up off the ground as a six-inch piece of jagged steel ripped into his pack.

The deafening noise gradually subsided, replaced by a rapid series of smaller explosions. Duan shouted to stay down, waiting for the debris that had been blown into the air to return to earth. A minute passed, then a ripping sound came from high above in the jungle canopy. It continued for thirty seconds, then the larger objects began to crash to the jungle floor. After that there was quiet, interspersed with spasmodic explosions of ammunition and the roar of the fuel fire.

Duan raised his head cautiously and looked around. Several men were crying and the rest whimpered and grunted, as all people do unconsciously when caught in bombing or artillery fire. He listened hard for another whisper of bombs, but heard none. He rose to his knees, peering warily around. He suddenly felt his pack slip from his back. He quickly swung it in front of him and saw that it was ripped straight down the middle and a piece of hot shrapnel had singed his spare uniform. He grabbed the hot metal and burned his fingers. Cursing, he poured water on it from his canteen, which created a billow of steam. Then he clutched his rifle and rose slowly, listening intently and muttering to the men over and over to stay down. When satisfied no more bombs were coming he said, "Stay down, but raise your heads and look at me." Slowly the men raised their mud-spattered, frightened faces and looked at Duan.

He searched the line for casualties. If anyone tried to get up he pushed them back down. He was startled to see the naked legs and pelvis of a body, charred black and smoldering alongside the trail. At first he thought a bomb must have hit among the platoon. Then he saw it was a woman's body, and he knew she must have been at the depot. He turned away, gagging at the smell of burning flesh. At the end of the column nearest the road he found one of his porters dead, with a small hole in the back of his head. He helped a dazed Ba to his feet and told him to get the platoon up and ready to go.

Moving cautiously, he crept out of the protection of the jungle back where he had left the three guides. The heat from the inferno at the fuel depot pushed against him, even though he was two hundred yards away. He found two of the guides lying on their backs, dead from concussion and multiple shrapnel wounds. The leader held a cigarette between his fingers; it was still burning. He called out for the third guide and found him whimpering, facedown in a small depression, ten feet from his comrades.

Duan said roughly, "We go," to the frightened man, who continued to sob and mutter incoherently. He didn't move. "We go, I said," repeated Duan, reaching down and pulling him to his feet. He looked him over and could see no wounds. The guide babbled on unintelligibly, as if insane. Duan slapped him and shouted, "We go, you son of a bitch." The guide looked at him blankly and Duan hit him again. "Get moving. Now." Finally the guide seemed to recognize Duan. He said weakly, "Where are my friends?"

"They're dead. They didn't do what I told them to do. They stood out in the open gawking like old women or children. If I were you I wouldn't make that mistake again. When I say go, you had better go if you want to live. We go! Fast!" He pointed with his rifle.

"What about my friends?" muttered the guide.

"Nothing we can do. The airplanes will be back soon. We must get out of this place of death. Get into the jungle. We go," he said flatly.

"The airplanes come again? We go," the guide repeated, still dazed. Then he began to run with a staggering gait, off toward the platoon.

Duan took the dead guides' weapons, ammunition, and packs and searched their pockets. He found two plastic bags of opium and a nice knife with a folding blade. Greedy bastards, he thought. They were going to try to sell the opium to the truck drivers and fuel-depot crew. That's why they didn't want to go. And it cost them their lives.

He left them in the bloody, twisted positions they had died in, thinking the Immortals would not welcome such men, for they had done evil. Too bad for them.

The porters now were filled with the elation of survivors. They talked and laughed excitedly, letting the tension out. The dead porter lay as if asleep on the trail. Duan handed the guides' rifles and gear to a porter, telling him to put them in a load. Then he barked orders to bring the platoon back to the task at hand. They wrapped the dead man in his vinyl poncho, and Duan gingerly rolled the still-smoldering remains of the unknown woman onto one of the guides' ponchos, and both were put in a hastily dug grave. The porter had been a good man, always smiling and willing. Duan said a Taoist prayer for him and asked the Immortals to welcome the woman, whoever she had been, and to elevate both their souls to the higher realms, for they had done no wrong. He cursed the cruel Americans and fervently asked the Immortals to blind them and their damned machines for eternity and to cause them pain and suffering equal to that they had inflicted. The men muttered in agreement.

Duan took the dead man's pack and quickly repacked his own gear, saving his ripped rucksack to be repaired later. It had been with him for a long time and twice had saved his life by stopping bullets and shrapnel. His attitude toward it was almost reverential because of the good fortune it had brought him. The pack was a close friend, and the thought of simply exchanging it was out of the question. It would change the balance of his *di may man*—luck—which had been particularly good on this day.

"We go," he repeated to the stunned guide, who headed off up the steep trail that eventually would take them to the 5,000-foot level of the Bolovens Plateau. It took three hours of hard climbing to reach the way station, set in a densely jungled streambed about halfway up to the plateau.

Duan and the guide reported the loss of the two other guides to the station commander and gave him one of the two rifles and a poncho, saying that was all they could find. The station commander's worried look told Duan that he had been part of the opium-selling scheme. The rest of the station crew were sullen people. Dinner that night consisted of rice mixed with Romanian cornmeal, which gave it a grainy consistency and a peculiar smell. There was nothing else to eat except tasteless boiled manioc roots. At least there were no mosquitoes at this altitude, and the rain had stopped, giving them a quiet night. But everyone was restless from the adrenaline rush they had received that afternoon.

Duan told Ba about the opium. Ba, still naive about a lot of things, was incensed that anyone would try to use their position in the Revolution for personal gain. Duan assured him it would only get worse farther south, pointing out that the Cambodian army and the Khmer Rouge were nothing more than armed gangs of cutthroats and bandits. They agreed to take turns staying awake during the night and to leave the way station as fast as possible in the morning. The platoon was now down to forty-eight men.

They were on the trail before first light. Once they reached the plateau the route flattened out, and they passed through the low-lying monsoon clouds into bright sunlight. Here the vegetation thinned, and they spent the day traveling nervously across open fields of thatch. They had to hide from airplanes three times. The guides and way stations in this area were in Zone 613 and reflected the attitude of their leadership. The trails were poorly maintained, the way station crews surly, the food lousy, and, worst of all, the guides were not trail-smart. Signs of poor discipline, lack of control, and low morale were everywhere.

Ba tried to square things away using his rank, which only incurred the wrath of the station teams. Duan told him not to waste his time, citing the hidden reason for what they were experiencing. This area encompassed the ancient opium-smuggling trails that led from the Golden Triangle in western Laos and Burma to the coastal city markets and the shipping lanes of the South China Sea. The station crews were more concerned with business than with the Revolution.

Movement was easy, if risky, on top of the plateau, but as they descended, the mud and rain began to make progress a major effort. They crossed the Kong River on a ferry and passed south of Muong May, Laos, taking trails that led southeast into Cambodia. They had again been routed off the main arteries and struggled on slippery hill trails that were the end of the Truong Son Mountains leading into northern Cambodia.

In three more days they reached the Cambodian border, where they lost two men, one to malaria and one to pneumonia. They had been on the trail for twenty-nine days, but counting the near-disastrous truck ride that had passed four way stations, they were on day thirty-three of their route card. They had lost fourteen porters, leaving a total of forty-six men. Six were extras, not matched to a load. They still carried twenty loads, having lost only one of the original twenty-one.

Many foot porter platoons had disintegrated completely by this point. Increment 1008's attrition rate at the end of the Truong Son Mountains was exceptionally low. The main reason for the platoon's low loss rate had been Duan's constant efforts at scrounging food, which by now had taken on the precise organization of a military operation. Once the platoon entered a way station, Ba and Duan would engage the station commander and the cooks in conversation. The guides were usually tired and squatted around the fire to dry out. The porters broke down the loads and cleaned and oiled parts, rewrapping them for the next day's march.

They would begin to call out softly, asking for permission to go into the jungle to relieve themselves or to search for herbal roots or vines to secure their loads. Ba and Duan would feign irritation and grant permission, which sent a dozen men in every direction searching for the station's hidden cache of food. It usually took half an hour or so of this fake activity for the food cache to be pinpointed.

Since all the camps put out security watches at night, several of the more light-fingered porters robbed the cache during the evening political indoctrination meeting, which everyone was required to attend.

Because of the weight of their loads they stole only enough to supplement their diet and keep up their strength. Sometimes they took only rice, which they distributed through everyone's packs. The high-protein items such as canned meat, condensed milk, dried fish, and American or Chinese rations were consumed as quickly as possible, usually that night in their hammocks or on the trail the following morning. Empty cans and wrappers were carefully collected and saved to be discarded on the trail. In this way they avoided the deadly equation of burning up more calories than they consumed, which spelled doom for so many on the trail.

Malnutrition was just one of the hazards they faced. Their digestive systems were also the target of a multitude of microscopic parasites that called the jungle and all intestines, human and animal, home. Even though water sources were abundant, Duan insisted that only boiled water go into their canteens. Most way stations provided water boiled with tea, but some did not. In such cases Duan put the platoon to work around the station fires, purifying their water. Even with these precautions most of the men's bowels were loose with diarrhea, but they managed to avoid dysentery—particularly the life-threatening amoebic kind. To bodies accustomed to high-carbohydrate, low-fat diets, the high-fat and protein content of American rations usually spelled severe stomach cramps and intestinal problems.

The hardships and adversities, along with the terror of the bombing raid, had served to fuse the porters into a very tight unit that instantly responded to orders. Load teams were permanently paired. By now Ky and Trang were inseparable. Both strong, quick-witted, natural leaders, they had helped keep the platoon together and moving through rough times. Duan had assigned them as chief scroungers in the way stations, and they helped Duan and Ba with river crossings and with keeping the teams moving over rough terrain. Each carried one of the spare rifles on the trail. They hid the rifles in their loads when they entered a way station at night, since porter platoons were not supposed to be armed—TG559 theoretically provided security. But Duan knew from bitter experience and long conversations with convalescing soldiers at the hospital in Hanoi that the Cambodian border depot areas were treacherous spider webs of bombs, artillery, booby traps, Cambodian and American ambushes, and periodic major ground incursions. Duan was a survivor, and the first rule of survival was to take care of yourself, because nobody else would.

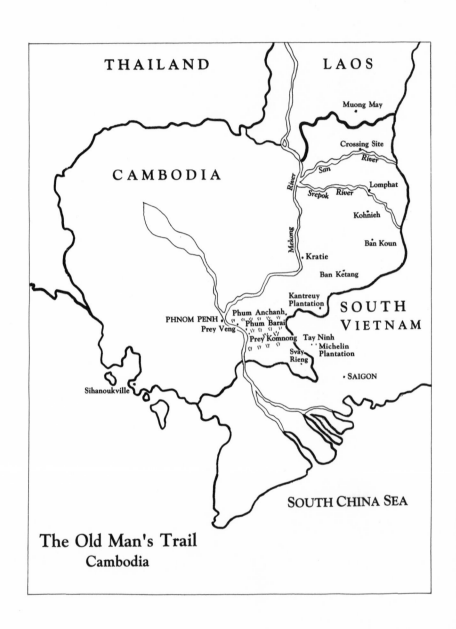

THAILAND                                        LAOS

                                                      Muong May

                                             Crossing Site
                                                     River
CAMBODIA                          San
                              Srepok    River        Lomphat

                                                     Kohnieh

                                                Ban Koun

                                    • Kratie

                                    Ban Ketang

                               Kantreuy
                               Plantation
PHNOM PENH •    Phum Anchanh,                    SOUTH
                    Phum Barai                   VIETNAM
   Prey Veng     Prey Komnong    Tay Ninh
                      Svay    •• Michelin
                      Rieng      Plantation

                                    • SAIGON
Sihanoukville •



                                    SOUTH CHINA SEA

The Old Man's Trail
Cambodia

# SIX

# Cambodia

## SAN RIVER, NORTHERN CAMBODIA

On their second day in Cambodia, the platoon crossed the rushing San River on a high rope footbridge. The weather remained overcast and rainy but it was warmer, which was a welcome relief from the wet and cold Truong Son Mountains. The terrain opened up, and they found themselves crossing wide stretches of thatch and rice fields that Duan insisted be accomplished at a fast jog. He was always anxious when there was no foliage overhead.

When they reached Boung Long, Cambodia—much to Duan's irritation—their route card directed them to take another loose-surface graded road, where they traveled again with other foot increments and vehicles that TG559 was pushing hard to get south before the weather lifted. Duan managed to talk his way out of riding in a convoy of ammunition trucks by promising to cover a particularly long stretch of trail between two way stations in a single day. It was a considerable distance, but twenty miles on a flat, graded road was easier than ten miles in the mountains. The platoon handled it well, but the guides grumbled about the fast pace.

They stayed at the expansive hub depot at Lomphat, Cambodia, in Zone 701. There was a big vehicle park filled with trucks and artillery, and four guns were set up in firing positions to support a battalion of Khmer Rouge and a battalion of Vietcong infantry that operated just to the west against the Cambodian army. That night the porters did some very successful scrounging, as they often did at the large bases, and added twenty pounds of dried freshwater prawns and three dozen loaves of bread to the platoon cache. Rice was plentiful, thanks to the Cambodian black market, and the porters gorged themselves. Bomb craters surrounding the base signified that the Americans had spotted the area. Duan noticed that the camouflage was neglected; obviously it hadn't been good enough to fool the enemy's spying devices. The depot commander apparently felt that he compensated for the poor camouflage with more than two dozen antiaircraft gun emplacements. A stupid but remarkably common error among my senior commanders, thought Duan. Anyone who did not know by now that guns would not stop airplanes was blind or a fool.

Ba and Duan roused the platoon early for a good breakfast of pork, cabbage, onion, and rice soup. Coffee was abundant in Cambodia, and the men drank it with a half-inch of condensed milk poured in the bottom of the cup for quick energy. They began moving while it was still dark toward the ferry site across the Srepok River and were the first increment in line to make the crossing.

As dawn broke they began to notice peculiar-looking objects floating in the wide brown river. There was also a strange, sickening smell in the air. Duan knew what the objects and the smells were and said nothing, but after awhile Ba asked the guide. He explained that the Cambodian government—*my nguy*—American Puppets—had declared all ethnic Vietnamese in Cambodia to be subversives and had begun systematically to exterminate them, throwing their bodies in the rivers to float into North Vietnamese base camps as reminders that Vietnamese were not welcome in Cambodia. The platoon overheard the conversation as they sat silently watching the bodies float by, some tied together in strings of thirty or forty. Their faces registered a mixture of rage and sorrow.

The ferry, an old barge, chugged across the river driven by four large smoke-belching Soviet-manufactured outboard engines. It beached at the loading point. The porters filed up a series of planks used for a gangway along with two other foot increments, in noticeably worse shape than Increment 1008. The men were emaciated, hollow-eyed, covered with running sores, and many had tubercular-sounding coughs. Their leaders didn't look much better.

To Duan's horror, two large trucks towing 130-mm artillery pieces drove up to the landing site and attempted to negotiate the wooden ramps, which promptly splintered. Duan cursed under his breath. Ba and the platoon watched the scene closely, wondering what to expect. To their surprise, Duan casually began talking to their guide, who seemed already committed to a long nap while the engineers figured a way to get the trucks and guns onto the barge. After a few moments the guide put on his bush hat, and he and Duan jumped off the barge and walked over to several officers who were not involved in the efforts to get enough timber gathered for the trucks to make it up over the high sides of the barge.

The porters watched Duan and the guide produce the platoon's route card and begin an intense conference with the officers. Apparently Duan was expressing grave concern that the platoon stay on schedule because of the deteriorating condition of his men. He pointed to one of the sorry-looking platoons, and the officers nodded. Clearly these men were on their last legs. Finally one of the officers gave the guide a piece of paper and told him to go around the bend in the river and collect several small fishing boats to ferry the platoon across.

An hour and a half later the last six porters had pushed off from the bank in a small boat, while mass confusion continued to reign at the barge. The loading party had managed to load both trucks and guns, but now the barge had settled to the bottom of the riverbank and its old motors did not have enough power to pull it free.

As they paddled across the river, the stench from the decomposing bodies became unbearable. The discolored water reeked, and almost everyone lost their substantial breakfast. At one point two boats got tangled in a rope linking the bodies of women and children, and the porters struggled frantically to free themselves. They reached the bank with the floating charnel house following them like silent ghosts while fish rippled the water, enjoying the unexpected feast.

The platoon set out from the south side of Srepok at a fast pace, trying, through physical exertion, to shake the horrible images from their minds. Things were quiet for several hours, and by noon they were making good time on the detested open road. Because of the traffic jam at the river crossing, they were alone. The rain had stopped and rays of sunlight filtered through the clouds as the weather cleared.

Ky was the first to hear the distant jet engines and gave warning. The platoon melted into the sparse jungle and took cover. The noise increased but was still distant, and they could hear planes going into shrieking dives as they hit the Lomphat depot and ferry site they had left several hours before. Four airplanes coming from the south streaked overhead to join the attack. It began to sound like a major battle. The platoon hid for an hour, periodically catching the glint of an aircraft wing in the now-bright sunlight. The planes arched high in the sky amid streams of green tracers from the ground, then dove back toward their targets. Antiaircraft guns still hammered away, but in fewer numbers than at the beginning of the battle.

Then, a faint sputtering noise. It grew louder, approaching their position. Suddenly a crippled jet, streaming black smoke, came into view following the trace of the road. When it was abreast of the platoon two streaks of white smoke arched from the airplane just before it exploded, and parachutes blossomed from the black objects on top of the white smoke plumes. The pilots drifted to earth, landing with a splash eight hundred yards away in the open rice paddies.

Several porters jumped up excitedly, to run out of the protective jungle to capture the pilots. Duan hissed after them, "Everyone stay where you are. It is more important now than before that we remain hidden. The Americans may fight for a bad cause, but they are good soldiers. They take care of their men like we do. Shortly they will come with helicopters and more airplanes to rescue those pilots out there. They will bomb us if they see us. Slowly cover yourselves with the vegetation around you. No abrupt movement, but be quick." The platoon began to follow his orders.

The guide, a young soldier not much older than the porters, spoke up. "Sergeant Major, our orders are to capture all American fliers we see. Let's go get them before the planes arrive."

Duan eyed him coldly. "You are welcome, my young comrade, to do as you wish. Your orders, of course, come from men who are stupid enough to let their camouflage rot and try to fight airplanes with guns. Those same men are probably dead now. If you wish to join them, please feel free to be a hero. But before you do, listen carefully." He cocked his head.

A faint sound became a deafening roar in a matter of seconds as two jets streaked over the rice field, arched high in the sky, and dove back toward the ground. They began to circle the area slowly. One plane, flying at an altitude of fifty feet, passed closely along the tree line where the platoon hid. Duan shouted above the engine's din, "Please, my young comrade, go and capture the Americans now," and ducked his head with a wry laugh.

Two prop-driven planes, with bombs under their wings, entered the area and began to circle below the jets. Then two big helicopters roared over their position. One pulled up steeply and orbited above the prop planes; the second dove low toward the downed pilots, banked sharply, pulling his nose high, and slowly set down in the rice paddy. They watched the pilots run and dive through a side door and the helicopter immediately lifted off, raising a geyser of water with its powerful rotor blades. It circled once and, joined by the orbiting helo, flew off toward the west.

The prop planes now circled higher and headed north, where they released their bombs over an unseen target. The jets streaked down and unloaded their ordnance on the same location. All four airplanes took turns strafing the unseen target. Ten minutes later they flew off to the west and everything was quiet.

"Guide," hissed Duan.

"Yes, Sergeant Major," he said meekly.

"Find us a jungle trail. No more of this damned road today. We should be thankful for the courage of our dead comrades, who foolishly tried to capture the American pilots and drew attention away from us." He pointed gravely toward the smoke to the north. "Learn a lesson in survival from this. You can capture pilots easily in the North, but in the South, you do so at your own peril. They always come after them with their endless supply of whoring helicopters and airplanes."

Everyone, including the guide, listened. Duan was a teacher, smart about things, and he would get them through. They trusted and feared him like a father. The porters, even the lazy ones, had been beaten, kicked, cajoled, and persuaded into the attitude that if you wanted to stay alive, you had to do hard things. Take the hard trails, lie in the mud, cling to the jungle like a beautiful woman, move fast at the slightest sign of danger, place comfort second, and always stay alert. The enemy was very clever, cunning, and cruel, and deserved close watching. A man could never let his guard down against such an enemy. If he did they would kill him. They were persistent and ruthless.

Neither Duan nor anyone else had more than a vague idea about how airplanes, radars, sensors, and cameras worked. Nor would they ever know. Duan taught them to learn from the patterns because the Americans had rules and procedures just like any other army. If their patterns were studied, a soldier could come up with his own rules for survival. Never venture into the open. Avoid cities, villages, base camps, roads, vehicles of any type, fuel dumps, ferries, antiaircraft guns, and artillery pieces, because they represented only one thing to the Americans: targets. Be a shadow, and they wouldn't waste time with you. To stay alive you needed to be cold and miserable most of the time. Comfort spelled danger. Avoid it. Survive. That was the important thing. These ideas had become their accepted creed. Duan and Ba, who had learned Duan's lessons well, made them live by the creed. The platoon had become like their sons and they the fathers. They were as one; they had the same goal.

It was 8:00 P.M. before they arrived at the next way station. The guide from the Lomphat base had violated his orders and stayed with them to the next way station, being afraid to go back. The station commander berated him, but as a long-term veteran of the trail system, he let it go at that. Good guides were getting hard to find, and he liked anyone who took initiative. Duan told him about what they had seen of the attack that day, and he passed the information along on a Russian field wire phone, talking to way stations farther south in violation of the strict security regulations. There would probably be at least a two-day delay before the way stations in this region would see any more increments passing south of Lomphat.

The food was good that night—rice, chicken, cabbage, cucumbers, *nuoc mam* with hot peppers, a dozen cans of captured American C-rations and ten big bottles of excellent Cambodian Angkor beer, split among the platoon. After their meal, when the platoon had turned in, the station commander confided to Ba and Duan, "I am getting a little edgy out here by myself with only eight men and one woman. The Americans are getting more aggressive with their airplanes, if that's possible. Even with the monsoon their planes are bombing targets from above the clouds, which terrifies everyone. The Cambodian army has always been a problem for small isolated stations like mine. They don't have the courage to fight the Vietcong or Khmer Rouge units. They like to sneak up on undefended stations like ours. We're easy prey. They loot and rape—it's their military specialty. Vietcong security platoons, and sometimes a whole company, patrol through my area, but we are alone most of the time."

Just then he received an order over his field phone, directing all increments to shift back to night instead of daylight movement. He and Duan, with the loathing of all field soldiers for high-ranking bureaucrats, sneered at the decision as once again being too little too late. The Lomphat attack must have cost them dearly, Duan decided. In any event, the platoon would get their first long break since leaving Van Xa and could sleep in the following morning.

Heeding the station commander's story, he set up a four-man guard, armed with the weapons they had picked up, to augment the station crew's security. It proved to be an uneventful night, and most of the men found themselves awake at the usual time. After breakfast, Duan explained in detail to the camp how the Americans used electronic devices dropped by their airplanes to pinpoint their movements. "I have found thirty-five or forty of the damn machines," he said. "They are cleverly camouflaged: their antennas are made of rubber to look like the jungle. You must be careful, because some are booby-trapped.

"However, never once have I seen Americans drop bombs or shoot artillery accurately on an infantry unit on a jungle trail. This may mean they don't know how to use the ones they drop in the jungle. The ones by the roads are different. I think they know very well how to use them. This is another reason to avoid roads at all times. In my experience, weather is not a factor for them. They can find you like a cat, day or night, in monsoon or bright sunlight. But in the jungle they can't make out if it's a herd of deer, a water buffalo, or a company of *bo doi*."

He borrowed some grenades from the station chief, and with several porters and half the station crew set booby traps in concentric circles five hundred, three hundred, and two hundred yards from the camp. Each had a different trip mechanism, and he showed the men how to set and disarm each type. The grateful station commander gave him two cases of American C-rations and some dried shrimp. Duan told the porters not to steal from this station, and when he caught one man doing so, he beat him with a tree limb.

They slept all afternoon. At sundown they set out under a clear sky with three guides on a relatively flat trail paralleling the main road. At a stream crossing they lost a man who yelled out and disappeared without a trace in the blackness. Halfway to the next station one of the guides became spooked and, mistaking guides from the next station for Cambodians, shot and killed one of them. A bitter argument ensued between the two guide teams, which could have turned into a shootout had Duan not stopped it. After a brutal and terrifying night, the platoon staggered into the next way station as the sun was rising.

It was 9:00 A.M. before their scratches and bruises had been cared for, leeches pulled off, and they had been fed. Exhausted, they collapsed in their hammocks. The talk around the camp was of the attack on Lomphat. Apparently the depot had virtually been destroyed. Casualty figures indicated around a hundred killed and twice that wounded. Duan showed neither sympathy nor sorrow, saying that only fools let their camouflage rot and try to fight airplanes with guns.

The platoon slept restlessly that day in the humid heat. Flies buzzed constantly and invaded their tattered mosquito nets. As they prepared to leave that night, one man came down with an attack of malaria and another couldn't march because of a knee injury. They left both with the way station crew, but there was no medic, so their futures were unsure. Duan ordered the porters to replace the stolen food before they left, for fear of reprisals against the two casualties.

They proceeded on level but treacherous trails that crossed numerous swollen streams. Any stream was dangerous to cross with a heavy load, and this was doubly true at night. Duan refused to let the guides rush him and he carefully organized each crossing so they wouldn't lose any more men. The guides were young and not very trail-wise. He cautioned them several times to move with more deliberation, but they ignored him. Three hours outside the way station, near Kohnieh one guide hit a Cambodian army booby trap and was killed instantly. The second was seriously wounded in the blast, and two porters were scratched and nicked. Duan quickly brought order out of chaos, imposing complete quiet. Movement and talking could be heard further south on the trail. The wounded guide was hoisted on a hammock hastily strung under a spare carrying pole, and Duan told the uninjured guide to pick up a small trail leading west through thicker jungle. He would catch up. The platoon filed down the path; after several minutes the thick undergrowth hid the sound of their movement.

Duan pulled Ba, Ky, and Trang aside and told them his plan. They positioned themselves with Ba and Ky on one side of the trail and Duan and Trang on the other, ten yards north of the guide's body so they would not fire at each other, and waited. After ten minutes they could hear the excited voices of four Cambodian soldiers approaching from the south. They were smoking cigarettes, their weapons slung over their shoulders. When they reached the dead guide they began searching his pockets and talking even louder.

Duan fired first. Ba, Trang, and Ky squeezed the triggers of their AK-47s and felt them rise back into their shoulders after each of their six short bursts. Ba had never fired a weapon in combat before, and it was the first time Ky or Trang had ever fired a rifle.

All four Cambodians were dead or mortally wounded before they hit the ground. Duan quickly moved over the bodies, shot one in the head who was still moaning and told the others to cut off the Cambodians' ears. Meanwhile he gathered the weapons, two American M1s and two carbines, and their ammunition belts. Ba, Trang, and Ky hesitated. Duan reached down and grabbed one man's ear and cut it off even with the skull. "See, it's easy. Just like cutting an onion."

Still they hesitated. Duan spoke softly in the dark. "The Khmer Rouge always cut the ears off the men, women, and children they kill. The Cambodians are terrified of them. When they find these bodies they'll run away and won't try to follow us. Go ahead. It's easy. They're dead." They hastily cut the ears off the remaining three men. The Cambodians had worn handkerchief amulets rolled tightly and tied around their necks. Inside the folds were notes, prayers, and good luck charms given to them by their friends and families. Duan took each handkerchief, cut it open, and stuffed the contents in the dead men's mouths to further terrify their unit when they found the bodies.

Next he passed around the four weapons and ammunition and picked up the body of the dead guide, draping it over his shoulders. "You did well in the ambush. You showed courage and shot straight." He smiled. "Now we go. Fast."

It took only half an hour to catch up to the platoon. They were moving much more carefully now, with the surviving guide in the lead. Duan called a halt and they rigged the dead man's body to another spare pole, which Ky and Trang carried. After an hour of walking they could hear wild shooting from the vicinity of the ambush. Duan smiled to himself. The Cambodian army hadn't changed much since he had fought them three years before.

The station crew at Kohnieh were very concerned when the platoon arrived just before dawn in a state of near exhaustion. They had heard the firing in the night. The wounded guide was put next to the fire and one of the men, who was not a medic, cleaned the wounds as best he could. The guide had a shrapnel hole in the side of his chest, which no one knew how to treat. There wasn't a doctor for fifty miles.

After breakfast Duan assembled the station crew and his porters to critique what had happened the night before. He explained how he had set up the ambush and why. He credited Ba, Trang, and Ky with killing the four Cambodians, and everyone applauded them. Then he showed them the ears, which awed and horrified them. The smooth trophies were gingerly passed around. The Cambodians' filthy, rusted weapons were shown as an example of how a soldier should never treat his best friend. One of the porters asked why the Cambodians were fighting the Revolution. He naively said he thought they were fighting only the American imperialists. Duan explained patiently, "The Cambodians are nothing more than *my nguy,* and if anyone raises his rifle against *Bac Ho* and the Revolution, the *bo doi* seldom ask why. We just kill them. Our job is to destroy those who stand in the way of the Revolution."

As usual Duan had a simple, logical answer to a complex problem. The porters nodded, accepting the answer to the question they had all been talking about.

They rested better that day. The sky was overcast, the air cooler. By mid-afternoon it had begun to mist. As they were eating dinner a Vietcong security platoon entered the station. They had come in response to the report of trouble with the Cambodians.

There was an air about the Vietcong that everyone noticed. They laughed easily as they greeted the station crew, whom they knew from other missions, but their eyes were constantly watchful; they sensed their surroundings with the wariness of wild animals. There were twenty men and two women. Most were in their mid-twenties but looked older. Five of the men were not much older than the porters, but their faces were hard and alert. They were heavily armed with AK-47 rifles, two RPD light machine guns, two American M-79s, and an RPG-7 grenade launcher. Their black cotton uniforms were old but mended, and their weapons glistened. Six men and one woman, the platoon's booby-trap expert, moved silently into the jungle to stand watch. The other woman, the platoon medic, looked at the wounded guide and said there was nothing she could do for him. He was in a coma.

The station commander, thankful for some protection, ordered extra food. Duan gave the Vietcong platoon leader his bowl of rice and the porters followed his lead and gave their rations to the platoon members, who graciously accepted. The station crew produced a bowl of papayas and four stalks of bananas they had cultivated in clearings around the station. The Vietcong complimented the delicious fruit, and a bowl was passed around to collect the big black banana seeds, which would be used to grow more trees.

All the porters squatted around the cook hut. The Vietcong rested their rifles between their legs while they ate, but they remained vigilant. Their accents identified them as South Vietnamese.

Duan talked with the platoon leader, trying to pick up as much information as possible. He knew the threats increased the farther south they moved. The last several days had confirmed this. He was told that indeed the American planes were bombing the big base areas along the border with more vengeance than usual. No, the Cambodian army was really more of a nuisance than a threat. The platoon leader assured Duan that by sunrise the next morning the Cambodian unit that had booby-trapped the trail would be hanging from trees minus their ears and disemboweled to remind others not to interfere with the Revolution's traffic on the Old Man's Trail. He said it matter-of-factly, with no trace of relish or revenge. These were his orders, and he followed orders.

After years of fighting the Cambodian army, the Vietcong had found that visible atrocities worked well as a tactic because of the Cambodians' almost total lack of discipline and other soldierly virtues. It was an army of mercenaries who sought the power that a gun and a uniform afforded. When they weren't paid, which was often, in order to stay alive their officers would turn them loose looting and raping, at which they had become quite skilled. Mutilated and disemboweled bodies hanging in strategic locations almost always signified a disorganized Cambodian retreat. Consequently, the Vietcong and the Khmer Rouge routinely fought Cambodian battalions with squads or platoons and won.

The platoon leader warned of a major American and South Vietnamese operation in and around Tay Ninh. They had heard that large units had crossed the border four days ago, and tanks and armored vehicles were involved. Duan asked about his old division, the Ninth Vietcong Division, the unit they were going to join. The platoon leader replied that, last he had heard, the division had been pushed out of their traditional operating area around the old Michelin rubber-tree plantation east of Tay Ninh City, and was reorganizing somewhere around Prey Veng, Cambodia. Reorganizing was the official description used for a unit that had been badly mauled and could no longer fight effectively. Duan alone understood the full meaning of the answer.

The platoon leader asked how many days the platoon had been on the Old Man's Trail, and Duan told him thirty-nine. He looked appreciatively at the young faces and complimented him on how well he had cared for his men. The Vietcong troops all smiled, knowing that Duan and Ba must be very clever to have gotten through in such good shape. They were used to seeing walking dead at this end of the trail.

Ba asked innocently about B-52 attacks. At the mention of the word all eyes jerked toward him. This was the only betrayal of apprehension that the Vietcong had shown. They glanced around nervously. Some darted their eyes toward the sky or cocked their heads as if to listen for the deadly whisper. Superstition dictated that you never mentioned B-52s. It was bad luck. Everyone shifted uneasily, and after an embarrassed silence the platoon leader said simply that there had been an increase in attacks over the past few months.

The Vietcong platoon finished their food and carefully washed out their bowls and spoons with water from a rain barrel. Each of them walked over and thanked the station commander for the hospitality. He gave them several rice balls, meat, and some fruit for the troops on watch. With no orders or instructions they adjusted their gear, formed up behind the point man and a machine gunner, and filed silently out of the station on their mission. The porters and station crew watched them go with a mixture of admiration, fear, and thankfulness that they were not the Cambodian unit they were after. That afternoon the wounded guide died, and the station commander dutifully filled out the death certificate.

As it was turning dark they formed up in the camp to leave. The two wounded men had been cleaned up and were well enough to travel. The station commanders at this end of the trail, isolated and vulnerable in their lonely jungle camps, welcomed the additional armed security Increment 1008 brought with them. Guides likewise appreciated the additional firepower on the long jungle trails. TG559 regulations against arming porter increments were disregarded in deference to the numerous threats that were present in Cambodia, giving credence to the proverb that inappropriate orders will be ignored. Duan positioned Ba and Ky with AK-47s behind the two lead guides, Trang marched with an AK-47 in the middle of the column, and he brought up the rear. Even though the Vietcong security platoon had assured them the trail was clear of booby traps and Cambodians, it always paid to be careful. The night's march was rough. A sudden thunderstorm came up, and the rain fell in a steady downpour. Two miles south of camp, whispers began to rustle down the column. As lightning flashed they could make out the decapitated and disemboweled bodies of three Cambodian soldiers hanging by their feet from a tree nearby, obviously the grisly work of the Vietcong platoon they had just had dinner with. Each man walked on hurriedly.

They fell on the slippery, winding trail and made slow time, but there were only three streams to cross. Shortly after sunrise they staggered into the next way station, covered with leeches. The station chief had bad news for them. Zone 740 headquarters, which controlled this section of the trail, had just issued orders to switch back to daylight movement because the monsoon had resumed throughout Vietnam, Cambodia, and Laos. Their orders were to eat and make it to the next way station by nightfall. They were too tired to complain, except for Duan, who demanded to know the route they were assigned for the day. Much to his dismay, the station commander assured him that they would travel on a nice, even, improved road, and maybe they could catch a ride with a convoy. Duan argued against it and demanded that they be rerouted on a parallel jungle trail of some sort. The commander consulted with his guides, who shook their heads gravely and said that was impossible. The streams that cut across the trails in the area were too swollen to cross. Duan accepted the situation reluctantly but insisted on a two-hour layover to rest. The men strung their hammocks in a spacious bunker and were asleep in minutes.

As they prepared to leave, one porter came down with a malaria attack and they left him behind with the way station crew; there was no medic or quinine.

At 9:30 A.M. the forty-two exhausted porters set out and joined other beleaguered-looking foot increments and vehicles in the dark downpour. They passed a convoy of twenty trucks, which had stopped while engineers repaired a washed-out culvert by a small bridge. Duan forced them into a slow jog to get past the pileup, which he knew could be bombed at any minute. He believed the Americans could see trucks regardless of the weather.

In spite of their exhaustion they made it to the way station at Ban Koun depot at 4:00 P.M., which made them the first increment in for the night. They ate, dried out their clothing, cared for the multiple leech bites, oiled the loads, and by sundown were sound asleep in a dry bunker. Ba and Duan searched the camp and came up with some canned goods and fruit that were not being watched. Another man was lost to malaria, which most often struck when they exhausted themselves. That night they heard heavy bombing off to the east, and the moan of the Gatling guns on the Thug gunships.

The next morning, to Duan's satisfaction, they set off on a wet and miserable jungle trail that they would follow for four days. The ground was horizontal, but they had to negotiate six to eight stream crossings a day. The leeches were horrible, and they attached themselves in swarms whenever the men were in the water. Other porter platoons traveled with them as they neared the end of the trail. Most of these units were thin with sunken eyes, and so weak they had to struggle just to lift their loads. They shivered helplessly in the rain, too exhausted and dazed to remove the leeches that sucked blood from their ankles and legs.

Increments piled up at stream crossings, and there were long waits. The other platoons sat shaking listlessly in the cold rain awaiting their turn to cross. Duan always pushed to the head of the line, assessed the situation, and usually ordered their guide to another crossing site. At one particularly wide stream, they watched in horror as a rickety bamboo footbridge holding eight men gave way. All were drowned and washed downstream.

Duan didn't hesitate to use the loss as a teaching point, explaining in a whisper loud enough for all to hear, "It's clear that the stupid *do khon nan* in charge killed his eight men when he allowed too many on the footbridge at one time."

Whether they started out first or last on the trail in the morning, they were always the first to reach the way station at night. Some increments moved so slowly that they had to sleep on the trail, which put them further outside the energy-expended versus food-taken-in equation of life and death on the Old Man's Trail. One increment they saw had been on the trail for ninety days. They had started out with eighty men and were now down to eighteen skeletons struggling to carry two of the twenty 12.7-mm antiaircraft machine guns and mounts they had started out with. Their political officer had died a month before and their noncommissioned officer, in as bad shape as his men, blamed the trail's lack of support for the miserable condition of his men. Duan patiently explained to him the basic rules of survival. Namely, you are on your own. Don't trust any higher headquarters. He gave the man some scrounged canned goods and was startled to see that he barely had the strength to open the cans.

TG559 was a cold and efficient logistics organization. Its major concern was to deliver tons of cargo to major depots supplying the war in South Vietnam. The loss of five trucks to bombing or a collapsed bridge was subject to investigation and severe reprimands for those responsible. But to lose two hundred men a day to illness, malnutrition, or other jungle hazards was considered an acceptable price of doing business. The only real problem was how to move the equipment after the assigned porters perished. Food for the way stations was seen in the same light as diesel or gasoline fuel for vehicles. So many porters times so many kilos and grams of rice and protein. All tidy, all easily managed. The Revolution had a lot more people than trucks. TG559's only human link with the suffering on the trail was the station crews. In Duan's opinion, it was the way station teams that made the trail work at all. TG559 would get the medals, but the real credit belonged to the thousands of men and women in the lonely stations stretched over 650 miles of forbidding jungle.

On the fourth morning of their trek to the Ban Ketang depot, they were scheduled to depart behind four beleaguered units who would be using the only open trail. Duan's sixth sense told him something was wrong as he watched the other units struggle out of the way station. He assembled the platoon and gave them another lecture on trail procedures, stream crossings, and the importance of helping each other. Even though it was the same lecture he always gave, the men listened intently. He held their attention. When their guide told them it was time to go, Duan told him to wait and they talked awhile about alternate routes. The guide finally said he thought there was another way they could get through, but they would miss their guides at the exchange point. It turned out he had worked from the Ban Ketang depot and knew the route all the way in. Next they talked with the station commander, who hesitated to disobey orders. Duan gave him and the guide half of the opium from one of the two bags that he had been saving for just such a moment, and they instantly agreed. The opium was worth a fortune. They would smoke some and barter the rest for luxuries. Duan had used it for the luxury of survival.

Even with a late start and longer trail they made it into the hub depot at Ban Ketang by 3:00 P.M. A security company of heavily armed and grim-faced Vietcong passed them, moving fast into the jungle in the direction they had come from. There was much excitement. Duan found out from an officer that four porter platoons had been ambushed and wiped out by an American deep-penetration patrol between Ban Ketang and station 740MZ, which they had just left. Duan said nothing to the platoon, but by the time they bedded down that night all of them had heard the story. As they went to sleep, every man knew that Duan had saved them again.

That night he became delirious with malaria.

# SEVEN

# Rumors

## CENTRAL OFFICE FOR SOUTH VIETNAM (COSVN) HEADQUARTERS, KANTREUY PLANTATION, CAMBODIA

The old Kantreuy Plantation looked deserted and peaceful. The once-elegant colonial mansions were still imposing, despite the ravages of war and the unrelenting encroachment of the jungle. The stately trees, laid out in perfectly symmetrical rows that stretched for miles in all directions, stood imperious in the steady rain that darkened their trunks, rich with rubber sap, which had not been tapped in years. The milky latex sap had been one of the chief enticements for the French to embark on a century of colonization in Indochina. The rubber—a necessity for modern industrialized nations—drove the extensive cultivation of plantations in the Cochin China region that had, much later, become most of South Vietnam and Cambodia.

The Western and Eastern views of most things had never coincided, and on the best uses for rubber plantations there had developed yet another divergent thought process. The French saw the obvious industrial and commercial utility of rubber, but the Vietnamese had found an entirely different use. Since war had dominated Vietnamese society for centuries, fortifications had always been important. They had discovered that the rock-hard trunks and root systems of the rubber tree were equivalent to thick armor plate in the ability to stop almost every type of modern ordnance. Since they had little access to armor plate, they gravitated to rubber trees for protection.

That protection had attracted the Central Office for South Vietnam headquarters to the Kantreuy Plantation early in 1959. Over the years the command complex had grown into a labyrinth of tunnels, storage bunkers, workshops, and chambers for living and working. The maze stretched for miles, all of it under the strong protective rubber-tree root system. From this crude, uncomfortable, and safe hiding place, the COSVN waged war.

The COSVN commander, distinguished-looking even in the standard Vietcong-issue black cotton shirt, shorts, and sandals fashioned from old rubber tires, sat on a rickety chair, devouring a bowl of rich rice and chicken soup with sweet red sausage expertly prepared by his cook and valet, who sat on an old camp stool across from him. Between them stood a small table fashioned from American artillery ammunition boxes. The two men had been inseparable for more than fifteen years. The cook was outstanding at his trade. He had learned his culinary skills in Paris and gone on to become chef at Saigon's exclusive Cercle Sportif Club before joining the Vietminh in 1952, where he had been assigned to the COSVN commander, who then commanded a battalion. Their relationship was more like that of brothers than of high-ranking commander and lowly cook and long-time valet.

They were on their second liter of Angkor beer as the commander tried to regain his strength after fighting off a severe malaria attack and a persistent case of dysentery. With each spoonful of the soup he carefully selected a fiery green or red pepper, dipped it in *nuoc mam*, and washed the food down with a big swallow of beer. The beer and peppers had been the final remedy his doctor prescribed, after all other treatments had failed. The peppers sometimes killed intestinal amoebas better than drugs—which were in short supply and of questionable quality due to the tropical conditions. The beer provided carbonation, which somehow aided the folk cure. In spite of his weakness, his eyes were alert. His handsome, stoic face did not betray the gnawing pain he felt in his intestines.

The cook, several years younger than his commander, was a testament to the axiom that proximity to power was power. Unassuming and ordinary, he went about his menial duties in a quiet, inconspicuous way, which gained him access to information that was of great value to his commander. Several missing teeth and a tubercular cough added to his peasant appearance.

For years his task had been to report meticulously the news floating in the torrid Vietnamese rumor channels. The COSVN commander was a Political Bureau member and ardent supporter of its strict policies concerning security of state secrets, and he had ordered executions for breach of those harsh regulations. He was also a pragmatist, however, who realized that nothing could stop the unauthorized flow of information. Therefore he had decided years ago to tap into the gossip mill, which gave him immediate access to events that could take weeks or months to reach him through official reports. This foreknowledge of events was indeed responsible for his ever-increasing power in the Political Bureau's inner circle. Nor had anyone ever guessed that his meek cook was his closest advisor on strategy and policy, as well as his source of information.

"And so, what have you heard at the market, my friend?" the commander said quietly to the cook, changing the subject from discussion of family and home, which neither man had seen in five years.

"Based on what I hear, either the American airplanes are getting much more aggressive or our commanders are becoming less skilled at tactics and camouflage," the cook responded, never raising his eyes from his bowl of soup.

"Which do you think it is?" said the commander between bites.

"I believe the causes of our recent losses are equally divided between us and the enemy."

"Tell me why you arrive at such a conclusion." The commander leaned back in his chair, which creaked ominously.

"Several stories I have heard lead me to believe this. A few weeks ago one of the new Thug aircraft caught a battery of artillery at night on a road south of Tchepone. The Zone 611 commander, instead of ordering a quick salvage operation, moved two batteries of 37-mm antiaircraft guns into position and tried to shoot down the American planes that came the next day. So, in addition to losing ten trucks and six artillery pieces we also lost sixteen antiaircraft guns and two hundred men and only got one American airplane in return," the cook said noncommittally between spoonfuls of soup.

"Go on," said the COSVN commander, again addressing himself to his soup.

"A few days later, in monsoon rain, the Americans wiped out the fuel depot at Ban Mun Lan. You remember we refueled there on our trip to the Political Bureau meeting last March. Tri, the depot commander who took such good care of us, was killed. That fueling depot had been there for four years and had never been bombed before. I do not believe that Tri let his camouflage rot. He was too good to allow that to happen. I think the enemy has some new means of detection working against us. A similar story comes from the depot at Lomphat. One morning the enemy unexpectedly makes an appearance in low clouds with thirty or forty planes and destroys the ferry, dozens of trucks and guns, and tons of ammunition. Some rumors say we lost over three hundred people. My sources say the camouflage was rotted. I believe that to be the case. We only shot down one American plane, and the pilots were rescued." The cook spoke in an even, unemotional tone. "All of these things, taken together, lead me to my conclusion. The enemy grows more clever and aggressive, making it even more difficult for our commanders to successfully counter their moves. What once worked for us—the antiaircraft ambush, heavy concentrations of antiaircraft guns to protect high-value depots, camouflage—are not working anymore."

The commander looked at his friend and smiled pleasantly. "Strange," he said. "TG559 has reported none of these incidents."

They continued eating in silence. Finally the cook said, "I have heard no rumors about the new SA-7 missile antiaircraft company that you told me to be alert for."

"Good. That is one secret I want kept a secret. When we use them it must be a total surprise to the Americans as well as to our own forces. The news will boost the morale of our troops." He sipped his beer and smiled. "The SA-7 company arrived at Prey Komnong depot this morning." They ate in silence for a while, each absorbed in his own thoughts.

Finally the commander posed the question that he asked of his trusted advisor at least once each day. "Do you still believe in our strategy to rid this land of the long-nosed bastards?"

"Yes sir, I do," came the swift, confident response, which belied the cook's humble and sickly appearance. "We can never defeat the Americans in open combat. They are too powerful and ruthless. Only in a protracted conflict that concentrates on inflicting maximum casualties, fighting their airplanes wherever they appear, and holding their pilots as pawns can we ever hope to win a negotiated withdrawal, and they will withdraw. They have no courage for the *truong chinh!* Besides, it is not their land. When the Americans are gone Saigon will crumble of its own corruption. We have only to push a little," he concluded, a zealot's smile radiating his gap-toothed face.

The commander did not return the smile but looked gravely at his friend. Without a word, he stood up and wrapped a thin issue blanket around his shoulders and lay down carefully in his hammock, strung between two sturdy coconut logs supporting the ceiling of their bunker, thirty feet below ground. It was cold and damp, which did little to help him shake the effects of his sickness. "Thank you, my friend, for the superb meal. You are truly a master chef." He said nothing about the information he had been provided.

The cook covered him with his own blanket and stroked his shoulder as if he were a sick child. The commander drifted into his usual fitful sleep.

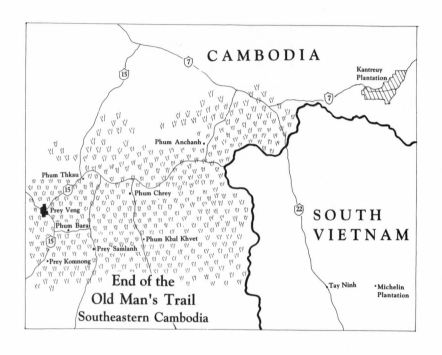

CAMBODIA

Kantreuy
Plantation

Phum Anchanh

Phum Thkau

Phum Chrey

Prey Veng

Phum Barai

Phum Kbal Khvet

SOUTH
VIETNAM

Prey Samianh

Prey Komnong

Tay Ninh

Michelin
Plantation

End of the
Old Man's Trail
Southeastern Cambodia

# EIGHT

# Enclave

## BAN KETANG, CAMBODIA

Ba, Ky, and Trang tended Duan throughout the night in his fits of fever. He called out for Su over and over again. His nightmares were always the same, with little variation. He was naked and had lost his rifle. The airplane, with the same pilot, was right behind him as he ran as fast as he could. Sometimes a banyan tree was there for him to hide behind, but sometimes he was on an open road running as the bombs fell, drifting from the wings of the airplane toward him. Or there was the worst variation of this nightmare. It was the re-creation of that terrible day on the open road west of Saigon as he fled the carnage of the aftermath of the Tet offensive. In his dream the American helicopter, like a giant flying insect, slowly approached them as they tried desperately to look innocent while fighting the instinct to dive for cover. The helicopter gradually closed in and he could see the grim faces of the pilots looking at him coldly through their dark eye shields. Mustering all his courage, he raised his hand casually and waved, and then there were white and yellow winks from gun muzzles and all around him the loud cracks of bullets. For some reason in the dream he always remained standing, feebly protecting himself with his arms. The helicopter moved off into the distance and there in the ditch was Tan, his friend and radioman for almost three years. "Tan, are you hurt? Are you hurt?" he heard himself say as he turned the body over. Tan's face was gone. There was just blood. "He was my friend," he screamed, "and I can't remember what he looked like. He was handsome and that is all I know." Then a powerful invisible hand threw him violently into the ditch with Tan. After that there was nothingness for a few moments and gradually he began to feel the searing, hot, piercing pain of the bullets and he awakened with a moan that sounded remarkably like the cry of a small child.

Ky wiped Duan's forehead with wet rags, trying to get some moisture into his mouth, watching him with calm black eyes. "Duan, I am here, and I will not let you die," he whispered softly. "You will not die. We need you."

In the morning the fever still had not broken. An arrogant, efficient TG559 scheduling lieutenant approached the platoon's crumbling and poorly camouflaged bunker. "You will go in thirty minutes," he said curtly to Ba.

"We are four days ahead on our route card. I will need two extra hours," responded Ba.

The lieutenant smiled maliciously and said the order stood. He strolled off to his bunker. The platoon moped as if they were at a funeral. Ba snapped them out of their depression by issuing the orders to move out. He noticed the smug lieutenant leave his bunker with some papers and walk casually off toward a column of trucks. He sent Ky and Trang into the bunker and they returned with a large plastic bag of bread and an American nylon blanket, which they quickly folded into the loads. They rigged Duan's hammock under a poncho draped over a carrying pole and followed the guide out of camp. In an hour, when the scheduling lieutenant discovered his loss, the platoon was out of sight in the jungle and rain. Duan was wrapped in the lieutenant's blanket and the platoon and their guide munched in silence on the bread, which was a little stale but still good.

The fever and delirium broke after two days on the trail, despite the lack of quinine or medics at the way stations. When he finally came around he was weak. The first thing he said was, "Are we in the jungle or on a main road?"

"Do not worry my friend, we have not seen the sky for two days," Ba reassured him. "We are in the second way station south of Ban Ketang."

The station crew, at the platoon's insistence, coaxed by some hard-to-find items in the platoon's cache, fixed Duan a rich herbal and meat broth, which did wonders to bring up his strength. They stood watches over him that night and fed him the broth whenever he awoke.

In the morning he was still too weak to walk but hungry enough to wolf down three bowls of rice, a can of sardines, two onions, and three whole bulbs of garlic. The garlic was believed to hold mysterious medicinal powers.

They carried him again that day, through the rain. After watching Ba for a while, he went to sleep knowing the platoon was in good hands. Ba could even talk like him after the past three months together, and Ky and Trang were capable leaders. Duan thought, Ba just might turn out to be a good officer after all. He has made it past the Srepok River, and I thought he wouldn't make it to the Kong.

He was glad Ba had come around. They had, in spite of their differences, become a very effective team. Idealistic, academic political cadres seldom did well in the mud, blood, and hardships of real war. It usually took a year or so for them to get tough and smart, or else they were killed. Ba had toughened up very fast.

Ba followed Duan's rules for survival precisely, refusing at each way station to take the easier and quicker graded road, which now included long sections of asphalt. The area they were in was the center of the main artery of the trail network leading south to Prey Veng and then east to Svay Rieng, Cambodia, and to the major base area at Zone 354, which sat astride the South Vietnam and Cambodian borders in what is called the Parrot's Beak and Fishhook areas. The trails in this area were in some places less than ten miles from the border. Fighting could be heard to the east day and night. The platoon had less than twelve days remaining on their route card, and after delivering their cargo, they would pass from the control of TG559 to the Ninth Vietcong Division. Based on the information Duan had received from the Vietcong platoon a week before, they might run into the division sooner, since they were reported to be regrouping around Prey Veng, only five days' march away.

On their forty-eighth day on the trail, at Station 354HV, Duan was able to walk and felt better. The way station was one of many that dotted the southern end of the trail where TG559 attempted to disperse military units, porter increments, and convoys, so as not to present too lucrative a target for the enemy, only a few miles away. There were two other porter platoons billeted with them in three large, well-constructed and camouflaged bunkers. The way station, like most close to the source of supply, was well-stocked and its fat, jovial commander treated them with great hospitality. The other two platoons in the station were in terrible shape, some of the men being too exhausted to eat. The station medic was busy tending them.

After dinner and their political indoctrination session, which had become more motivational than political at this point, the platoon bedded down. Duan and Ba talked for several hours, working out a strategy to keep them out of the murderous clutches of the scheduling bureaucrats who would, the next morning, certainly herd them as fast as possible onto Route 7 or Route 15, the local main roads. This time the miserable weather didn't comfort Duan. He doubted it would deceive the all-seeing Americans, particularly in open rice paddies like Prey Veng, which was situated just east of the Mekong River flowing southeast toward Saigon.

That night malaria claimed two more men, and the loss put them down to thirty-nine porters. A persuasive conversation with the station chief got them a phone call and two replacement porters who had been left at a nearby dispensary by their original increments several weeks before. The next morning the platoon rose early and huddled in the gloomy downpour under their vinyl ponchos eating rice balls and chicken. Duan talked to the scheduling NCO. "It's going to be at least an hour before the other platoons are ready, and we need to get moving." The NCO nodded and talked to the station medic, who said it was unlikely the other two increments would be able to move at all that day. The station chief agreed with Duan and gave them two guides. They set off on a wide, flat trail.

By first light they had left the jungle and broken out into vast rice fields dotted with villages and people working the paddies in the rain. This was the largest civilian population they had encountered on their journey. Most were ethnic Vietnamese who had fled persecution in other parts of Cambodia or the war in Vietnam and tilled the fields here under the protection of the major Communist forces that had occupied the enclave for several years.

Before noon they reached the wide east-west roadbed of Route 7, crossed it, and picked up a paved road that was well hidden under the jungle canopy. They passed huge, heavily camouflaged vehicle parks where hundreds of trucks, guns, and tanks were staged. Camouflaged bunkers and huts on stilts covered the landscape as far as they could see in the overcast gloom. Fenced pens teemed with chickens, ducks, and pigs, indicating that food would be plentiful again. Even Duan, who had seen just about everything, gawked when they came to a concrete apron next to the road where six massive Soviet-manufactured helicopters sat with the red, blue, and yellow NLF flag painted on their fuselages. One was doing an engine check, rotors turning.

It took them two hours of steady marching to pass through the depot area. Duan turned down three offers to ride in truck convoys, claiming he was punishing the platoon for their lack of discipline. At 4:00 P.M., still under dark clouds and rainy weather, they arrived at their way station at Phum Anchanh, which was at the southern end of the depot complex.

They ate in a big mess hall built in a bunker. The cooks had obviously benefited from the fertile rice fields and farms of the region and the depot's abundance of food. The meal was a banquet. There were delicious meat and herbal soups, designed to put exhausted, starving men on the road to recovery after their tortuous journey. The menu rivaled the send-off meal they had been given at Van Xa almost two months before.

The platoon was the only foot increment able to do the feast jus-
tice. There is a difference between a hungry and a starving man. The
other porter platoons were pathetic, ghostly in their appearance. Some
were down to sixty or seventy pounds. They had seen and experienced
privations unimagined before they had started their *truong chinh*.
Duan couldn't bring himself to look at them. He knew he had looked
like that after his first trip, but he refused to remember.

The starving porters sat as if alone and would slowly put a spoonful of the life-restoring broth in their mouths and then savor the flavor
before swallowing. Then another slow-motion movement from bowl
to mouth. Some sat sipping broth for two or three hours, gradually trying to bring themselves back to life. Duan's platoon was just hungry,
due to his leadership and his determination to beat a system that paid
little regard to human suffering.

Old habits die hard. When Duan's porters headed for their billet
bunker, pockets were stuffed with stolen bread, potatoes, dried shrimp,
and fruit. In spite of the sounds of fighting just off to the east, they slept
like babies. Ba and Duan found a helpful mess sergeant, who gave them
six big bottles of South Vietnamese La Rue beer. Ba's stomach didn't get
upset this time. As the alcohol coursed through his exhausted system
he confided to Duan, "The platoon and I are convinced that we would
not have made it without your great skill and leadership. You are the
reason we have survived this ordeal, Duan."

Duan was humble and quietly thanked his friend. In his line of
work, appreciation and encouragement were things a man learned to
live without. The beer, and an elated feeling of almost being finished
with the trail and the despised loads, led him to drop his guard for the
first time since leaving North Vietnam.

# NINE

# Convoy

## CONVOY STAGING AREA, TG559 DEPOT, PHUM ANCHANH, CAMBODIA

The next morning Duan stood in the rain with bleary eyes and a throbbing head, cursing himself for his stupidity in not making route arrangements the night before instead of getting drunk. In his mind, what made his dereliction even worse was that he had understood they were not among real soldiers but supply and transportation bureaucrats who let themselves be herded like docile farm animals toward the inevitable slaughter by the powerful and persistent Americans. From Duan's point of view, the TG559 organization so loved their comforts, schedules, and routine that these things came before life itself. He repeatedly cursed himself for not acting on his instincts, which were remarkably accurate.

His frustration was justified: the convoy commander, a smug transportation major, had assigned them to ride on the last three trucks in a fifty-vehicle convoy scheduled to move to Prey Veng that day. The trucks were already loaded with artillery and mortar ammunition. When Duan and Ba tried to persuade him to change their orders, he cut them off. "There will be no discussion," he said. "TG559 will deliver Increment 1008's cargo early, thereby showing the great efficiency of our logistics organization." He smiled benignly.

As the major, obviously quite pleased with himself, strode away toward the head of the convoy, Duan weighed his chances of shooting him in the back and getting away with it. The high probability of being caught was the only thing that stopped him. He looked around like a caged animal seeking a way out. There was none. The idea was obviously to rush as much cargo south as possible under cover of the bad weather. Duan knew that not only were the Americans good at finding the trucks or artillery that were their favorite targets, but that sometimes they randomly bombed locations in which they merely suspected activity. A major artery such as the road they would take was a prime target that could be hit at any time. But today he had no choice.

The front of the convoy was almost a quarter mile ahead of their three assigned trucks. Vehicles of every description were lined up bumper to bumper. Ten-wheeled trucks, flatbed tractor-trailers loaded with Russian-manufactured bulldozers, trucks towing 130-mm artillery pieces, and a battery of 57-mm antiaircraft guns stretched out in front of them. The drivers casually walked around talking, smoking, inspecting their vehicles. Ten trucks were loaded with a troop unit. Thirty young *bo doi* rode in the backs of the vehicles looking unconcerned. Duan cursed their officers and NCOs for not seeing the danger.

After what seemed like hours, the convoy began to move from under the camouflage onto the raised roadbed and into the rain. Movement was excruciatingly slow. After an hour they began to average about five miles per hour as they inched their way south on the wet and muddy roads. At the end of the convoy, the three trucks carrying Duan's platoon alternated between long delays and brief periods of racing to catch up.

At noon the whole convoy stopped on the open road for lunch, while drivers and passengers stretched and moved around in the rain with apparent unconcern. Duan was furious. He moved the platoon into the open rice paddies to get away from the vehicles, and he swore at the convoy commander's stupidity. As they were preparing to move again, the rain stopped and sunlight broke through the clouds far to the west. The efficient TG559 major suddenly recognized the presence of danger and tried to get the trucks going.

Duan stood in the middle of the rice paddy screaming the worst obscenities he could think of at the convoy commander; fortunately they were drowned out by the roar of engines. Several of the men snickered and Duan viciously kicked them into silence.

Ba tried to calm him down. Duan spit, "These bastards have only gotten worse over the years. They have lost their senses. You cannot give the Americans even a brief glimpse of you. They are too good, too clever, too cunning and will kill you every time. You must hide, Ba. Don't ever forget. These miserable supply *do cho de* will kill us if they can. I tell you, they will kill us. Look at this road. Look at the sky. This is what the Americans have but one name for. They call this a target, and so would I if I were them. Nothing but a target, Ba. May their souls be tormented for a thousand years. May their sons be born slaves and their daughters whores. May their children spit upon them in life and on their graves in death. Let their rice bowls be full of shit." He stopped and glared at the situation, enraged that he had no control over it or over his own destiny this day.

The drivers yelled for them to come on. The lead vehicles were already starting to move as the platoon scrambled into the truck beds. Duan ordered everyone to keep their eyes on him for a signal to dismount, because his voice would be drowned out by the truck engines.

The convoy gained speed and again became strung out. The trucks moved sporadically for half an hour and then ground to a halt as each laboriously negotiated a bypass around a small washed-out bridge. Gradually they inched their way up to the detour as the sky darkened once more and it began to rain.

As the lead vehicles of the convoy negotiated the bypass, they eroded the primitive earthwork engineering fashioned by a hundred women working as a road crew with wide-bladed hoes. In trying to drive through the muddy defile, the truck in front of them buried itself up to its rear axles as it attempted to regain the road surface. The woman in charge of the road crew motioned to a man with a team of water buffalo, who yoked the resentful beasts to the front axle of the stranded truck with three plaited ropes and painstakingly pulled it out of the mud. The convoy had moved a mile east and stopped to deal with the last stream bypass before picking up Route 15, which would take them safely into Prey Veng.

At the rear of the convoy, Duan worried and fumed.

Unseen and silent at 30,000 feet, a cell of three B-52 bombers, each carrying 105 MK84 750-pound bombs, followed the radar beacon. Instructions from ground controllers beamed from the immense American air base at Bien Hoa in South Vietnam. The ground controller would give each aircraft the precise location and time to drop the lethal loads, which today were targeted to crater the improved east-west road branching off Route 15 at the small village of Phum Thkau. The raid had been ordered by Task Force Alpha, operating out of their Surveillance Center headquarters at Nakhon Phanom, Thailand.

The frag order for the B-52s was borne of Task Force Alpha's frustration with the mounting pressure from their superiors to interdict the trail. This was their job, but bad weather over nearly every air base in Thailand and South Vietnam had reduced the number of airplanes that could get off the ground to barely enough assets for immediate support of ongoing ground operations. None were left over for interdiction. Pinpointing targets had also become a problem. There hadn't been a good aerial photo or ground surveillance radar run in ten days, and even the usually reliable sensor strings were of no use, since sensor links required airborne relay aircraft, grounded along with everything else. The southern Cambodia section of the trail had never been a good area for sensors anyway, because of the high population density and extensive rice paddies. In desperation the targeters had picked this particular section of road, principally because it had never been bombed before and ground surveillance radars on recon aircraft had picked up some truck traffic during the preceding week. The expense involved in B-52 raids usually dictated that they be targeted against hard, fully confirmed enemy positions. This road-cratering raid would be an exception to the policy in an attempt to get some safe interdiction sorties up on the tally boards. No one knew that a convoy of fifty vehicles would happen to be passing through the impact area. Later that would be counted as merely good fortune, even though several intelligence analysts would claim that they had predicted the traffic.

The planning for the raid and target assessments had been carried out in close-hold, top-secret, compartmented intelligence channels, because Cambodia was theoretically neutral and bombing raids in this area were not announced to the press. They were directed against the Vietnamese enclave, so the Cambodians never complained. Such missions had the added advantage of being low-risk, since no anti-aircraft or radar activity had ever been reported in the area. The conclusion was that the North Vietnamese were equally interested in keeping their enclave a secret.

As the B-52s crossed their Initial Point, twenty miles west of the target, two American F-105 Wild Weasel aircraft flew ahead on the same course at 3,500 feet. Their mission was to suppress and attack any enemy fire direction radar that might activate, using the ARM missiles slung under their wings. A single ELINT-66 airplane flew parallel to the bombers' flight path, ready to jam any radars that might come up and lock onto the B-52s. As Task Force Alpha had predicted, there were no radar activations, and the three mission-support airplanes, after clearing the bombers into the target, assumed circular flight paths to the north and south.

The B-52 cell, after receiving the all-clear signal from the support airplanes, approached the target in column formation. The lead bomber began to release his load in three distinct ripples, beginning with the two wing bomb racks, followed by the bomb bay ordnance. The release technique put most of the bombs down along the center axis of the road, or within fifty yards of it. The other two B-52s followed suit.

At the bypass, the sound of the F-105s had passed above the clouds and continued to the east. Several women had looked up, but instinct told them there was no danger as the sound of the engines faded. Then, a few minutes later, they heard another sound, the oscillating, hissing sound of bombs mixed with the splattering noise caused by the rain, which combined quickly into an unearthly blast. Almost in unison they raised their heads toward the sky and stood momentarily still while their minds tried to identify the source of the noise. Suddenly one woman yelled a warning and everyone began to scatter in whatever direction their intuition told them offered safety. In a few moments some would live and others die, based on the keenness of that intuition.

The ill-tuned, idling diesel engines of the trucks in the convoy delayed the sound from reaching the platoon for several more seconds, but Duan reacted as soon as he saw the first woman begin to run. He yelled, "Get out of the trucks. Down, on the ground!"

He signaled frantically to Ba and the others in the last two trucks to get to the side of the road as they had practiced. There followed twenty seconds of mad scrambling, as men and loads were flung down and the first string of bombs augered into the soft, wet earth two miles west of their trucks along the axis of the road. Brilliant flashes of red and yellow were followed by great geysers of mud, water, and steam, forming a thick black cloud. A few seconds passed and shock waves of successive, crunching explosions reached them. The thunderous concussion and heat of the bombs could be felt even at that distance. The ground shook.

The platoon lay facedown along the north side of the road, heads covered with their arms. Duan watched the explosions and sensed they were off at a distance that spelled no grave danger at that moment. One of two things would now happen. Either the second string of bombs would fall to the west of the first or to the east. His speculation was cut short as more bombs exploded on the near side of the first impact area. A few moments' pause, and another string of bombs walked into the lead vehicles of the convoy. Steel, bodies, ammunition, and fuel were consumed in the crunching explosions, releasing more dark clouds of smoke, steam, and mud.

In an instant Duan was on his feet yelling and kicking the platoon into action. This was his nightmare, except he couldn't see the pilot's laughing face. The dream always had two outcomes. He was in the open, but at least he wasn't naked, and he had his rifle.

He motioned for Ba to lead them north along the narrow stream-bed that flowed into the washed-out bridge culvert. Struggling through the slow-motion feeling that accompanies life-and-death situations, the platoon clawed their way off the road, dragging their loads. Once they reached the streambed a five-foot embankment stood between them and the bombing pattern, which was moving toward them from the west. As the bombs approached, the sound began to hurt their ears. Duan pushed them farther up the streambed, away from the road. A group of women cowered against the embankment directly off the road. Duan glanced back at the truck they had ridden in and saw the driver still sitting behind the wheel, paralyzed with fright as certain death came toward him.

By the time the bombs started bursting among the last vehicles of the convoy, the platoon had turned a slight bend in the streambed, putting the roadbed out of sight. The thundering, soul-shattering din now mingled with spasmodic detonations of exploding ammunition and fuel on the destroyed trucks. Duan frantically assessed their cover and was horrified to see that to their rear, only a two-foot rise sheltered them. They could look out over sweeping rice paddies to their east and see the raised roadbed as it curved around.

The bombs continued to impact along the axis of the road. The trucks they had been riding in disappeared in a blinding flash of red, yellow, and black. From their position behind the bend in the streambed, they could feel the force of the rapid explosions in their bowels. The sound was maddening. It engulfed them in a pocket of horrendous noises, lifting them helplessly out of the mud and slam-ming them back down again. A wave of water and debris blew down the streambed. Three smoldering crates of artillery shells bounced end-over-end and finally stopped, steaming in the water several feet from where they clung to the embankment. The bodies of half a dozen women flew down the stream like rag dolls and then lay still, with their heads and bodies twisted at inhuman angles clearly indicating instant death.

The last bombs fell with a terrifying roar to the east of their position. The two-foot embankment to their east left them exposed to most of the blast just several hundred yards away. The overcast sky now went black as night as huge, billowing clouds of mud and debris engulfed them.

From their pathetic hiding place rose the sound of the porters' moans, cries, grunts, and incoherent phrases of mixed curses and prayers. The eerie, deathly whine of steel was everywhere. The nauseating thud of shrapnel impacting their open sanctuary became a series of rapid-fire sounds as shards from bombs to their east reached them in a wave. Men cried out as they were hit by the hot, jagged metal. Those fortunate enough to have a position below the rear stream embankment could hear and feel the blazing steel hit in the muddy embankment over their heads and sizzle as it generated steam from the wet earth.

The crunching, high-pitched explosions of the bombs were now replaced by the roar of burning fuel and a continuous series of dull, thudding blasts as ammunition randomly blew up from one end of the convoy to the other. The moaning sound that the platoon made was now almost a steady wail and took on a weird quality of its own, like souls being tormented in hell.

The whole attack had taken only a few minutes, from the first bomb impact to the last. It had seemed like a lifetime. Now the fallout began to ripple through the paddies. First came bits of rock and steel, which sounded like handfuls of pebbles being thrown in the rice paddies and the stream. Then larger objects began to fall in succession. An intact set of tandem wheels and a truck axle hit the ground, bounced high in the air, and rolled heavily down the shallow stream. The barrel of an anti-aircraft gun cartwheeled over their heads, followed by a cluster of anti-aircraft ammunition and a naked, blackened, decapitated body. One of the water buffalo from the bypass fell from the sky and landed in the stream with a thump, sending up a geyser of water. He lay on his side and blinked slowly, jaw moving. Then his jaw stopped and he passed a long emission of gas and emptied his bowels for the last time. Falling debris splashed into the stream around them for a full minute. No one looked or raised their heads. Then there was silence, punctuated only by the crackling of burning fuel, vehicles, human flesh, and the occasional smack of exploding ammunition.

Duan rose carefully to a crouched position, holding his rifle at the ready, as if it would protect him. He gazed around in the sooty darkness at the destruction and yelled for the platoon to stay down. His mind raced through his experiences with enemy aircraft. There was only one thing that stuck in his mind. B-52s never bombed the same target twice. The safest place after an attack was the impact area. His old battalion commander had shown them that trick when they had begun to bomb the Tay Ninh Forest years before. Now he knew what to do. "Push fear aside and think," he whispered to himself. It took all his willpower and concentration to formulate a plan of action.

"Raise your heads. Look at me. Now!" he said, trying to steady his voice, which seemed to come from another person. He noticed that he could not hear.

The low wailing continued as though the men hadn't heard him. Louder this time, he shouted, "Look at me. Now!"

Only a few heads came up and gazed at him with dazed expressions. He saw blood running from their ears. He ran his finger in his own ear and felt the slick liquid. He looked at the blood on his finger for a moment and said a few words to himself, which sounded distant and strange. He could understand himself only through the vibrations of his vocal chords. It was as if his voice were not a part of him but came from a great distance.

Urgently he worked his way down the line, shaking each man hard by the shoulders. The response was almost uniform. After several violent shakes the man would jerk his head up, wild-eyed as if he had just awakened from a nightmare.

Five porters were dead or dying and two were seriously wounded. The ones who had not been hit bad were scratched and dazed. They looked about as if they didn't know where they were. He yelled as loud as he could, "Everyone who can hear me, raise your hand. Now." The hands came up, except for those of three men who still looked around confused.

Using his voice, foot, and hand signals, he began to get them on their feet. Most could now hear the burning convoy and exploding ammunition, but it sounded strange and far away. Three were stone deaf. Ba had been hit in the arm and was bleeding from both ears. He noted the names of the dead men. There wasn't time to bury them, so they left them where they were.

Next he ordered the loads gathered up. They could find only fifteen. Luckily they had all six mortars. Duan had always made sure that only the best and strongest teams carried them and it had paid off in this attack. Out of the forty-one men that had embarked in the convoy that morning, Duan counted thirty-four capable of marching, plus two wounded, who had to be carried. He slit the ropes on two loads of ammunition and they rigged hammocks for the wounded. The spare poles had been lost with the trucks. Suddenly a box of artillery ammunition blew up a hundred yards from them and everyone flattened themselves in the streambed. No one moved until Duan kicked them to their feet.

"We will now get out of this damned place as quickly as we can. You will follow me, and you will not stop until I say," he said. He moved down the line yelling the instructions over and over until he got at least a vague indication of understanding from each man. The only thing their minds really comprehended was that they trusted him completely. Wherever he took them, they would go. Today it would be through the doors of hell.

He led them slowly down the streambed. They passed the women of the road crew. Most were dead, but a few survivors moaned and appeared dazed. The blast had blown through their position unabated by the turn in the streambed that had saved the platoon. The water ran red with blood. Several reached out to Duan for help. He ignored them. There was no time except to save themselves. Several women staggered to their feet and followed along, not knowing where they were going but unable to think of anything else to do.

At the road Duan turned west. The scene that greeted him was one of complete destruction. Mountains of black smoke billowed from burning vehicles. A steady ripple of explosions punctuated the scene with flashes of gray, yellow, and red. The smoke from burning diesel fuel caused them to gag and cough. Every fifty yards or so they had to walk down into deep craters twenty yards wide. They stumbled and fell in the dirt and mud. Some depressions contained bloody unrecognizable masses of human flesh. When they fell, the ground burned their skin. Hot water at the bottom of the craters scalded their ankles, but they barely noticed it in their anxiety to reach level ground again and get away from the carnage and heat. Each hole was like a descent into hell.

When they had moved up to the main body of the roasting convoy, Duan stopped to reassess his plan. The heat and continuing explosions made following the road impossible. As they paused, the revoltingly sweet smell of burning flesh reached out and surrounded them. Duan gagged and vomited. Most of the men followed suit. He collected himself and watched the smoke drift off south of the road, then ordered the men to head for the rice paddies to the north of the road. The bomb pattern had created several craters off the center line of the road. They had filled with water that still gurgled and bubbled, and Duan led them around these holes, which put them off the small dikes and into the sucking mud of the paddies. Bodies floated everywhere in the mire. Some wounded and dazed people sat expressionless on the dikes, not noticing their passing.

Duan's senses were gradually coming back now, even though he still couldn't hear. He began to carefully pick their route, leading the platoon on a zigzag course that kept them on the paddy dikes and out of the mud. Detonations continued to ripple through the convoy. They could see bodies still sitting upright, burning fiercely in the backs of trucks. Duan had to kick several arms and legs off the dikes so they could pass.

After an hour of torturous movement they came to the head of the destroyed convoy. Duan recognized the commander's vehicle. It lay overturned in the rice paddy a hundred yards from the roadbed. He searched the area for the efficient major who had ordered them into this slaughter. Then he saw a knee rising from the water. He peered down and, just under the surface, saw the major's face looking up through the murky water, eyes and mouth open, a crab feasting on the nose. "You bastard," Duan said quietly. "I hope your soul is burning. You killed these good men and women, you pompous son of a whore. But you didn't kill me, even though you tried. See? I still live!" He spit in the water and kicked the body viciously. Then he took the dead officer's pistol and holster and had a man put it in his pack.

Now he looked around, trying to get his mind functioning again. It seemed to slip in and out of rational thought. He couldn't seem to control it. He sized up the platoon standing obediently and watching him, scared, patient, waiting for his decision. They were a ragged-looking bunch. Skinny, covered with mud, their uniforms in shreds, stunned expressions, bloody ears. Six women from the road crew followed along at the end of the column. They also looked disoriented, and two cried hysterically. Duan noticed how dry his mouth was, the result of the adrenaline rush his body had received. After a moment he signaled for a break and told them to drink. He was unable to think of anything else to do.

The water from his canteen tasted sweet and cooling to his parched mouth and throat. He drank deeply, feeling it seep into his body. Ba walked up to him and said calmly, "Look, Duan. The sun is out." He pointed to the almost cloudless sky, with rain clouds moving off to the east. Duan looked up and smiled and continued gulping the last of the water. Then he came to his senses. His smile disappeared and he looked around at the clear day that he hadn't even noticed. He cursed several times and was relieved to notice his mind clicking over options. "Think," he said out loud. Ba pointed south to a tree line and said,

"There's a small hamlet over there. Maybe a thousand yards. Looks like the dikes will take us there. Let's get out of this damned place, my friend."

"You take the lead, Ba. Ky, Trang, and I will get them going." He moved with smooth motions down the line, talking loudly to the platoon, consoling them with his touch. He saw that they were all in the same shape and having difficulty thinking. Soon they were following Ba in a zigzag pattern on the dikes, heading south. The sun was hot and dried them out quickly, but the moisture was replaced by sweat. They made it to the tree line by the small hamlet in forty-five minutes.

# TEN

# Escape

## RICE FIELDS SOUTHEAST OF PHUM THKAU, CAMBODIA

The hamlet was inhabited by ethnic Vietnamese farmers, not part of TG559's organization. Ba and Duan spoke courteously to the only man among the four families living in three mud-and-thatch huts. The villagers had been terrified by the bombing raid and were just now cautiously emerging from their underground bunkers. Duan suggested quietly, "We all need to get back in the bunkers, because soon the American planes will return, now that the skies are clear." The advice was instantly heeded.

It was still far off, but even with his hearing impaired Duan could hear the distant hum of inbound aircraft. Duan and Ba hid the loads carefully inside the houses and herded the platoon into the bunkers and trenches not being used by the villagers. All houses in that part of Cambodia were fortified. Any wise home builder first dug a deep bunker and then laid his floor on top of the coconut logs that comprised the bunker roof. In the event of attack, the tree line around the hamlet was laced with deep, narrow trenches that had been dug by the people or various military units, on both sides, who had passed through this much-contested and bloody locality. Duan and Ba jumped into a trench line.

They could hear the sound of children crying and whimpering in the bunkers as they sensed their parents' fear.

An American photo reconnaissance plane had done a Bomb Damage Assessment following the B-52 attack. The call that a whole convoy was smoldering in the open, under clear skies, sent twenty fighter bombers off the runways in Thailand as fast as their pilots could get them in the air.

The towering cloud could be seen from thirty miles away, and the first four planes came straight in without a pause to orient themselves on the target. They dropped their bombs down the axis of the smoldering convoy and then pulled up sharply, engines screaming for altitude to avoid antiaircraft fire. There was none. Two more planes came in and dropped napalm further down the convoy. The remaining aircraft followed in on the target in rapid succession.

Duan and Ba peered through a firing port cut between two big logs and were surprised to see a number of men from the trucks now beginning to scramble for safety. In their movement past the convoy, which had been at a distance of no more than two hundred yards, they had noticed only a few signs of life. Now a hundred or more people were making dashes for cover. Several planes began to make strafing runs on those exposed in the rice paddies and streambeds. Duan shook his head and whispered to Ba, "If you are going to move, never move after they have attacked you. Pick a spot to hide and don't move. We must remember this, Ba. The B-52s may not bomb in the same place twice, but if the bastards hit something big, they will send the smaller bombers. We were lucky today. Those planes could have come while we were in the open. Learn a valuable lesson at the expense of our dying comrades out there." Ba nodded solemnly.

For a half hour they grimly watched the Americans slaughter the survivors of the B-52 attack. One of the planes now flew directly for the small hamlet. Duan and Ba watched as it approached them head-on like a bird, silently floating on the wind, its engine hum slowly increasing. They dropped to the water in the bottom of the trench and covered their heads. First there was a series of high-pitched cracks from machine-gun bullets, then the aircraft burst over their heads with a deafening roar. The plane pulled up into a climb, then lazily dropped a wing and dove back toward the three-hut hamlet. This time he passed over and did not fire, apparently satisfied that there were no useful targets in that area.

The other planes circled and then flew off to the west. Again all was still, except for intermittent eruptions from the convoy. Women and children could be heard weeping in the bunkers. Duan left the trench, clutching his rifle for protection. It was still the most powerful thing he knew, but each time he was attacked by airplanes he subconsciously knew his rifle was weak and useless. As always he forced these thoughts away, because in his line of work relative power was the margin and measure of survival. A soldier had to believe in the might available to him.

By now it was midafternoon, and the day remained sunny. Duan and Ba got the platoon out of the bunkers and inventoried the loads in the shade under the wide eaves of a thatched roof. They had six mortars and seven ammunition loads, thirty-four able porters, and two wounded.

There was crying and confusion among the civilians. Finally they brought a woman and her six-month-old baby out of a bunker, both dead. A round from the airplane had found a slit in the coconut logs and the .50-caliber bullet had passed cleanly through both of them as she held the child close to her breast. Duan ordered two men to find a couple of hoes and help the people dig a grave in the cemetery mound fifty yards out in the rice paddy. It was marked by a small Buddhist stone monument. There were already four fresh graves there as death, from a multitude of sources, was always among the rice farmers.

The man of the hamlet was stunned by the unexpected violence. The dead woman had been one of his wives and the child his sixth and youngest. He wrapped their bodies in a single vinyl poncho and laid them in a common grave. He shed his tears quietly, then regained his composure. He had lost two wives and three children over the past two years to war and disease and had not become accustomed to it. But he had learned to put tragedy behind him as quickly as possible and resume his work, with so many other mouths to feed.

He told the women to start cooking for the platoon. This was a routine ritual when a military unit passed through, regardless of which side they fought for. But Duan stopped him and ordered the porters to break out the spare rations they had stolen the night before, plus twenty kilos of rice to put in the community cooking pot. The bread, potatoes, dried shrimp, and fruit supplemented the rice, which, in this part of the country, was cooked with the hot red peppers that grew abundantly along the rice paddy dikes. Big chunks of dried coconut meat provided a sweet dessert. After awhile everyone began to laugh, releasing the horror of the day.

Six women from the road crew waited on Ba and Duan, thanking them profusely for saving their lives. Two women were still sobbing, but were quieter now. Duan talked to them and both had the same explanation: they had lost aunts, sisters, or friends in the bombing raid. He consoled them but knew the truth was that their nerves had been shattered by the violence of the bombing and their minds had come close to snapping. He had seen it before. Sometimes the victims would come around; some would live the rest of their lives wearing these vacant stares. They usually became outcasts in a society that required everyone to contribute and take care of themselves. Duan told the oldest woman of the group what symptoms to look for, and she nodded gravely. One of the girls was her younger sister.

The women were part of the TG559 organization. Duan talked to them for a long time, leading them skillfully toward the answers he needed to form a plan. He was following a longstanding rule of survival. Whenever an individual or organization threatened his life needlessly through their stupidity, he figured a way to keep himself from ever getting in their grasp again. His two trips on the Old Man's Trail had been among his worst experiences with survival. To have almost completed such an arduous journey only to be attacked by B-52s in the open was unacceptable. The events of the day could have been avoided if someone had only thought like a soldier. He would not give TG559 another chance. The B-52 raid had been one of the closest and most terrifying calls of his life, which contained a remarkably large number of close, terrifying calls. At this point the platoon was on their own, outside TG559 control. Duan's plan was to go back into that system as close to their destination as possible, thereby minimizing the chances they would have to kill him.

The women had repaired a fifteen-mile stretch of road around their home village of Phum Chrey. Sixteen miles to the southwest was the Prey Veng market, the largest in the area. Like all such markets, it formed the backbone of the local economy and was a great source of gossip, much of it related to TG559. The women had intimate knowledge of military activities in the area and they all talked freely.

After two hours Duan had learned that their last stop on the trail likely would be the TG559 base area at Prey Komnong, ten miles south of Prey Veng. One of the young women, named Hai, spoke wistfully of a young soldier there with whom she had been involved. He had come with his unit from Tay Ninh, South Vietnam, after a major battle with the Americans. He helped guard the Prey Komnong base area. The young woman and her mother, Thu, both hoped he would propose marriage, because her last meeting with him had left her pregnant. They had arranged to meet at the Prey Veng market on Saturday, which was two days hence.

Based on this information and what he had learned from the Vietcong platoon the week before, Duan concluded that the soldier was probably from the Ninth Vietcong Division. "It's a perfect plan," he told Ba. "Report one morning to the TG559 bureaucrats and by afternoon, we will pass under the comforting command of real soldiers who are intent on surviving."

They talked quietly, working out details. Although the idea was risky it was better, in both their minds, than turning themselves over to the TG559 organization and being herded onto trucks only to be bombed again and maybe killed. They would stay in the hamlet that night and the next day. The villagers would hide them from the rescue and salvage teams that would probably begin to comb the area that night. The following night, Thu and Hai would guide them south on known porter trails paralleling the main artery of Route 15. On Saturday they would lay over in a small village southeast of Prey Veng where Thu's brother was the village chief. Hai would rendezvous with her young soldier, and that night Duan would enlist him in guiding them on the last leg of their journey. The only thing wrong with the plan was the possibility that the two wounded men might not survive that long. Duan decided that since both had been hit in the legs with shrapnel and were not bleeding badly, they would just have to bear the pain. Their wounds had been dressed as well as possible by two of the women, but soon they would need a doctor to remove the deeply imbedded metal fragments. Until then they would have to make do with four aspirin a day and some rice wine to deaden the pain.

At nightfall Duan issued his orders. Everyone's ears still ached, but most had regained their hearing. Three men remained completely deaf. Duan sent Ky and Trang and half a dozen of the shrewdest scroungers out to the smoldering convoy with orders to return with as much food and as many weapons as they could find. Two hours after sundown the recovery vehicles and work crews could be heard out on the road. The scrounging party returned with almost fifty kilos of rice taken from the packs of dead soldiers, along with dried shrimp, potatoes, and six live chickens that apparently withstood bombs better than humans. They also brought in twenty new Russian-manufactured AK-47 rifles, two dozen magazines, and several hundred rounds of ammunition. Duan gave most of the food to the man of the hamlet and tried to give him a couple of rifles, but the man refused, citing the strict law prohibiting civilians from having weapons. The punishment was death. Surrounded by the violence of war, he felt safer being unarmed.

To ensure his continued support, Duan gave him half of the opium from one of the bags he had taken off the dead guides several weeks before. The man was overwhelmed by the gift. Opium was worth an immense amount of money in this part of Cambodia. Duan was pleased that he would sell it for the profit of his small band of people and not smoke it. If he had shown an interest in smoking the opium,

Duan was prepared to kill him. His cooperation was too important to the plan. Duan had found you couldn't trust men who used the sap of the poppy plant.

Around 10:00 P.M., two TG559 officers from the salvage crew came over to the now dark and quiet hamlet and demanded to know if any survivors from the convoy had taken refuge there. The man offered them tea and related in detail the events of the day, assuring them that no one could have survived the two attacks. The officers left, apparently satisfied and warned him sternly not to repeat what he had seen that day. Duan smiled to himself in the dark of a bunker and whispered to Ba, "By morning Increment 1008 will be scratched from the bureaucrats' intricate schedules, which is precisely what we wanted." It had started to rain again.

He silently eased out of the bunker and crept to where Thu slept between two straw mats under the wide eave of a house. He woke her and slipped the other half of the opium stash into her hand, whispering what it was. There was a long silence while she felt the precious plastic bag, and then she began to cry silently. She told him that things had been very bad for her since the death of her husband and sons two years before. She knew precisely what this treasure would bring at the market, and it was more than she had had in her life. Duan reached out to pat her shoulder and then moved to leave. Her small hand grasped his and pressed it against one of her breasts. She raised herself on one elbow and whispered, "I would be honored to repay you for his gift with whatever pleasure my body might bring you. Besides, it has been a long time since I have been with a man." Duan considered this in silence for a moment, then eased under the straw mat next to her. With the sound of the rain as a curtain they shared a rare experience of enjoyment in lives that were driven mostly by the hard things required to survive. Several times during the night she began to weep, softly thanking him again for the opium, and her sobs mingled with those rising from the other huts in the hamlet. Fear, loss, and tears had become daily rituals for these people.

At dawn a slow rain continued. Duan, who was not easily impressed, was amazed to find that the road had been cleared of all burned-out vehicles by the night salvage crews. Grudgingly he conceded that it was an impressive effort. TG559 was efficient at salvage, he decided, but lousy at anticipating the enemy. Since he cared nothing for salvage, he would continue his judgment of them on how well they could protect him. They had very low marks in that all-important category.

They rested that day. The Americans, no doubt flush with success, sent in three B-52s off to the east to bomb blind again through the heavy cloud cover. By the sound of it they were randomly bombing the road in that area, hoping for another big kill. But Duan heard no secondary explosions and assumed the Americans had missed netting another lucrative target.

The women from the road crew were uneasy, because the bombing sounded as if it were near their village. The four who were not involved in Duan's plan decided to return home. Two were still unable to stop crying.

That night the platoon lined up in the rain—Ba, Duan, thirty-four porters, two wounded men in hammocks strung under carrying poles, Thu, and Hai. The villagers had fed them well late in the afternoon, and much food remained from what Duan had given them. They thanked the platoon and said goodbye. It had been the most generous unit to pass through their hamlet since a platoon of Vietcong had billeted overnight six months before.

Even though it was raining, a full moon glowed through the thin clouds and they made good time. At a tree line two miles south of the hamlet they were challenged by a Vietcong security patrol. Thu quickly explained the situation. She and her daughter had been pressed into service as guides after the B-52 raid the day before and they were guiding this increment to Prey Komnong. Duan and Ba talked to the platoon leader who, after listening to them and checking their route card, relaxed and confirmed that indeed the Ninth Vietcong Division was regrouping around the depot. Duan was pleased to have his analysis of the overall military situation in southeastern Cambodia confirmed. At dawn, without further incident, they arrived in the village of Phum Barai, and Thu's brother, Manh, welcomed them warmly.

Phum Barai was a village of around a hundred ethnic Vietnamese families, numbering six hundred men, women, and children. They belonged to the prized North Vietnamese and Khmer Rouge Cambodian enclave east of the mighty Mekong River. Beginning its tortuous trek to the South China Sea, 2,600 miles to the northwest on the Tibetan Plateau, the Mekong's ebb and flow produced one of the most fertile rice deltas in the world. This area, the *Tien Giang*—Upper Mekong River—was home to thousands of ethnic Vietnamese who had, over the years, migrated to inhabit the area. They had fled from northern and western Cambodia to escape the increasing terror of the Cambodian persecutions in those regions, and from South Vietnam to escape the intensifying war. Even though the war had followed them here, they were living a much better life than they had known elsewhere.

Prosperity in Southeast Asia even in the best of times required intellect, judgment, and cunning, and in all these Manh was well endowed. Timed by the endless cycle of monsoons and the rising and falling of the river, the village produced three rice crops a year. Two went to the Revolution, and the farmers kept one for themselves. Rice byproducts were used to supplement feed for big pens of pigs, ducks, chickens, and rabbits. The split on the livestock was the same. Two parts went to the Revolution, one to the village. Families cultivated plots of corn, tomatoes, peppers, beans, and herbs around their houses and along the rice-paddy dikes, and the split here was reversed: two for them and one for the Revolution.

Phum Barai also boasted a heavy industry: an iron-smelting operation that was Manh's special enterprise. Iron ore and other metals found in abundance throughout Indochina, but that remained unexploited on a large scale, were shipped from North Vietnam to Cambodia on Soviet or Chinese ships that off-loaded at the Cambodian port of Sihanoukville. The ore was then transported by truck to numerous smelting locations scattered throughout the Vietnamese enclave in southeastern Cambodia. Phum Barai received an allocation of four truckloads a week.

Using a dozen small furnaces fired by coal, which was also plentiful, the village produced a weekly quota of 500 steel fragmentation heads for grenades, which were trucked off to TG559 Zone 354 factories for final assembly. Because of the village chief's skill with iron and steel, the Revolution also allowed him to make farm and cooking implements, which were sold mostly to the Vietnamese farmers for the profit of the villagers. Phum Barai was a major consumer of scrap metal, which is always plentiful in a war zone, and the people had become highly skilled craftsmen in durable alloy metal fabrications. Hoes, pitch-forks, plow blades, cooking pots, and utensils with the Phum Barai mark were highly sought-after items throughout the area and brought top prices.

When it came to cash, the Revolution had a peculiar aspect to it. Through numerous sources such as taxes, extortion, robbery, and counterfeiting, cash was never in short supply. War materiel was always precious and as a result was watched and hoarded closely by every echelon of command. Since money was of little value to the hard-core Communist, doctrinally and institutionally the organization paid only scant attention to it. That is not to say that this high philosophical view affected individuals within the Revolution. All people love money, and the Vietnamese were no different. It became especially important to the people of Phum Barai, in view of the fact that most lived their lives on a narrow line between subsistence and poverty.

The cash generated from the smelting business was handled by the village chief in a communistic way. He used some of it as a fund for the general welfare of the people. A community herd of twenty prized water buffaloes shortened the hours required in the fields, allowing extra time to be devoted to the more lucrative market economy. To be sure, he kept a portion for himself and his family, but that was agreed to by the villagers. Each family did the same thing, putting aside small amounts from the sale of vegetables and metal utensils they made themselves and sold at the market. The people of Phum Barai were prosperous and happy. They knew from bitter experience that this could vanish quickly in the fortunes of war, and each hoarded a small family treasury for just such an occurrence.

Strangely enough, all transactions were made in South Vietnamese piasters, dollars, or American Military Payment Certificates, the only paper money considered to have value. North Vietnamese and Vietcong *dong* were viewed as worthless, which they were.

The platoon was split up and shown to billets in four well-constructed community bunkers. Ky and Trang led the men in breaking down the loads, cleaning, and oiling all parts in anticipation of the final inventory. Manh treated Duan, Ba, Thu, and Hai to a breakfast of *pho,* rice noodle soup with paper-thin slices of pork cooked in the hot broth, green onions, and strong *cafe sua*—coffee sweetened with thick condensed milk.

In spite of the obvious prosperity of the village, Duan ordered the porters to empty their packs of hoarded rice and other food to compensate Manh for the inconvenience of feeding the extra mouths. The village was part of TG559's logistics organization, and, since their plan called for them to move independently, they had to ensure Manh's silence and cooperation. The entree from his sister and sharing the food contributed to these all-important ends.

After they had talked for an hour, Duan was confident that he could trust Manh. Duan judged him to be like all successful men in his precarious line of work: a quick and accurate judge of character, a consummate politician, a master of the art of give-and-take. He was a great talker, a generous host, and he had cultivated numerous political alliances within the area.

As soon as they had arrived Manh had put an old Hmong midwife and healer in charge of the two wounded men. Surrounded by a rapt crowd, she deftly worked on them while both men slept contentedly, drugged by a special potion of hallucinogenic roots and herbs. She had applied acupuncture needles to strategic body locations, further blocking the pain. As she extracted the jagged pieces of metal from their festering wounds using a fire-sterilized pair of American needle-nose pliers, she kept up a running monologue about what marvelously fine steel the Americans used in their bombs. She carefully placed each piece in a soup bowl to be melted later into some special steel molding. The pure metal was a handsome payment for her services. After cleaning each wound, she cauterized it with a red-hot poker and smeared on a salve made of a herbal tree sap and salt. So effective were her anesthesia blocks that neither man was disturbed by her rough probing and cauterizing.

In the Vietnamese hamlet society the local healer and midwife was, in most instances, the only recourse the people had to medical attention. Similar to trained medical doctors, some healers were better than others. The well-being and prosperity of a people very often depended on the healer's skills. If people couldn't work the fields, walk long distances to market, fight off the ever-present diseases, parasites, and amoebas, and generally keep themselves physically fit, they quickly became poor and hungry. It was that sort of hard life.

The Hmong woman examined the three deaf men and applied a salve to their ears. She gave Duan a bottle of foul-tasting herbal medicine with instructions that they should each drink five small doses before sundown. She sternly admonished Duan, in pidgin Vietnamese, "You will personally return the bottle after administering the last dose to your men. Do you understand?" He smiled and startled her by thanking her in her own language for helping his men. "The bottle is safe with me, and your assistance will not be forgotten," he said, as she beamed a toothless smile.

Duan admired and trusted Manh even more after watching the old woman's miraculous operation on his men. He had seen Vietcong doctors with degrees from the great European medical schools who could not have done as capable and painless a job as this unschooled, uneducated village healer. He wished he had had her services during his recuperation a year earlier in the overcrowded military hospital in Hanoi. Pain, fear, and depression were his strongest recollections. He quickly banished them from his mind.

Manh confided that he had only found and enticed her to take care of his village two years before. The arrangement, expensive by rice-farmer standards, had been well worth the cost.

Duan and Ba inspected the loads, and each man washed out his least-tattered uniform, and they were hung in half a dozen kitchens to dry by the cook fires. After a filling breakfast of *pho*, the platoon was ordered into their hammocks. Manh and Thu decided that it would be safest for him to accompany the two women to market. The sale of the opium was illegal and tricky, but with his connections there would be no difficulties. Hai was anxious to get moving. Markets were loosely run affairs with complex unwritten rules, the first of which was to show up early and leave late, and it was now almost 7:00 A.M. Hai was young, pretty, and well-mannered, but anxious and embarrassed. If her young soldier didn't show up she would be taken care of but she and her child would still struggle without a father's name. In spite of the lack of formal written records and such, a fatherless child was difficult to disguise. Hai's shame would be based not on moral grounds, but rather on her having a lack of judgment and common sense. These things were valued in Vietnamese society above all else.

After the three departed for market, Duan and Ba set a watch in case of betrayal or accidental discovery. Far to the northeast they could hear the rolling thunder of air strikes and artillery. The people working the rice fields for the next planting never even raised their heads. The sound had become a backdrop to daily life.

Late that afternoon Duan spotted, through the light rain, a rarely seen *xich lo*—motorcycle—slowly splashing toward the village, dodging chug holes in the dirt road. As it approached he carefully counted the passengers and noted there were four. He smiled. The plan was working out. One of the riders had a rifle and was no doubt the young soldier. As the *xich lo* got closer he eased into the bunker under Manh's house.

The *xich lo*, engine sputtering, careened along at maximum speed of slightly less than ten miles per hour, seeming to defy gravity as the passengers shifted their weight in unison to counter the precarious tilts caused by the numerous potholes in the muddy road. The vehicle came to an abrupt stop on the path in front of Manh's house. Thu paid the driver and the four of them dashed into the dry comfort of the big bamboo, thatch, and mud home. The welcome smell of cooking rice and pork filled the rooms.

Thu and Hai carried four big baskets full of produce and a large goose to the kitchen, while Hinh, the young soldier, looked around warily in the strange surroundings. Manh, Duan, and Ba put him at ease over strong, sweet tea, and began systematically to extract as much information as possible. Like all Vietcong, Hinh was remarkably well-informed on military and civil affairs and very talkative.

Hinh told them that the Prey Komnong base was a big TG559 logistics facility constructed almost entirely underground, and it doubled as a refitting area for badly mauled units that were withdrawn from the South Vietnamese front. Duan's face lit up when Hinh told them he was from the 272d Regiment of the Ninth Vietcong Division, Duan's old regiment. He listened quietly as the young man told of the battle with the Americans two months before at the Michelin rubber plantation, east of Tay Ninh City. He told of the waves of helicopters and airplanes raining fire and death for two full days and nights. Of the incessant artillery. Of how the regiment had held out, not revealing their positions in spite of the mounting casualties. Of the American infantry finally moving in, confident that nothing could live through the continuous bombardment, only to walk into the regiment's trap and be cut down in a withering crossfire like thatch under a sharp scythe. And finally, he told of the eerie quiet that had suddenly been shattered by the tons of bombs dropped by the B-52s that crisscrossed their position for two full hours. Hinh was visibly shaken as he told his story. He confided at the end that he had been one of the four surviving members of his company.

Duan reeled off a series of names, and Hinh repeated monotonously, "*Giet*—killed." Duan's face remained impassive.

Then Hinh brightened and confided proudly that since then, his unit had been training hard on antiaircraft tactics, and that the division now had a battalion of antiaircraft guns and dozens of new shoulder-held antiaircraft missiles. Duan swore under his breath at this information. He almost launched into his theory that the best life-preserving tactic was to hide and dig; shoot at an airplane and the Americans would black out the sun with fighters and bombers trying to get the guns. But now was not the time.

Manh called for more tea, which Thu brought from the kitchen. She also brought four packages wrapped in brown paper and tied with string. One contained a bottle of whiskey, which she presented to her brother. Duan's contained an American plastic hairbrush and metal mirror. Ba and Hinh each received a carton of French Gauloise Bleue cigarettes. These were lavish gifts by Vietnamese standards. She thanked each man for his help in a singsong voice, bowing, her hands clasped together below her chin. They thanked her in return, each rising and taking her hands. Only Hinh didn't know the source of his future mother-in-law's affluence, but he was suitably impressed. Each man had brought her good fortune over the past three days. She was overwhelmed by her *di may man* and anxious to ensure that it continued after so many years of heartbreak, loss, and poverty. She was also perplexed by the fact that it had all begun when she was caught in a B-52 raid, which was considered to be the worst fate that could befall a person.

Acting as the head of his sister's family, Manh turned the conversation to marriage and asked Hinh, "Is there something you would like to ask?" Taking his cue, Hinh formally interjected the traditional Vietnamese marriage proposal, which was just as quickly accepted, and Hai, who had been listening to every word from an alcove just off the kitchen, made her entrance. Everyone stood and applauded as the couple blushed and smiled, embarrassed by the sudden attention. Manh uncorked his new bottle of black-market Johnny Walker whiskey and they toasted the couple.

Hinh said that he had asked for and received permission from his commanding officer to take a wife. Duan and Ba listened closely as the young man explained in detail the NLF's policy for the marriage of soldiers during times of war and revolution, which had been the case for decades and would remain so for the forseeable future. His commander would perform the ceremony when Hinh presented his wife-to-be, if she met the criteria, which were that she couldn't be American, Cambodian, or capitalistic Vietnamese, and she must be willing to join the Revolution.

Later Duan and Ba took Thu and Hinh aside and went over the plan one last time, questioning Hinh closely on the details of security and how they would get into the Prey Komnong base. Hinh assured them there would be no problems. Everyone had the required documentation, which base security would check closely, and then Hinh would lead them to the TG559 headquarters tunnel complex.

Duan and Ba began to shake the platoon out of their hammocks and lined up the remaining loads under the wide eaves of Manh's house. The two wounded men slept deeply thanks to the healer's potion, and the porters rigged their hammocks under carrying poles.

Duan assembled the platoon and carefully explained the strategy to them. The fact that they had only seven or eight miles to go on their journey brought a round of laughter and backslapping. Duan jerked them back to their task, pointing out that they looked like poverty-stricken woodcutters, which they did. He had a strong reputation and fully intended to expand on it by bringing in the platoon in good shape, which was an unheard-of occurrence for a foot increment at this end of the Old Man's Trail. The clean-up of their battered and bruised bodies would proceed with military precision. The village barber set up his chair under a small bamboo-and-thatch stall by the village well and each man was given a haircut, including Duan and Ba. Then they proceeded to the well and took a cold bucket bath using one of the two bars of soap Manh provided. Afterward, they dutifully lined up while Duan and Ba inspected their torsos for open wounds, applying the healer's salve. Their lower legs and feet were covered with infected leech bites and unattended scratches and abrasions. The worst of the leech bites had left dark circular marks that would heal leaving scars. The men then put on clean and dry uniforms and proceeded to the kitchen, where they received large bowls of rice with hot peppers, several chunks of grilled pork, greens, fresh bread, and cane-sweetened tea. All in all they looked better than they had in the last two months, but they were exhausted and haggard. Their eyes had developed the animal wariness that marks anyone whose life has been seriously threatened and who now intends to survive. They were still fifteen years old but looked much older.

Duan administered the last dose of foul-tasting potion to the three deaf men and then went to look for the Hmong healer to return her bottle. He told her that the men still couldn't hear. She patted him and said, with a toothless smile, "Don't worry. Tomorrow morning they will hear." The effects of the medicine would cause them to run a low fever that she patiently explained was part of the healing process. He gave her four packs of cigarettes donated by Ba, and thanked her for her help.

At nightfall Duan and Ba thanked Manh for his gracious hospitality. Duan gave him the very nice Russian TT-33 pistol that he had taken off the dead convoy commander several days before. It was cleaned and oiled and the handmade Yugoslavian leather holster was brightly buffed with leather soap. Unlike the man in the small hamlet, Manh deeply appreciated the gift and proudly added it to his personal arsenal, which contained an AK-47, an SKS semiautomatic carbine, and a Soviet SVD sniper rifle, all neatly hidden in a hollow bamboo wall.

A light haze veiled the full moon as they departed the village. Thu and Hinh had selected a route south that would parallel Route 15 on rice paddy dikes and several small dirt roads. The route was designed to avoid hamlets and villages and known patrol areas.

At 8:00 P.M. Duan enthusiastically gave the platoon their marching orders for the night. For the first time in several weeks the porters responded in unison with a crisp, "*Tien len!*" They picked up the loads and headed south on the last leg of their *truong chinh*.

# ELEVEN

# Spectre

## NAKHON PHANOM, THAILAND

As the platoon left Phum Barai, a U.S. Air Force AC-130 Spectre gunship began its roll-out down the runway at the American base at Nakhon Phanom, Thailand. The four-engine converted cargo plane weighed eighty-seven tons empty, and with the addition of two and a half tons of armor plate, several tons of ammunition, two 40-mm automatic cannons, two 20-mm and two 7.62-mm Gatling guns, a flare dispenser, a vast array of ground search radars and night optical sensors and related control consoles, two ECM pods, a full load of fuel, and a crew of fourteen, it weighed considerably more. The aircraft combined state-of-the-art target acquisition equipment, devastating firepower, and long loiter time over the target, which made it the outstanding night interdiction weapon that the Americans employed against the Old Man's Trail. The Spectre gunship had earned the fear and respect of the North Vietnamese, who had dubbed it the Thug. In fact, the airplane had only two weaknesses: first, it was slow, and second, to engage targets it had to fly at relatively low altitudes, which made it vulnerable to ground fire and antiaircraft missiles.

A slight break in the weather had put Task Force Alpha back in the interdiction business. General Kendal, U.S. Air Force, commanding, had called for a maximum effort. With signal relay aircraft already over the trail, the sensor readout consoles at the Surveillance Center in Nakhon Phanom pulsated with lights indicating large truck convoys south of Nape and Tchepone, Laos. Finding and destroying trucks along the Old Man's Trail was precisely what the AC-130 had been designed for. As it struggled to gain altitude, sensor-activation data was fed electronically into its on-board computers. At 20,000 feet, Spectre 7, which was the plane's call sign, set a course east toward its assigned target area, a fifty-mile stretch of trail south of Tchepone.

Forty-five minutes later, Spectre 7's crew entered their assigned target area only to find that cumulus clouds and thunderheads, reaching to 9,000 feet, had beat them to it. From that altitude the bright moon revealed a solid gray-and-white carpet of clouds as far as the eye could see. Spectre 7's sensor readout consoles revealed more than a hundred trucks moving on the trail, which was corroborated by the Black Crow ignition detector mounted on the forward fuselage. The Black Crow picked up electro-static emissions from truck engines. Spectre 7's crew worked feverishly trying to put together a target solution but could not compute one, due to the altitude they had to maintain over the clouds and the resulting range to the targets. To make matters worse the Black Crow sensor signals suddenly ceased as all the trucks turned off their engines, which was TG559's only meager countermeasure against the Thug. Without the capacity of the Black Crow sensor to locate the target, Spectre 7 could not compute a precise target solution. In defiance, using the airplane's remarkable instrumentation, the pilot lined up a pylon turn that brought the aircraft around in a tight circle, left wing down, pointed the weapons on a direct line to the target, and fired a salvo from all guns. The crew could not even see the impact of the tracers as they were swallowed up by the clouds. The sensors on the ground transmitted the sound of impacting rounds, but no secondary explosions were recorded. The pilot radioed his situation to Nakhon Phanom and received information that all clear targets were well covered and under attack by a dozen Spectre AC-130 aircraft and fifty fixed-wing bombers included in the night's frag order. Spectre 7 was ordered to follow the trace of the trail south with instructions to search for breaks in the monsoon cloud cover and to attack any targets of opportunity they might encounter.

That night Duan ordered the platoon to move slowly, minimizing chances of mishaps. They had lost almost half their number over the past two months, and he intended to bring in the remaining thirty-six men and their loads in good shape. The loads had become a part of their existence. Their exhausted bodies had become accustomed to the unrelenting weight, but after a day of rest the poles felt lighter than usual. Spirits were high, and at first Duan silenced them with whispered fatherly admonishments. He explained, "We must be quiet, otherwise a Vietcong patrol might take us for undisciplined Cambodian or South Vietnamese troops." When laughter broke out in the column, he reverted to his more accustomed role of tyrant and restored strict discipline with the back of his hand and foot.

After the first rest stop the platoon moved out of the jungle and began to cross half a mile of open rice paddy. Duan stopped the column and questioned Thu and Hinh about alternative routes. There were villages and patrol areas in the jungle on either side of the rice paddies, they said. Either way had its drawbacks. After studying the clouds and rain a moment and judging the rumble of war to be at least twenty-five miles to the east, Duan decided to cross the paddies, but he ordered them to move fast. Instructions were whispered down the line and the platoon took off at a brisk walk on a wide, raised path that crossed the flooded rice fields.

Spectre 7 flew south vainly seeking a break in the cloud cover. The southern end of the Truong Son Mountains and the Bolovens Plateau were shrouded in a gray fog. East of Kratie, Cambodia, the clouds thinned out, and weather checks with U Tapao, Thailand, and Ton Son Nhut, South Vietnam, indicated a 5,000-foot ceiling prevailing over most of southern Cambodia. Spectre 7's pilot, anxious for his crew not to be shut out on their first interdiction mission in three weeks, asked for and received permission to drop below the cloud cover and hunt for targets. Since Spectre 7 was a lone aircraft with no supporting planes and was flying in an area not targeted for that night's interdiction attack, it took ten minutes for the request to be approved. General Kendal finally agreed based on two factors: first, he needed to show some significant truck kills in order to get the chain of command off his back. Second, he had long believed that they should apply additional interdiction assets to southern Cambodia other than the occasional B-52 raid. He had been prevented from doing so by the lack of unmanned remote sensor fields for pinpointing targets and the high civilian population density. Without sensors there was no way, other than using photos, ground surveillance radar readings from recon aircraft, or satellites, to confirm military targets. Since he had been ordered to conduct a "tactical emergency—maximum interdiction" effort, he felt justified in employing Spectre 7 outside its normally authorized operating areas. This would show his command's aggressiveness, something he had been accused of not displaying over the last several weeks. If there were repercussions, he could always point to the big convoy they had accidentally hit three days before as justification for going back into the area. He ordered two F-4s on strip alert at Ubon, Thailand, to launch and provide backup for the mission, even though there had never been any reports of antiaircraft weapons or air search radars in the area.

Spectre 7's pilot found the cloud layer hanging at precisely 5,000 feet, just as the weather beagles had predicted. He also found that visibility was greatly obscured beneath the clouds. The crew used Spectre 7's array of sensors to search for targets. Soon the first activations popped up on the Black Crow truck ignition detector system, which had a range of ten miles. The screen showed a convoy of twenty trucks driving south on an improved road.

As Spectre 7 altered course and lumbered toward the indicated location of the convoy, the Black Crow console screen suddenly went blank. The North Vietnamese commander had heard the telltale drone of the airplane in the distance as the convoy had stopped to fix a flat.

He had been attacked by Thugs before. He ordered his drivers to shut off their engines. They sat still on an open stretch of muddy road west of the village of Phum Kbal Khvet.

The gunship's pilot fixed on the last location the Black Crow system had given him and in ninety seconds flew directly over the convoy. The airplane's low-light television cameras and infrared imaging sensors clearly showed the twenty vehicles and approximately forty men standing alongside the road. The console operators scanned the vehicles for antiaircraft weapons and reported to the pilot that there were none in sight.

The convoy had been on a routine run from the big depot at Phum Anchanh to the TG559 base at Prey Komnong carrying a mixed cargo of rice, ammunition, and small arms. When the Thug roared overhead like the shadow of a gigantic black fish in dark waters, the convoy commander ordered the drivers and the six-man Vietcong security squad to leave the vehicles. He held no illusions and knew precisely what was now going to happen. They scurried into the rice paddies on either side of the road.

Overhead, the low-light television operator aboard Spectre 7 notified the pilot that troops were running from the vehicles and that he had positively identified Soviet-manufactured two-and-a-half-ton cargo trucks. The pilot ordered his crew to prepare to attack, and his computer gave him a target solution indicating the exact position and angle of his pylon turn. He brought the airplane back around and over the convoy and, dropping his left wing, entered the turn precisely as the computer dictated. He aligned the heads-up display gun sight with a computer image of the target and fired his weapons. The airplane lurched violently from the recoil of six guns simultaneously firing thousands of rounds of ammunition. The burst of fire lasted only three seconds. The pilot immediately asked for a target damage assessment from the infrared and low-light television operators, who reported eight trucks destroyed and burning. The crew could now see them through the rain.

On the ground, most of the men had managed to put a hundred yards or so between themselves and the trucks and had taken refuge behind the paddy dikes. So accurate was the fire from Spectre 7 that no rounds had hit more than fifty yards off the road. This was most of the men's first encounter with a Thug. They burrowed into the mud and prayed they would not be the next target. None had ever seen or heard such a terrifying and massive display of raw firepower, except for a few who had survived B-52 raids.

The young Vietcong security squad leader, Toan, was as disoriented and frightened by the attack as his men. But he had been meticulously trained in what to do in shooting situations with the enemy. The first thing that came to mind was to work out a plan and rehearse it. He quickly discarded this doctrine as not fitting his current situation. The second thought, and the only one that seemed to stick in his mind, was to return fire and gain fire superiority. The fact that an RPD light machine gun, three SKS carbines, and two AK-47s could in no way match the Thug's firepower never crossed his mind. He searched for the convoy commander and could not find him. He decided to follow the rule that all leaders would continue to push the attack when out of contact with their commanders, and he moved along the rice paddy dike issuing orders to his men.

To the west of the convoy, Duan was startled by the sudden bright light of red tracers descending from a point near the horizon to his east and hitting the ground. It took him a moment to register what was happening. He had heard no airplane engines; Spectre 7's orbit was far enough to the east and its engines had been muffled by the rain. After a few seconds the sound of wailing guns reached them. The platoon paused and looked at the light. Then Ba whispered loudly, "We're in the open, Duan. Let's get to some cover, quick."

Duan yelled, "*Chung ta ra di!*" violating his own order for quiet. The platoon broke into a rapid shuffle, which was the best they could do in the sticky mud.

Meanwhile, crouched along the dikes, the convoy drivers and Vietcong security squad heard the Thug circle once more over the twelve remaining trucks and fire another burst from all weapons. Ten trucks exploded in flames. Overhead the Spectre 7 pilot ordered a target solution for the remaining vehicles.

No rounds fell into the men. Toan had lined up his security squad along a dike with their weapons pointing skyward in the direction of the most recent rain of fire, which had come from west of the road. All they could see above the arch of light coming from the burning trucks was blackness and rain. Because the Thug was slow, they could generally track its location by the sound of its engines.

The pilot again aligned his gun sight with the target image, and with careful concentration because of the smallness of his target, fired his weapons. Only the two 20-mm Gatling guns were selected this time, to conserve on ammunition. The plane vibrated with the recoil of the short, two-second burst.

Toan was startled when the Thug's third round of fire came from behind his position to the east; his hearing had placed the plane between him and the road. He turned his head quickly and in the light from muzzle flashes caught a glimpse of the fuselage outline and wings moving through the night. Then he could see nothing but blackness and rain. The two lead trucks burst into flames and mortar ammunition began to detonate in bright flashes. After that Toan could see nothing in the black night.

The sensor operators on Spectre 7 reported the hits to the pilot, but because of the random ammunition explosions their screens were blinking madly, making it difficult to record the final destruction, which the Task Force Alpha staff required as proof of the mission's success. The pilot broke off his pylon turn and leveled out in a wide circle around his smoldering prey.

Two U.S. Air Force F-4s arrived over the target and checked in with Spectre 7, who would act as mission commander for the three aircraft. Each fighter carried napalm and 500-pound bombs. The pilot of Spectre 7 briefed the fighters and coordinated their altitudes. The F-4s moved to an orbit 500 feet above Spectre 7 and could now see the fires on the ground, as the exploding ammunition lit the scene. Spectre 7 expanded its orbit to search for additional targets. None presented themselves even though there were more than two hundred vehicles on the roads around Svay Rieng, which was out of range for the gunship's equipment.

Spectre 7 had turned what would have been a shut-out mission into a productive one, with twenty truck kills in an area not normally targeted by Task Force Alpha. Its crew had proved that with no cuing from remote, unmanned sensor fields or an airborne forward air controller, an AC-130, which had only recently replaced the much less capable AC-47, could be productive using only the onboard target acquisition suite in marginal weather. The Surveillance Center staff were elated by the outcome. Task Force Alpha ultimately would destroy ninety-eight trucks on this night, and more than 20 percent of them had been bagged by Spectre 7. Several staff officers were put to work preparing a "Lessons Learned" message to the entire chain of command, which would unashamedly point to the aggressiveness and innovativeness of Task Force Alpha and its versatile flight crews.

# TWELVE

# Grail

## KANTREUY PLANTATION, CAMBODIA

In the COSVN's underground headquarters at the Kantreuy Plantation, fifty miles northeast of the burning convoy, five men, all wearing
Vietcong-issue black cotton shirts, pants, and rubber-soled sandals,
squatted on their haunches around a cast-iron pot of rice and dishes
filled with fish and vegetables, an assortment of greens, red peppers,
and *nuoc mam*. The rice pot and all the dishes bore the Phum Barai
mark. Two fire-blackened American metal canteens containing freshly
brewed tea were balanced on the edge of the straw mat that served as
their dinner table. Each man held a delicately painted blue-and-white
porcelain rice bowl and matching tea cup, the only signs of elegance.
They ate with bamboo chopsticks that had been expertly carved by the
cook. The COSVN commander was their host.

Squatting to his left was the TG559 commander of all logistic and
combat forces in the Vietnamese enclave in southern Cambodia, who
was directly subordinate to the COSVN. To the host's right was the
commander of Military Region 5, the honored guest for the evening.
His command included all of *Trung Bo*, the North Vietnamese name
for Central South Vietnam and the South Vietnamese coastal provinces. Facing them from across the straw mat were the Military Re-

gion 5 deputy commander and chief political officer and the cook.

The guests complimented the cook lavishly on his meal. His skill was renowned among the NVA and Vietcong, and an invitation to the COSVN commander's table was as much coveted for the food as for the access to great power.

The host quietly turned the conversation to business, and in a conciliatory tone told the TG559 commander, "I have interceded up the chain of command, and there will be no repercussions for your loss of the fifty-truck convoy. I have explained that it was merely an unfortunate accident."

The commander thanked the COSVN but adamantly accepted full blame for the loss. He insisted that it was at least partially preventable, had the convoy been spread out in small increments of ten to fifteen trucks each, which had been his orders to the staff. The Communist practice of public self-criticism permeated to the very top of the organization.

The TG559 commander understood very well that a recurrence of such a significant loss of equipment would not be so easily explained. There was no mention of the men killed. Men could be replaced. Equipment could not, except with great effort.

It was now his turn to change the subject. "I have just received a report that an American Thug aircraft has been firing in my area of responsibility." This was news as such activity had never before occurred. He did not yet know that he had lost another twenty trucks and their cargo. That information would not reach him until the following morning.

The COSVN commander recognized that his subordinate was fishing for some guidance on how to handle the increased air activity in his area of responsibility. He took over the conversation and recounted in precise detail his strategy for the Cambodian enclave. "It has worked remarkably well for several years," he pointed out. "Whereas numerous modern antiaircraft weapons have passed through our Cambodian enclave, I have maintained a strict policy that none would be used to attack aircraft, nor would any of the increasingly sophisticated radar equipment flowing to the south be activated while in the enclave. This passive tactic has put the Americans in a quandary, and, when combined with their preoccupation with world and domestic public opinion and pseudo-legalities, has stymied them into inaction. As a result we have suffered only periodic air attacks and have greatly expedited the flow of supplies east to the war zone."

The Region 5 commander complimented his host on the wisdom of his policy and expressed gratitude for his support.

"However," the commander continued, "our good fortune may be changing. These recent B-52 and Thug attacks may signal a shift in the Americans' tactics and capability. The Thug seems to be able to find targets in the dark and through cloud cover, without the benefit of sensor reports. If the Thugs start coming here with regularity, then the Americans will soon discover the extent of the traffic inside the enclave at night and during the monsoon."

He turned again to the local TG559 commander, who was, by two echelons of command, the junior man present. He asked him, with a benevolent smile, "What would be your recommendation about my longstanding policy in view of the recent Thug threat and B-52 attacks?"

The young commander confidently launched into his analysis. He praised the COSVN's strategy, then pointed out, "We know that eventually the Americans will step up their attacks in our enclave. The Revolution's greatest task is to ensure that this does not occur soon. The Americans are not fools. They know that the COSVN and TG559 run major logistics operations in this area. Should they begin to target Thugs against us, that would not stop the flow of our supplies, but it would make it far more difficult and costly." He dismissed the B-52s' long-term effectiveness, because they had to have a hard fix on a target. He reasoned that if the Americans knew where his depots were, they would have bombed them long ago.

"The Americans have always appeared reluctant to use the B-52s in heavily populated areas because of the saturation effect of the bombing patterns," he said. "Therefore I believe that the Thug aircraft are our immediate problem. If Thugs appear in our area, we should use the recently arrived antiaircraft company armed with the new SA-7 Grail shoulder-fired antiaircraft weapons against those airplanes. Our strategic objective should be to put as many enemy aircraft on the ground as possible and then mount a world-press offensive that the Americans are targeting civilian population areas in neutral Cambodia." He paused and added, "I would, of course, arrange for the SA-7s to fire from positions adjacent to civilian population areas and away from any of our depots."

The older men all smiled approvingly and nodded. They admired his plan.

The host asked for more fish, which was deliciously cooked in a spicy hot-pepper sauce. When the cook produced another large portion, everyone ate appreciatively.

The strategy conversation continued.

# THIRTEEN

# The Golden BB

## DESTROYED TG559 CONVOY, PHUM KBAL KHVET, CAMBODIA

Duan's platoon had finally made it to the relative safety of the tree line when they heard the two F-4s fly into the target from the west, passing several miles to their north. A yellow glow had lit the horizon, reflecting off the clouds, and the sound of the intermittent explosions had reached them as they moved into the jungle. They walked several hundred yards along a narrow path. Duan went to the head of the column and stopped Thu and Hinh. The platoon was breathing heavily and needed a break. Duan and Ba moved down the line silently checking the men and their loads. Then they waited.

Unable to find additional targets in the rain, Spectre 7's pilot decided to terminate the mission. He briefed the F-4 pilots that he would illuminate the target with a string of parachute flares and then they would put their lethal ordnance on the burning convoy, ensuring that nothing but scrap metal would be left for the salvage crews. Afterward, Spectre 7 would let the fires die down and then make a last photo run to record the destruction on the infrared and low-light television equipment. Then they would head for home.

From his position along the dike Toan squatted behind his men, whom he had reoriented with their backs to the road facing east, the last direction the Thug had fired from. They had instinctively dug deeper into the soft mud when they had heard the roar of the F-4 engines. They heard splashing in front of them in the paddies as some of the drivers took advantage of the lull to move farther from the road. The Thug's deadly drone grew louder, and Toan alerted his men to get ready to fire on his command. He cautioned them to fire in front of the noise of the aircraft.

Suddenly the gunship was behind them, flying on the west side of the roadbed. They heard a series of loud pops, and bright flares ignited, swaying gently beneath white parachutes. The squad was completely exposed in the sudden light. They ducked lower in the meager protection of their dike. The screaming noise of a diving F-4 followed almost immediately and two giant balls of flame erupted as napalm tanks exploded among the burning trucks. They felt the intense heat on their exposed backs, and they burrowed for protection into the dike. The second F-4 followed closely farther down the road; two more napalm explosions erupted.

Several men complained to Toan that they were on the wrong side of the dike and in danger of being killed. He told them to shut up and hold their position. They stopped grumbling and lay still in the bright light.

Another pause, and again they heard the scream of an F-4 diving low over the convoy, followed by the terrifying crack of 500-pound bombs among the blazing vehicles. Shrapnel whistled around them, rippling the water. A small jagged piece tore silently into a rifleman's back, lodging in his heart and killing him instantly. A second F-4 dropped its load farther down the convoy.

Spectre 7 flew off a few miles to the south and turned to make his photo run on a due north heading at 3,000 feet. That altitude would place him above the effective range of small arms, which should be the only possible threat remaining.

Toan sensed he had missed his chance to fire at the Americans. The jets could barely be heard above the rain and the crackle of the burning trucks, and the Thug's engines were hardly audible to the south. It seemed to be over—but then he heard the AC-130 coming back. He ordered his squad to get in their firing positions, still facing east away from the road. He guessed that the plane would pass to their east, in front of them, as it had done once before. The engines grew louder as he tried to make out its shape in the black night. Suddenly there it was, its fearsome sharklike fuselage barely visible, moving fast directly in front of them, just as he had predicted. Toan reminded them again to fire in front of the target and then he ordered them to shoot. All weapons opened up at once, green tracers from the RPD light-machine gun arching into the night.

Spectre 7's course allowed its sensor operators to adjust their focus as they approached the convoy. As they flew by, one camera took a panoramic shot while a second took close-ups of each smoldering vehicle. As the aircraft drew abreast of the convoy, the weapons officer, peering through a gun port, reported, "We have several muzzle flashes and some tracers coming our way from the rice paddies to the east of the road." The pilot acknowledged and instinctively applied power and began to climb. The crew was not particularly concerned, because if the shots had been close they would have heard high-pitched static cracks in their headsets.

The squad continued to fire as long as they could see the vague black shape in the sky. The RPD gunner, seeing his green tracers falling well behind the Thug, raised himself to his knees and arched his last twenty-five rounds high above the vague shape of the airplane and far out in front. The other riflemen, without the aid of tracers, did not even come close to the big but elusive target.

As Spectre 7 pulled away, the last two rounds fired by the RPD gunner hit the left outboard engine's inlet cowl blow-in door, which offered no resistance other than to deflect the bullets into the first-stage compression chamber fan, where they slammed into and snapped off two of the hard but extremely brittle titanium turbine blades. The two broken blades instantly were pulled into the second-stage compression chamber, where they wedged and began rapidly to snap off dozens of turbine blades, which were then pulled into the third-stage compression chamber with the same catastrophic effect. As the blades in all three chambers began breaking in rapid succession, the centrifugal force shot them in all directions, cutting the hydraulic and fuel lines around the engine. Then the engine caught fire. As the outboard engine continued to disintegrate, hundreds of the hard titanium fragments peppered the cowling of the inboard left engine with the same force of a direct antiaircraft hit, severing the oil and fuel lines. The lack of oil, combined with the massive number of fragments simultaneously penetrating all three compression chambers on the inboard engine, caused the engine to seize as if it suddenly had been put in a giant clamp. It rapidly turned into a superheated glob of metal.

The pilot had instantly noticed the drop in power and lift as the fully functioning right-wing engines began to force the plane into a left turn. Even before the left inboard engine had seized, the pilot began to apply right rudder, and the copilot, who had spotted the flickering fire in the outboard engine, slammed down the engine fire button, which released fire retardant into the engine pod. All eyes in the cockpit were scanning the instrument panel when the inboard engine's drive shaft abruptly froze, which did not stop the propeller freewheeling in the airstream, which instantly sheared off the frozen drive shaft. The sudden loss of all power from the left engines caused the plane to lurch to the left. The freewheeling, severed half-ton propeller tore into the side of the cockpit. The pilot and engineer were killed instantly as the big blades sliced through the fuselage with sudden and terrifying force. The copilot's left arm was broken and two fingers severed, and the navigator was sprayed with high-speed fragments and knocked unconscious at the navigation table.

High-velocity wind and rain spewed into the cockpit from the gashes in the fuselage and a dozen broken windshield panels. In the turbulence, glass, jagged metal, rivets, screws, papers, and books swirled around, buffeting the copilot, who had the presence of mind to lower the eyescreen of his flight helmet to partially protect his face. The flight-control yokes were forced back into his lap, erratically raising the plane's nose.

As Spectre 7 continued to turn left and climb, warning lights and buzzers went off, indicating an imminent stall. With his good right arm, the copilot slowly forced the control yoke forward, applied full right rudder, and felt the airplane respond as it leveled out. In agony, he reached over and shut down both of the left engines and released fire retardant into the inboard engine pod.

The gun and sensor crews in the cargo bay had been violently battered by the airplane's sudden turn. The first two men to regain their feet tried to reach the elevated flight deck but were injured by debris when they attempted to climb the stepladder leading to the cockpit. Finally, three of the crew managed to crawl to the cockpit and remove the dead pilot and crew chief from their chairs.

By this time the copilot was on the verge of shock, which would be closely followed by unconsciousness. The weapons officer had taken over the pilot's controls, but even with his helmet eye shield down he was having difficulty following the copilot's instructions, as the full force of wind and rain blew directly into his face through the broken windshield and the gashed side of the fuselage. The aircraft was still moving in an erratic but level left turn when the copilot passed out. The weapons officer came up on the emergency frequency and gave the first distress call, which brought the F-4s down to look for the crippled aircraft.

At the Surveillance Center, Task Force Alpha mobilized rescue and attack aircraft for what most pilots considered their worst nightmare: an inclement-weather night rescue in enemy territory. Even worse, they had no experience with downed air crews in the North Vietnamese enclave in southern Cambodia.

Task Force Alpha patched through Spectre 7's squadron commander, who was on the ground at Nakhon Phanom, Thailand. The commander began talking Spectre 7's weapons officer through a procedure to get the aircraft out of its increasingly erratic left turn. By applying right rudder and varying the power and propeller pitch on the remaining two right engines, gradually the weapons officer brought the aircraft around to a reasonably steady westerly heading. The problem of maintaining a steady course was further compounded by several cut hydraulic lines to the left-wing control surfaces, which made the control yokes in the cockpit hard to move. In the confusion, Spectre 7 had drifted west and lost altitude. The altimeter read 1,600 feet.

The F-4s had stayed close and quickly joined Spectre 7 on the emergency frequency. The gunship was barely staying above stall speed on two engines. The F-4s circled 500 feet above. The AC-130 squadron commander concentrated on talking the weapons officer onto an even heading for home and trying to gain some altitude. The sensor officer now occupied the co-pilot's seat.

Spectre 7 continued to lose altitude. The men in the cockpit were being soaked by rain, and water was collecting on the cabin floor. Finally the water reached a damaged electrical outlet, which shorted out the instrument panel lights, leaving them in the dark. A flashlight revealed that the instruments still worked. The altimeter read 1,500 feet and showed the airplane slowly descending.

The weapons officer, who was in command, now made a fateful decision. He said steadily to Task Force Alpha and the squadron commander, "I have no confidence in my ability to keep this damaged airplane in the air nor to get it home. I want the F-4s to mark our location, and I will put the plane into a turn and my nine able crew members will bail out. This should put them within a quarter mile of each other on the ground, which will help with the rescue efforts. Then I will put the plane back on course and try to get it home with the two KIA I have and my wounded navigator and copilot. I realize this is a desperate plan, but I want you to know that so is our situation. If I lose any more altitude, we will be too low for parachutes to open. I cannot jeopardize the lives of everyone on the slim chance I can fly this damn thing." Task Force Alpha acknowledged his transmission.

Duan's platoon had been squatting quietly on the trail, listening to the sounds of the convoy being destroyed. Duan had searched for better cover deeper in the jungle and had found a good spot twenty yards off the trail. Unfortunately, with better cover came an overwhelming attack of leeches and mosquitoes.

A leech's first bite doesn't hurt, so the only way to find them in the dark was to search every inch of skin with the hands. It was pulling them off that hurt. Leeches make most people squeamish and fidgety; the urge is to cry out or run, even though neither does any good. Duan cautioned them to get the parasites off as quickly as possible and then kill them on the ground. Otherwise they would slither right up somebody else's leg.

The porters worked in twos, methodically removing the leeches from each other's bodies. They made considerable noise during this process, so Duan moved them another hundred yards off the trail to somewhat drier ground. He ordered Thu and Hinh to stand watch on the trail. In the distance they could hear small-arms fire, and then quiet except for the rain falling.

Duan heard no more firing for a while except for some distant artillery along the border, but he could hear the steady hum of aircraft above the rain. The sound of the planes and vulnerable location of the platoon on the trail both bothered him.

He barely heard the Thug to their east. The sound of the jets was much clearer, because their wider circles brought them closer to the platoon's hiding place. Obviously the planes were circling something, but Duan couldn't figure out why they hadn't started shooting. "The Americans love to shoot and never seem to be concerned about ammunition, so why this peculiar behavior?" he whispered to Ba, who shrugged his shoulders. Meanwhile, in the small hamlet of Prey Samlanh, a company from the Ninth Vietcong Division wondered the same thing. They had been ordered to occupy their defensive trench line in preparation for an attack by the Thug and the F-4s.

No one in the entire chain of command liked Spectre 7's weapons officer's desperate proposal, but no one would override him. He was the guy in the seat, as the saying went. In an emergency, unless you are looking through the canopy yourself, you will never see what the pilot sees.

Two HH-53 Jolly Green Giant search-and-rescue helicopters had been airborne for twenty minutes when the plan was approved. Four A-1 Sandys with full bomb loads and an OV-10 observation airplane with a forward air controller at the controls had taken off with the helicopters. Spectre 15, another AC-130, was diverted from its target over Lomphat, Cambodia, to provide flare support. Four F-4s and four F-105s were uploaded with ordnance and put on strip alert. To conserve fuel, four planes would take off when the rescue package was thirty minutes out from the recovery area. The others would remain as backup.

In Spectre 7's cockpit, the weapons officer had traded seats with the sensor officer, putting him out of the direct force of the wind and rain. All officers in an AC-130 crew were given rudimentary training in flying the aircraft in anticipation of just such an emergency. But even an experienced pilot would have had difficulty flying with the damage that Spectre 7 had sustained. The aircraft was getting more difficult to control and they were barely able to keep it above 1,500 feet, even though holding a wide turn was easier than trying to steer a straight course. The rear cargo ramp had been lowered and the crew had pushed two tons of ammunition out to lighten the aircraft. The ramp was left open for the crew to bail out. The orbit gradually worked the airplane west. The F-4s now reported low fuel, and the first group of four replacement escort planes launched.

Duan was confused by the situation. While taking turns pulling off leeches with Thu, Hinh, and Ba, his mind was engrossed in solving the mystery of the airplanes to the east. The leeches were a nuisance but not life-threatening. Airplanes killed. The others were focused on the maddening blood-suckers. They had heard the jets, and the drone of the Thug was now closer. The sounds indicated the planes were still circling. Hinh added to the mystery by pointing out that the B-52 raid several days earlier had been the first American air activity in the area during the three months he had been stationed at the Prey Komnong base.

Most officers and troops in his company had attributed this low level of activity to the monsoon, but there could be other reasons.

After a time Duan said quietly, "We will stay where we are until the intent of the airplanes to our east is determined. They never just fly in circles at low altitude. Something peculiar is happening." There was no further discussion of the matter. They waited.

Spectre 7's final crisis came when water shorted the instrument panel and the radios went dead. Cut off from the outside world, the weapons officer gave the signal for the nine able crew members to bail out. In desperation, he ordered two men to jump with the unconscious navigator and copilot and try to pull their rip cords, figuring they would have a better chance that way than with the airplane. He put the plane into as flat a left turn as he could manage and tried to gain as much altitude as possible. With no altimeter he prayed that he was high enough for their chutes to open. All eleven men went off the ramp almost simultaneously. Only ten parachutes opened; one young ordnance man panicked and failed to pull his rip-cord ring in time for the chute to open. The copilot and navigator's chutes both opened, but they landed, still unconscious, in the flooded rice paddies and drowned before they were found. The eight survivors landed close to each other and promptly joined up, taking refuge along a rice-paddy dike. They turned on their survival radio transmitters. The signals were immediately picked up by the F-4 crews, who reported a clear and strong beeper location. Spectre 7's sensor officer was now in command of the downed crew and began calmly to talk through their situation with the F-4s, who relayed the information to TFA, the inbound rescue helos, and the A-1 attack planes. One of the fighters dropped down and vainly searched for Spectre 7.

The spot where the crew had landed represented their first piece of luck in the last hour. They sat in the middle of a rectangular rice field a full mile square. The nearest tree lines and villages were well out of sight, and after ten minutes it appeared no one had seen their parachutes. The orbiting F-4s moved their position several miles north so as not to mark their location precisely. The rescue helicopters were still half an hour away. The crew huddled together in the mud for warmth. It was cold, and the rain fell in a slow but steady drizzle. Each man clutched his pistol, now their only weapons other than survival knives. They had become vulnerable prey. Each had undergone courses in survival training, but no training prepared a man for this situation.

The weapons officer, still on board Spectre 7, now faced a hopeless situation. He was too low to bail out. His instrument panel and radios were out. Gamely, he lined up the magnetic compass, which was still functioning, and tried to fly a straight westerly course. In the dark he did not even see the surface of the rice field when his crippled aircraft flew directly into the ground at such a steep angle that it only moved a hundred yards along the ground before abruptly stopping and bursting into flames.

Duan had instantly noticed the rapidly increasing sound from the Thug's engines when it turned west. The noise grew louder as Spectre 7 approached the rice field near their hiding place on the trail. Then he noticed a whistling sound as if the airplane was diving. He hissed, "Down—now—forget the leeches! Down!" The platoon instantly flattened in the mud.

The Thug's blast sounded like it was coming straight for them. It crashed four hundred yards south of their location. The fireball lit up the area like a floodlight for a full thirty seconds.

The F-4 searching for Spectre 7 picked up the brightness and reported it up the chain of command. The crew on the ground saw the flash on the horizon and knew instantly what had happened. After another ten minutes, with no additional survival-radio transmissions, the weapons officer was presumed dead.

The American military system was remarkably methodical, analytical, and driven by the fundamental belief that everything, including war, was best managed. The fact that the ultimate anarchy of war undercut this doctrine was denied in the mountains of regulations and orders that governed virtually every conceivable event. Nowhere was this passion for efficiency more evident than in the requirement calling for reams of documentation to explain the loss of a multimillion-dollar aircraft.

It would be months before Task Force Alpha would release its final report on the loss of Spectre 7. The document, after hundreds of pages of tedious details and trivia, would conclude that a "Golden BB" had downed the formidably armed, armor-plated aircraft. The Golden BB was a theory claiming that a child armed with a Daisy BB gun could down any aircraft that flew, if the BB just happened to hit a particularly vulnerable spot.

The report would not be well-received in the upper reaches of the chain of command. The reasons were simple. After the millions of dollars and years of painstaking design work that had gone into the AC-130, it was a politically unacceptable conclusion that some barefoot Oriental soldier in a flooded rice paddy in the black of night could place two bullets worth maybe ten cents in just the right spot to destroy the highly prized, much-touted AC-130. The fact that this was the truth was irrelevant to the flurry of charges and countercharges of incompetence and cover-up that emanated from the controversy. Two cheap bullets in exchange for a multimillion-dollar airplane was clearly not a cost-effective trade—therefore the explanation was unacceptable.

The three bodies that were left in the destroyed fuselage caused much less furor until years later, during the turmoil of the MIA controversy. The efficient American system, strangely enough, accepted the frailty of human life much more readily than it did the vulnerability of its finest machines of war.

# FOURTEEN

# Hornets' Nest

### RICE FIELDS SOUTH OF PHUM BARAI, CAMBODIA

In the aftermath of the crash, Duan was bewildered. An American Thug had crashed in an open rice paddy four hundred yards from his platoon. He lay in the mud, trying to grasp the situation. As the fire died down he crawled over to Ba and they moved to where Hinh, Thu, Ky, and Trang lay on the trail. Hai was sobbing quietly.

Everyone whispered excitedly about the crash, no one making any sense. Duan quieted them down and summarized the situation. "We have a crashed American airplane burning in our path to the Komnong base. The *My*—Americans—will now come to rescue the crew of the plane who are dead, killed in the crash. They don't know that they are dead yet. They will do whatever it takes to find out. We must get away from that damned airplane now. This area will be a hornets' nest in a snap of your fingers. Where we are is certain death. We can't go due south but must find another way. And we must stay in the jungle or along tree lines. No open rice paddies." He paused and looked at the vague outlines of their faces in the dark. "Understood?" he asked. No one responded. He reached out and grabbed Hinh by his shirt front and hissed, "Do you understand, my fine young Revolutionary Brother?"

Hinh, brought back to the harsh discipline of the Vietcong, said steadily, "Yes, Commander." Duan leaned close to him and said, "If you want to taste the beautiful dragon-toothed jade gate of your bride-to-be ever again, you had better get us out of here fast!"

Hinh responded in a strong voice that they could count on him. They all smiled as Hinh, Ky, and Trang jogged down the trail to look for a route around the burning airplane.

The tension was broken. Thu and her daughter smiled and then began to giggle. Duan had accorded the young woman the highest accolade in the Taoist tradition by referring to her vagina as the dragon's tooth, the name of the most desirable of all female organs. Both women were vastly pleased by his compliment.

The scouts returned shortly and reported that they had found a covered path that skirted the site of the crash. Hinh told Duan he was almost certain they would run into Vietcong patrols or reaction teams moving to the plane crash in the direction they were heading. Duan decided quickly that if that were to occur it would be more bad than good, and he told Hinh to be careful. Duan and Ba moved down the line explaining the plan to each man. Finally Duan whispered in a voice loud enough for everyone to hear, "We will make it; I promise you that. We have not come this far to be killed a few miles from our goal by the damned Americans. Follow your orders, keep up, no talking. *Tien len.*"

They moved off with Hinh, Thu, and Hai in the lead. Ky and Trang, tireless workers, took one of the poles carrying a wounded man and headed off behind the guides and the three deaf men. The rest of the platoon followed.

The surviving members of the Spectre 7 crew huddled together against the dike pulling off leeches. The bodies of the three dead men lay on the dike. The sensor officer talked to the search-and-rescue team commander in the lead HH-53 helicopter. To the west they heard the far-off drone of helicopter engines heading toward them. Spectre 15 had taken up an orbit at 4,500 feet, just under the cloud ceiling and slightly to the north of the stranded crew on the ground. The A-1s and the OV-10 observation aircraft, which were short on night-flying aids, held orbits half a mile to the north of the AC-130. As the helos approached, Spectre 15 dropped a string of parachute flares in a semicircular pattern, turning the night into day. From the air the ground was visible but heavily shadowed by the clouds and rain in the artificial, oscillating light of the flares.

The rescue commander asked for a strobe light, which the sensor officer aimed toward the sound of the engines. The bright, pulsating light was shielded so that it was not visible from the ground. The rescue helicopter headed straight for it.

The Vietcong security company from the Ninth Vietcong Division, in the small hamlet of Prey Samlanh, had been confused when the dreaded Thug, and what sounded like two jets, had circled overhead for a long time and not fired. Their confusion deepened when they heard heavy objects landing in the rice paddies to their north. The commander assessed the sound as dud bombs. Later American ammunition boxes would be found. The Thug finally flew west and all had breathed a little easier, and then they had seen the fireball of the crash. The company commander, with no other orders, had held his position. But when Spectre 15's flares threw the open rice field a mile to their west into stark light and the helicopter engines could be heard, he decided he had to do something. His standing orders were to attack the enemy wherever he encountered them.

He moved his eighty-five men at a run toward the slowly descending flares and sent a runner with a message to his battalion commander, telling him of the situation and what action he was taking. He requested reinforcements.

The string of flares several miles to Duan's platoon's east cast a faint light behind the treetops. Duan paused, studied the light, and heard the helicopter rotors in the same area. Suddenly he understood. The crew of the Thug had used parachutes to escape their disabled airplane and were now being rescued. He estimated the distance from their position and concluded that it was not far enough, particularly if some overzealous commander fired at the airplanes. He knew that the Americans ex-

pended extraordinary effort in protecting downed airmen. Keep moving south. Get away from this place, he thought over and over.

The HH-53, call sign Low Bird, was the primary rescue helicopter.
It made a fast loop at 1,500 feet to the south of the descending parachute flares, trying to gain a sighting of the downed airmen and a grasp
of the terrain. The strobe light was clearly visible but in the rain and
clouds the flares cast eerie shadows, which made it difficult to see the
crew huddled against the narrow dike. Following the trace of the original flare string, Spectre 15 dropped another dozen flares to ensure light
for the entire rescue.

The Vietcong company moved fast along the dikes, heading toward
the lights. Low Bird flew directly overhead but did not see them in the
dark. Three hundred and fifty yards from the downed aircrew the Vietcong came to a wide, rain-swollen canal. The footbridge that crossed it
was 500 yards farther north, so the commander ordered his men into
firing position on a line along a raised earthen embankment running
parallel to the canal.

The helicopter's rotors began to make a dull, popping sound as the
aircraft descended rapidly to land on a small raised burial plot, seventy-
five yards from the downed crew. The four A-1s and the OV-10, now
able to see the target, took up a racetrack pattern just above the descending flares. The jet fighter-bombers orbited to the north. Low Bird
turned on a shielded strobe on the top of the aircraft that located his
position for the fixed-wing aircraft above.

Duan heard the hornets' nest of airplanes assembling for the rescue and knew exactly what would happen. Someplace, somehow, someone from his old division would find it impossible to keep from taking
a shot at the airplanes. In mid-thought, he heard the distinct crackle of
small arms fire and yelled with no regard for security, "Let's get out of
here!" They broke into a shuffling run.

Still unnoticed in the dark and rain, the Vietcong company had
opened fire on the perfectly silhouetted helicopter as it hovered a few
feet above the burial mound. The bullets hit the helicopter with such

sudden force that for a few moments the crew didn't realize what was happening. The heavy armor plate protected them from the small-arms rounds that rattled off the airplane's tough skin, but there was no armor plate on the exposed rotor blades. Bullets tore through the rotating blades, and they immediately disintegrated as the balance of the rotor hub was broken. The helicopter rotated on the axis of the now-unbalanced rotor shaft, which rapidly began to overheat as the transmission mechanism to the tail rotor began to lose power. In seconds the helicopter began uncontrollably to turn and lose adequate lift, and it slowly rolled over and crashed on its side. The blades still turned, throwing up a circular fountain of water. They kept churning into the mud and water, lifting the fuselage up and down, thrashing it on the ground like a rag doll in the invisible hands of a giant. Finally the helicopter ceased its death throes and sat steaming in three feet of water. The pilot, who had been shot down before, expertly went through shutdown procedure and there was no fire. The plane's tough armor plate had saved the crew.

The downed crew of Spectre 7 had begun moving toward the HH-53 when it had gone into its landing hover. Their run to safety had been nightmarishly difficult going in the water and sucking mud of the rice paddy, dragging three dead men. At first the HH-53's engines had drowned out the sound of enemy fire. But they knew something was wrong when the helo's fuselage began to flash with white-and-green twinkling lights, which were the bullets ricocheting off the armor plate. They stared as the helo staggered like a wounded animal and rolled over on its side. Reality set in when a rotor blade whizzed just above their heads. Instinctively they ducked down and lay in the filthy water of the paddy. None of them noticed the smell, or the leeches slithering inside their flight suits.

The pilot of the OV-10 observation airplane had gradually lowered his altitude as the flares descended. It was no accident of military bureaucracy that the pilot's call sign was Fast Dog. Fast Dog had never flown a routine mission in his life. As he put it, "Every one of 'em is the Super Bowl, and if ya ain't playin' 'em that way, we'll be a-toastin' ya here some night soon." The frequent toasts to fallen comrades, which Fast Dog always led, concluded with the sage epitaph, "And Lord forgive him for freezin' up and forgettin' everything he ever knew at the most important time."

Within seconds of the Vietcong company's opening salvo, Fast Dog's 20/05 eyesight had a hard fix on their position. As he threw maximum power to his two engines and rolled in toward the line of muzzle flashes, he instructed the lead A-1 to drop all his ordnance on the marking rocket he had fired squarely into the middle of the Vietcong. The A-1 that followed Fast Dog down went in low, laying a string of napalm and 500-pound bombs along the line of the embankment where the company hammered away at the wounded helicopter. The remaining three A-1s now dove and, in the span of two minutes, the Vietcong company ceased to exist as a cohesive fighting unit. The withering fire on the downed crew and the crashed HH-53 abruptly ceased.

Fast Dog dove directly behind the last A-1, going in on the target and skillfully placing a marking rocket at each end of the line of fire he had observed. Spectre 15 dropped another string of flares and crossed over to a firing position parallel to the target. Lining up his sight and computer target image, the big gunship fired at maximum volume for a full five seconds, placing a solid sheet of lethal steel between the two marker rounds. Only seven members of the Vietcong company had survived the air attacks.

The platoon listened as the sound of small arms was replaced by that of diving airplanes and exploding bombs. The moan of Spectre 15's guns terrified them. Adrenaline propelled their exhausted young bodies through the jungle tree line. The cracks of the 20- and 40-mm rounds echoed like thunder under the low clouds. Duan chanted, "*Tien len*," at the rear of the column. They found strength they hadn't felt since leaving Van Xa two months before. Ky and Trang set a fast pace behind the guides, and no one fell. An intense physical dexterity comes to most people when confronted with extinction.

Meanwhile, all five crew members of the crashed helo crawled out of the wreckage shaken and bruised but otherwise unharmed, and huddled on the burial mound. Command of the rescue automatically had passed to High Bird, the call sign of the second helicopter's pilot, when Low Bird crashed.

In the air-conditioned Surveillance Center at Nakhon Phanom, there was pandemonium. The numerous staff tried vainly to piece together what was happening. In the span of an hour they had lost two aircraft with at least six men dead and another thirteen on the ground requiring rescue. Over the target they had four fighter-bombers, four A-1s, one AC-130, one HH-53 helicopter, and an OV-10 observation aircraft.

After heated discussion, General Kendal decided that control of the operation belonged to High Bird until the downed crews were rescued. Later he would decide the best course of action. The hundred-man intelligence section was put to work documenting the fact that there had never been reports of antiaircraft fire in the Prey Veng area of Cambodia. General Kendal correctly anticipated severe repercussion for his losses. The reality that uncoordinated attacks by small infantry units had inflicted their casualties would never be fully accepted by the Task Force Alpha staff or by higher headquarters.

Kendal now made several phone calls to alert his superiors that he had run into some trouble. They were not pleased.

At the Kantreuy Plantation, as the COSVN commander and his guests continued their unhurried meal and strategy discussion, another report arrived for the commander of TG559. Relayed over five separate field telephone lines, the report had taken only six minutes to be transmitted from the Ninth Vietcong Division command post at Prey Komnong, a distance of over seventy miles. The report indicated that the Thug aircraft that had been reported earlier possibly had crashed, and that the area around Prey Samlanh was lit up with flares. At least half a dozen American planes, including helicopters, were attacking anything in sight. The TG559 commander read the message aloud and peered inquisitively at the older and more senior men around the straw mat.

The host returned the inquiring look with a smile and asked, "What would you recommend in this situation?" His placid face did not betray his churning, cramped intestines.

The officer persuasively followed the basic idea he had broached earlier. "I believe the emerging tactical situation, with several slow and low-flying aircraft involved in what appears to be a rescue attempt, is a perfect chance to surprise the Americans with the presence of the SA-7 Grail missiles, while putting the enemy government in an international propaganda bind with pictures of their war planes crashed on neutral Cambodian soil." He paused and looked at his host.

No one spoke, deferring their answer to the host while they casually selected morsels of food with their chopsticks.

The commander extended his chopsticks and selected a bean, which he dipped in *nuoc mam*. He paused halfway to his mouth with the food, smiled, and said, "You are authorized to implement your plan and use the SA-7s against the American airplanes. Since the missiles are infrared and seek the heat of an aircraft's engine, there is no radar signature, which leaves my original policy intact." He smiled again at his guests.

Everyone registered surprise, but there were no objections. Usually any new initiative required considerable discussion and deliberation. What the guests didn't know was that COSVN had received a directive from Hanoi to employ the SA-7s as soon as possible in order to provide the Soviets with actual combat evaluation of their latest weapon. The COSVN commander was very deliberate in giving his subordinates the impression of great powers of decision and insightfulness.

The TG559 commander scribbled a message and handed it to a waiting runner. It took less than three minutes for the message to travel the seventy miles over the field-phone relay system. Each operator immediately recognized its significance and forwarded the order as quickly as possible.

The porter platoon struggled along an overgrown trail, partially lit by the flares shining over the treetops. They were now over half a mile from the still-burning AC-130. They could see the fire through gaps in the jungle. Duan's mind was racing, trying to figure the American's next move.

High Bird knew from experience that surprise perished with time, and speed and surprise were the keys to successful search-and-rescue operations. The noise of the airplanes and the light from the flares had given the enemy precise targets to home in on. If he waited longer it could mean captivity or death for the stranded crews on the ground. He ordered Fast Dog to start working the fighter-bombers in on likely enemy positions to create a diversion and threat for any enemy commander who decided to take another shot at the rescue attempt. Fast Dog already had his targets picked. A likely spot was the tree line close to the burning wreckage of Spectre 7.

The porter platoon heard the OV-10 circling behind them. It sounded closer than it was, and the men anxiously stepped faster. No one looked back. They bowed their backs and necks and used all their strength to keep moving. The weight of the loads was unrelenting on their bruised and calloused shoulders. Never forget the rules you have learned at such a dear price, Duan reminded himself. They have never once found the *bo doi* in the jungle with their damned machines. Stick to the jungle and you will live. Besides, there is nothing to do but put as much distance between you and the crashed airplane as possible. "*Tien len*," he hissed loud enough for everyone to hear.

High Bird was a veteran of this very risky business, and pressure only made him calmer. Like all great combat pilots, he had learned to use fear productively to solve the frequent life-threatening emergencies he faced. Fast Dog's epitaph rang in his mind—"Don't forget all ya ever knew at the most important time." He knew the men on the ground were terrified. To move them all to a dry spot would take at least half an hour. The only suitable landing site within 500 yards where he could touch his wheels down was useless—the crashed HH-53 lay partially on top of the burial mound. He radioed his instructions calmly, his heart pounding. He would hover and winch each man up individually, starting with the Spectre 7 crew. The hover would have to be above a hundred feet to avoid sucking up a geyser of water through the rotor blades. He outlined the plan to Fast Dog and Spectre 15, who were instructed to move the flares to the peripheral areas and attack likely enemy positions within range of the rescue area. High Bird would then do his extraction in the dark, homing on the downed crew's strobe lights and using his landing lights if necessary.

The flares that lit the rescue area went out as they hit the water in the rice paddies, and everything again went dark. Just then Spectre 15 dropped a string of six flares two miles south of Duan's platoon, and Fast Dog rolled in and placed a marking rocket. A single fighter bomber went in on the target, laying napalm directly through the platoon's last hiding place. The leeches wouldn't bother anyone again.

Duan heard the drone of the Thug's engines as it passed close by, heading south. As the sound faded, the platoon was startled by a series of pops followed by a bright light, then the loud swoosh-bang of the marking rocket behind them. The brilliant string of flares descended to the southeast; it was so bright they could see their shadows. Duan stopped and watched. Suddenly he yelled, "Down!" The reaction was instantaneous, except for the guides and the three deaf men in the lead, who ran on for fifty yards before they noticed there was no noise behind them. They quickly doubled back to the platoon and Duan hissed them down to the ground. He whispered, "The airplanes can see us in the light. We will stay down until the flares go out." Thankfully there were no leeches, but the mosquitoes were as zealous in their quest for blood as the Americans.

At the Prey Komnong base, the commander of the Ninth Vietcong Division had moved out of his underground bunker and into a tree line that gave him a good view of the flares to the northeast. He and his operations officer had identified the sound of a Thug, several prop-driven airplanes, a helicopter, at least four jets, and an observation airplane. They had heard the small-arms fire and the prop-driven airplanes attack a target that they had correctly assumed was their company. A panting runner had delivered TG559's order to attack the airplanes with the new SA-7s. Both men were surprised at the directive. They briefly discussed authenticating the message and decided time did not permit being cautious. Besides, the order made sense. Seldom did slow, low-flying American aircraft appear in this area. The operations officer ordered the newly organized antiaircraft battalion to dispatch five SA-7 missile teams and a company of security forces to the vicinity of the flares and engage the American airplanes. In minutes the attack force was running northeast along the dikes toward the lights.

High Bird hovered over the Spectre 7 crew. The flight mechanic operated the hoist, and the pararescue man descended to the ground and began to send up the crew one at a time. Tree lines to the south shielded them from the full light of the flares, and they worked feverishly in the rain and semidarkness. The downed crew from Low Bird, deciding they had time, worked their way over to the hover spot. It was hard going in the sucking mud. The helicopter's engines and blades made a deafening noise and churned the water into waves. The men on the ground helped the pararescue man. They ascended in reverse seniority, with the lowest-ranking going first. It was a tedious process. High Bird felt streams of sweat run down his face and back as he held a steady zero airspeed and a hundred feet on the altimeter while following the instructions of the flight mechanic, who kept the hoist centered over the men on the ground.

Fast Dog shifted his diversion operation to the northwest and marked another tree line that faced on the open rice paddy. He worked Spectre 15 into a position where his flares would give enough illumination for the pilots to see the target but would not throw direct light on High Bird in his rescue hover. The A-1s expended the last of their ordnance on Fast Dog's marker, and Fast Dog radioed Task Force Alpha for at least four more airplanes. Only four fighters and Spectre 15 remained to divert attention from the slow-moving rescue. The four strip alert planes took off immediately from the American base at Ubon, Thailand, and flew at maximum speed toward the rescue area.

Duan watched the nearby flares drift slowly into the water and go out just as the airplane engines faded to the north. But then another ten flares popped several miles to the north. The light only illuminated the tree tops. Duan ordered the platoon up and told Hinh and Thu to put some distance between them and the terrifying American activity. They heaved their loads and shuffled down the overgrown trail.

Fast Dog had developed a keen intuition for how the enemy operated. He knew they would try to approach the rescue helicopters using for cover the tree lines that crisscrossed the paddies. Since he had no information on enemy ground units in the area, he relied on his instincts. By moving the flares he had shifted the point of action north, placing two large paddies and half a dozen tree lines between the light and the rescue. Since he was using his available firepower only on likely avenues of approach, he decided to save the fighter bombers' heavy ordnance in case a hard target materialized. Instead, he would use Spectre 15's guns. As the flares drifted slowly toward the ground, Fast Dog dove and strained his eyes to glimpse signs of enemy activity. He saw none. He placed a marking rocket on the edge of a tree line facing an open rice field.

The villagers of Phum Barai had occupied the substantial bunkers that each family had painstakingly constructed under their homes when the first moaning wail of the Thug's guns had pierced the quiet night more than two hours before. In spite of the accumulated water and dampness in the bunkers, hammocks had been quickly strung and most of the people had tried to get some sleep. At first the Thug was far enough away that they were not concerned. Then the night had suddenly begun to fill with the noises of war as they heard low-flying jets pass overhead, moving east. Then they had heard small-arms fire and bombing. Some had nervously looked out of the bunker entrances and noticed the flares to their east. Manh had called a hasty meeting of the village elders to assess the situation. There was but one course open to them: stay in the bunkers and seal the entrances. It was good to talk, though, and the people agreed promptly with the village council's decision. They rolled coconut logs into place and sealed most of the bunkers tight.

Three men, who were known for their laziness, now wished fervently that they had positioned logs to cover the entrances to their family bunkers like everyone had told them to do. The sound of these men's wives berating them for their lack of foresight was the only human sound coming from the bunkers. The pop of the flares over the village and Fast Dog's marking rocket chilled the people's hearts. The children began to cry.

Spectre 15 maneuvered into firing position. Fast Dog instructed him to use only his 7.62-mm and 20-mm Gatling guns and to save his 40-mm ammunition for later. Spectre 15 fired a three-second burst and walked the rounds perfectly down the edge of the tree line for several hundred yards. The Thug's guns wailed and bullets ricocheted and exploded on the ground, tracing the edge of Phum Barai, which was hidden from the aircraft by the wide, overhanging leaves of the coconut trees.

As suddenly as it had started, it was over. A brief, intensely violent moment followed by complete silence. The people in the bunkers held their breaths, waiting for the rushing sound of bombs. After a full two minutes of quiet, excited talking broke out as the sound of the airplanes drifted farther off in the night. Manh and his assistants checked each home for casualties. One house on the edge of the village had been hit by half a dozen 20-mm rounds, and the thatch roof, in spite of being rain-soaked, caught fire. The man of the house, who had not prepared his bunker properly, had been seriously wounded by one of the explosive rounds and the village healer could do nothing for him. He died shortly after the attack. Everyone interpreted his death the same way. The Immortals had used him as an example against laziness and recalcitrance. He had brought about his own death. The Thug was only an instrument to teach the living an enduring lesson. Do not begin to dig a well after you have become thirsty. And build your bunker before the enemy attacks your house. He had violated this axiom and paid the just price.

Fast Dog banked his aircraft into a steep dive and passed close to the tree line, spotting the roof of the burning house that lit up several adjacent houses. He knew the enemy frequently used villages as cover, but since there was no return fire, he announced his intention to shift the diversion operation away from this area. Many fighter-attack pilots developed an abstract view of the damage they inflicted with their bombs: at a thousand feet or more and speed in excess of four hundred miles an hour, all terrain looked essentially the same. Very seldom were pilots capable of seeing their targets in any detail, or of assessing the damage they had done.

Forward air controllers, who flew much slower airplanes closer to the ground, were not afflicted with this abstract view. They saw things up close, and even the most hardened among them seldom ran strikes on villages unless hostile intent was evident, which always meant a heavy volume of enemy fire. Even though the political persuasion of the population in this area was clear, Fast Dog had no intention of randomly attacking civilians regardless of which side they were on. It was just something he and his kind didn't do. As he flew south he mumbled to himself, "Be more careful. You should have noticed the houses." He shook his head. He didn't like making mistakes, particularly ones like that.

The roar of Fast Dog's engines passed low over the porter platoon, which struggled south on a muddy but open path. The sound of the engines frightened the men. Duan calculated that the flares to the north would not reveal their movement and whispered, "*Tien len.*" Fast Dog's engines passed to their east, flying south, followed closely by the Thug.

In the rice paddy the rescue operation continued to go smoothly. The pararescue man was the last one up the hoist, behind the sensor officer. After he had been pulled through the door, High Bird slightly dropped the nose of his straining aircraft and began a gradual climb in the dark and rain, spiraling up to 3,000 feet and setting a westerly course for home. There was jubilation among the men rescued, which soon died out as the HH-53 crew dutifully began to put the three twisted corpses of their friends into body bags. Then they methodically set about pulling off leeches.

With the rescue almost complete, Fast Dog had decided to put in the ordnance on the fighter-bombers. He banked north and worked Spectre 15 over an area to the southwest of Spectre 7's burning wreckage. Spectre 15 dropped a short string of flares and Fast Dog dove toward a sparse tree line, reminding himself to check closely for houses.

The sound of the Thug was coming straight for the platoon. The aircraft passed directly overhead. Duan yelled, "Down!" Everyone instantly went into the mud. "Completely still," he yelled. "No movement. Don't look up."

The flares went off directly over their heads, and their hiding place was bathed in bright light. The temptation to panic and run for cover was overwhelming, but they held their positions. They had learned always to trust Duan. That trust, which he had never betrayed, was now stronger than the powerful urge to get away from this place. Duan would get them through. The loud sound of the prop-driven spotter airplane now came straight for them. No one moved a muscle.

The antiaircraft company from the Ninth Vietcong Division was startled to see the flares burst a short distance to their north. The commander stopped his men and called the five SA-7 teams forward for a clear view of the target area.

Each of the SA-7 gunners was a veteran of North Vietnamese antiaircraft forces. Each had fought airplanes with various weapons that were being supplied in increasing numbers and equally growing calibers by the Soviets and Chinese. They had undergone extensive training, even though it was hardly required because of the weapon's simplicity. Weighing just twenty-three pounds, the SA-7 was a product of the Soviets' feverish and intense technological espionage and was almost identical to the American Redeye infantry antiaircraft missile. All the gunner was required to do was to place his optical sight on the target aircraft and squeeze the trigger to a half-way position. When the red light in the weapons sight turned green, it told the gunner that the missile's heat-seeking sensor was locked onto the heat of the plane's engine exhaust. The gunner then merely squeezed the trigger through the remainder of the firing cycle, and a two-stage rocket motor boosted the missile to over 750 miles per hour—fast enough to catch most ground attack planes on any battlefield. It was particularly effective against low-flying, slower aircraft.

The antiaircraft company spread out along a thinly vegetated, raised cart path. The flares were close enough to cast shadows as the troops set up their defensive line. The two-man SA-7 crews broke out their weapons from the protective wrappings and activated the launcher systems. The gunners, almost in unison, reported to the company commander that the situation was not good. The flares gave an alternate heat source that caused the firing mechanisms on the SA-7s to show instantly green, or ready to fire, regardless of what they were pointing at.

The commander, a former dry-goods shopkeeper from Haiphong, had never understood the SA-7. He was well-accustomed to 12.7-mm antiaircraft machine guns, which the gunner aimed, fired, and then adjusted the path of its tracers to coincide with the flight path of the target aircraft. He did not really understand a weapon over which a gunner had no control after it was fired.

He abrasively told the gunners that his orders were to shoot down an American airplane, and that was what he intended to do. The discipline of the Vietcong compelled them not to argue, even though they knew he didn't understand the SA-7. Each crew attempted to gain a target solution on the enemy airplanes in the shifting light of the flares.

Fast Dog dove his aircraft for the narrow tree line, which was now well-lit by the descending flares. He slowed and passed fifty feet over the platoon which lay motionless on the trail. In the shadowy light he glimpsed what he thought were four men lying facedown. The loads and their carrying poles registered with him as possibly long antiaircraft machine guns, but he was not sure. "Make sure what you saw was not women and kids," he cautioned himself. He pulled up the airplane in a high arch, passed through 500 feet and dove back toward the platoon. He flew directly over the antiaircraft company, who were invisible in the dark. Three of the gunners caught a glimpse of the shape of the OV-10 in the light, and one saw his red sight flash green. But he didn't pull the trigger; he was still confused as to whether he was locked onto the airplane or the flares.

The sound of the airplane became an overwhelming din as it dove back toward the platoon sprawled on the open trail. Duan lay still with his head turned in the mud so that one eye could see. The string of flares floated down directly toward them. He felt naked and helpless in the light. His mind raced for options. This hell was worse than his darkest dream. There were only two possibilities, and both would probably end in death. Stay still and be slaughtered by the airplanes. Or try to run out of the light when the spotter plane was off in the distance. But the loads slowed them down too much. Leaving them behind was not much better; there was no jungle to hide in, and they had to carry their wounded. Vegetation was sparse. Staying still remained the best option, but that was looking worse as he saw the underbelly and wings of the gray airplane flash close to the ground.

Fast Dog dove back toward the platoon keeping a close eye on the ground and the descending flares. He cut the power on his engines to slow his speed and banked sharply for a clear view of the narrow trail in the sparse jungle. There they were. Prone figures lying motionless next to what still appeared to be the long barrels of weapons. This time he saw at least ten men. Throwing power to his engines, he arched into a climb and leveled off at 2,000 feet, putting him out of small-arms range.

The flares drifted slowly toward the ground. The platoon held their frozen positions, obeying orders. One of the flares directly overhead malfunctioned, burned through the parachute cords, and fell to the trail. The free-falling canister hit Trang on the head, knocking him unconscious and sending spurts of blood from a six-inch cut along the top of his skull.

Fast Dog fixed the target in his mind and now began methodically to set up the strike. He directed Spectre 15 south of the target and ordered him to drop a string of flares so as not to interfere with the bombers' run on the target, which would run east to west. The new flare string popped just a minute after the first one burned out.

The flare canister that had hit Trang lay on the trail throwing hot sparks. It slowly went out, glowing reddish-yellow. Ky stayed still, obeying orders. "Ky! Roll over to Trang and see how he is," Duan instructed.

Then the new flare string ignited to their south. Duan breathed a little easier—maybe they had not been spotted. At least they were not directly under the bright light of the flares. He raised his head slowly and tried to piece together the situation. From the sound of it the planes were north of their position, except for the Thug, which was off to the south. An old *bo doi* adage rushed to his mind. He had not thought of it before. It said, Any cover was better than no cover at all. That was it, he thought.

He rose to one knee clutching his rifle and spoke in a loud whisper. "Look at me!" All eyes were on him. "Crawl slowly to the edge of this raised ground and slip into the rice paddies. Leave your loads. Leave the poles for the wounded, and drag them with you. Now."

Duan and Ba crawled over to Trang and helped Ky drag his limp body toward the short drop-off into the rice paddies. The rest of the platoon crawled on elbows and knees and slipped down the three-foot embankment into the cold muddy water up to their necks. They were horrified to feel the water surface ripple with the rush of leeches swarming toward their bodies. They began their private battles with the horrifyingly aggressive and agile parasites. They were so bad that even Duan lost his concentration and wildly searched with his hands to keep the slimy bloodsuckers from his body. The water and leeches revived the two wounded men who had slept through most of the night's chilling events. Holding Trang's head out of the water left Ky unable to defend himself against the parasites.

The Vietcong antiaircraft company commander had assessed the situation and did not like his conclusion. The flares, now half a mile to his southeast, had revealed his unit's position along the exposed dike and cart path. He ordered his platoon commanders to disperse and camouflage their men. Each man wore a handmade mesh cape tied with a loop of rope around his neck. Normally the capes were recamouflaged three times a day with foliage. Each had a similarly camouflaged hood. The squad leaders positioned their men along the south side of the cart path and each man pulled on his cape and flipped up his hood. The prone troops, their weapons barely visible over the top of the dike, blended in so well with the ground vegetation that even an observer a few yards away would take them for part of the ground. An aerial observer would find it impossible to see them.

The company commander now had only two major problems to overcome. First, the SA-7 gunners had to kneel or stand erect to fire their missiles because of the backblast. Second, the leeches were swarming out of the water and had begun to attack his troops. He called his platoon commanders around him and issued his final order.

Fast Dog knew speed and altitude were the best defense against ground fire, so he threw maximum power to his aircraft and circled the area once, then banked into a steep dive from 2,500 feet toward his target.

As the platoon fought the unrelenting leeches, they heard the roar of the prop airplane diving straight for them. Duan had been right to put them on this side of the raised strip of scrub bushes and trees. They leaned into the muddy embankment, forgetting the leeches in the face of a more lethal threat.

Fast Dog fired a marking rocket toward the center of the target. The rocket hit and its smoke charge exploded, followed by a loud detonation as a load of mortar rounds exploded. Still in his dive, Fast Dog pulled up on his stick and leveled out, avoiding the exploding ammunition. Only then did he know for sure he had a hard military target. He radioed the fighter-bombers that they were cleared in hot, which meant they should put their bombs on the rocket marker.

Fast Dog's course took him directly over the antiaircraft company, which he did not see. As his airplane passed overhead, the five SA-7 gunners moved up on top of the exposed cart path and followed him with their sights. As he banked back east and passed in front of the flares, their weapons sights wildly flashed red and green. Fast Dog turned north again and descended below 1,000 feet, which was the pull-out altitude for the fighter-bombers in their bombing runs on the target. As he flew low toward the north he noticed several evenly spaced short tree-like objects in the vague light. He did not realize that what he had mistaken for trees were SA-7 gunners waiting for him to pass over their position.

As the first fighter-bomber dove toward the marked target, the most experienced SA-7 gunner, who had been designated to fire first, saw his sight reticle turn green as he aimed at Fast Dog's plane. He pulled the trigger through the last half of the firing sequence and the long slender weapon roughly kicked back against his shoulder. The deafening rush of the rocket motor propelled the small, pipe-size missile toward its target, leaving an uneven white trail of smoke as its guidance mechanism adjusted to Fast Dog's engine exhaust.

Out of the corner of his eye, the pilot of the lead fighter diving toward the platoon caught the distinctive white smoke of the missile snaking upward toward Fast Dog's airplane. It immediately registered with him as being a missile. He pulled off the target and radioed to Fast Dog that he had a SAM chasing him at six o'clock.

The missile had been fired by the gunner toward the retreating tail of Fast Dog's airplane. Fast Dog had no defensive warning system for a heat-seeking missile. The pilot had to acquire the threat visually.

Fast Dog, who had survived for years by trusting his instincts, asked no questions when he heard the warning. He threw his throttles to maximum emergency power and in a split second decided to dive, using the agility of his airplane to elude the sudden threat. Going to full power was his fatal error. The missile, like a leech, remorselessly bored in on its target, which became more distinct when Fast Dog applied full power.

He went into a shallow dive, banking sharply to the south, as the missile raced up to his left engine exhaust and detonated its five-and-a-half-pound charge of explosive, which tore apart the engine exhaust manifold, crushed the inboard flaps and ailerons and immediately rendered the airplane unflyable.

In a flash Fast Dog knew his life had ended. Like all men, he clung hardest to the hope of life at the most desperate moment, and he pulled his ejection-seat trigger, which blew him out the canopy just as the airplane hit the rice paddy. His chute didn't open and Fast Dog died in a giant geyser of water, 200 yards from his crashed airplane.

The pilot of the lead F-105 pulled out of his dive at 2,000 feet, threw his throttle forward, and dove toward the spot where he had seen the missile rise from the ground. In less than a second he saw the missile explode next to Fast Dog's wing, and in another blink-of-the-eye image saw Fast Dog explode into the rice paddy.

He banked toward the raised cart path.

The antiaircraft company troops spontaneously cheered when the SA-7 exploded and the American airplane staggered for a moment and crashed. None of them had ever seen anything quite as spectacular. They stood on the cart path and slapped the successful gunner on the back.

The company commander jerked them back to reality. He yelled a warning as he heard the approaching F-105. The SA-7 gunners began to fumble their weapons into firing position. In the light from the flares they could see the F-105 heading straight for them. Two gunners squeezed the triggers to the half-way point, holding the F-105 in the center. The sight lights spasmodically flashed green and red because there was not a constant heat source coming from the front of the airplane. One man panicked and fired anyway, sending his missile straight for the onrushing plane.

Then the platoon commander made a fatal error. He ordered his men to open fire with their small arms, and the muzzle flashes gave away their position.

The F-105 pilot, with his wing man diving close behind him, saw the erratic smoke trail rising to meet him. Even though he had never encountered an SA-7, he had figured it must have been a heat-seeker that killed Fast Dog. The fact that his SAM radar warning equipment had not activated corroborated his conclusion. Still the missile flew directly for his airplane. He radioed two words to his wing man, "SAM. Break." The aircraft banked sharply right and left, each pilot careful not to expose his jet tailpipe. The missile, with no constant heat source to guide it, picked up the heat from the still-hot load of exploded ammunition, dove rapidly toward the trail where Duan's platoon had left their loads, and exploded harmlessly.

Then the lead F-105 saw the winking muzzle flashes along the ribbon of cart path and noticed some figures standing on top. He banked hard right and came in straight down the long axis of the target, rippling napalm tanks and 500-pound bombs among the exposed troops. A few seconds later his wing man dropped his ordnance in the same place. The string of flares to the south burned out and threw the area back into darkness, vaguely illuminated by the smoldering napalm and the burning wreckage of Fast Dog's airplane.

The antiaircraft company commander lay dead, along with most of his men. Moans and cries of the wounded and burned mingled with the crackling of smoldering napalm. The SA-7 launchers were destroyed. Their dead gunners were hardly recognizable as human.

Everything was clearly visible from the platoon's hiding place in the rice paddy. Only a few had managed the courage to look. The marking rocket, the igniting ammunition, the startling rush of the SA-7 rocket engines, the exploding airplane, the ripple of small-arms fire from their south, the jets racing over their position, the resounding crack of the missile into the smoldering ammunition load, and then somehow, miraculously, the American planes had not dropped their bombs on them. Most of the men lay whimpering in the mud, oblivious to the leeches ravenously eating their blood.

Like a boxer, Duan had trained himself never to close his eyes, even in the worst situations. He had been amazed by what he had seen. Most spectacular had been the missile that had downed the American spotter plane. The only missiles he had ever seen were the big surface-to-air SA-2s in the north. He incorrectly concluded that they must have some set up here in southern Cambodia. He had seen the towed launchers on the trail several months before but hadn't known their destination. The picture he had in his mind was of four or five of the big launchers set up less than a mile from their position. That meant grave danger. The Americans would find and destroy them, and anyone nearby would suffer the same fate. He checked the line for casualties. There were no new ones except for a few severe cases of nerves. Several men were crying. Duan gave very specific instructions. He told them to pair off and move out of the rice paddy, strip off their clothes, and clean their bodies of leeches. The bites admitted all water-borne parasites and diseases directly into the bloodstream. It took no encouragement to get them out of their hellhole of a hiding place. Thu grabbed Duan's hand and asked him to help her with the leeches. Vietnamese modesty precluded her from being naked in the dark with a strange man.

There were only the sounds of muttered curses and expressions of disgust and pain as they pulled the persistent and squirming creatures from every conceivable part of their bodies. It was fully understood and unspoken that each person would clear his own crotch. The ones in the crotch area were by far the most painful.

Ky, almost in a trance, had worked on himself and Trang, who was still limp. Duan came over to help pull off leeches and saw that Trang was dead. Ky kept talking to his friend as if he could hear. Duan said nothing. After five minutes he ordered everyone to get dressed and return to their loads. The detonated mortar ammunition still glowed in the dark. Each team quickly found their poles; they had a familiar feel to them. Duan put the two wounded men at the head of the column with the guides, along with Ky, who had draped Trang over his shoulder. He told them to keep up in spite of their injuries because time was critical to their survival. He had them help the three deaf men, whose faces betrayed their confusion over the rapid series of events spanning the last three hours. Duan told Hinh and Thu to find some overhead cover, skirt the area from which the missiles had been fired, and find the TG559 depot as soon as possible.

The depot now struck Duan as a sanctuary. He considered for a moment that it might have been better if he had turned his unit in to the TG559 salvage crew at the site of the B-52 strike. But he dismissed the thought. To stay alive a soldier must make the best decisions possible under the circumstances, and if he did so, then there was no need to question his instincts. His mind reviewed the past two months and briefly flashed a picture of Su, in her sensual beauty. He pushed the thought from his mind but could not prevent his lips from silently forming her name. He shook his head and forced himself to concentrate on the present situation. "*Tien len,*" he said in a loud whisper.

There was no response. The exhausted and terrified platoon began struggling south again.

The Task Force Alpha staff at the Surveillance Center had been stunned into silence when they received the message that Fast Dog had crashed, apparently shot down by a SAM of unknown type. The staff demanded three confirmations that there had been no parachute cited. Pilots over the area patiently confirmed that Fast Dog had not gotten out in time and, more important, that there had been no rescue beeper signal.

The startling events of the night were made even more depressing with the news of Fast Dog's loss. He had been a living legend among the pilots and staff, most of whom had flown with him as their forward air controller at some time over the years. His earthy and wise counsel, delivered with wit and a twinkling eye, had been practical advice that many of them had lived by for years. They had believed him indestructible. Attack pilots very often relied for their survival solely on the skill of the controllers who ran the mission. Fast Dog never left them unnecessarily exposed and always managed to bring them back. It was part of the legend that he had never lost a pilot. Even though some had been shot down, he had always managed to coordinate a successful rescue. It was a bitter irony that the only pilot Fast Dog ever lost was himself.

The count for the night of ninety-six enemy trucks destroyed seemed to be completely offset by the seven dead Americans and the loss of an

AC-130, an HH-53, and Fast Dog's OV-10. The phones rang incessant-ly with increasingly demanding orders for an explanation of the disas-ter. Gradually the activity at the vast command center returned to its usual efficient hum.

General Kendal's boss called and heatedly demanded to know what he intended to do about retrieving the state-of-the-art, top-secret sens-ing equipment that had been aboard Spectre 7. Both men knew the an-swer. It couldn't be retrieved, so it had to be completely destroyed.

Spectre 15 was directed to hold on station and put the four in-bound F-105s in on the wreckage of Spectre 7. When the order was is-sued the men who heard it turned away. The body of the weapons of-ficer, pilot, and flight engineer were still in the plane. Everyone knew they were dead and that the sensor suite must be kept out of enemy hands. Still it seemed ghoulish to intentionally destroy the bodies of brave men. Kendal reluctantly directed that the crashed HH-53 and Fast Dog's OV-10 also be destroyed and left the Surveillance Center with instructions to tell any callers he was on the flight line. He dis-missed his jeep driver and began walking with his operations and in-telligence colonels, discussing how they had blundered into this mess. The responsibility now rested on his shoulders.

After half an hour the platoon reached a stand of jungle with good overhead cover. It was pitch-dark under the low canopy, and Duan called a halt. He and Ba worked down the line checking each man with touches and whispers. The two wounded men at the front of the col-umn were keeping the pace well. Each of the three deaf men told Duan their hearing was beginning to return, but they still were dazed because of the fevers. Duan loudly whispered orders in their ears. He told them he couldn't wait for them if they couldn't keep up. Each man under-stood and said he would make it. The situation, plain and simple, was survival, and Duan would get as many through as could help them-selves. Ky, in a choked voice, told Duan he would keep up with Trang still draped over his shoulders. Trang's body had become stiff with rig-or mortis. Ky still whispered to him as if he were alive.

For the first time in years Duan took counsel of his fears. American airplanes had flown over them for three solid hours. He feared that somehow the Americans had devised a new, diabolical machine that could find *bo doi* in the jungle. He and Ba squatted on the path trying to sort out the events and find a clue. Possessing no real knowledge of sensor technology, Duan's analysis was based purely on the logic of move and countermove. His thoughts were clouded by the adrenaline that coursed through his system in massive quantities. Talking made it easier to think through what had occurred. After ten minutes of monologue interspersed with several corrections from Ba, Duan had his answer. "The only time we were specifically targeted was when the spotter plane shot a rocket at us," he said. "I am certain the pilot had spotted us visually before this, because I distinctly saw the spotter airplane at low altitude and slow speed drop his wing for a better view. Then the marking rocket came." He smiled. "Our survival rules are still intact. They have to see us before they can kill us. Stay hidden and we can survive. The rest has just been bad luck."

That's encouraging, thought Ba. All that bad fortune is difficult to imagine. Since there are few men who have had that much bad luck, it seems the Immortals should now send us good luck. He smiled at the thought.

The quiet night was broken by the sound of the F-105s returning to the area north of the platoon. At the sudden flickering light of the flares the porters reached for their poles in anticipation of the order to move.

"*Tien len*" was passed down the line. Duan cautioned the guides to stay in the best jungle they could find, regardless of how thick it was or how far it might take them out of their way. They moved south with the irregular light of the flares casting shadows in the jungle. The airplane engines helped quicken their steps.

Above, Spectre 15 briefed the attack pilots on the situation and first illuminated Spectre 7's burning wreckage. Two bombers dove and placed napalm and 500-pound bombs on the wreckage. Spectre 15 took pictures of the scene to prove that little had been left to enemy intelligence. They followed the same procedure with the other two crashed airplanes. The HH-53 was the most difficult to destroy because it had not caught fire in the crash. A 20-mm cannon burst finally caught the ammunition storage cases, and it blew up in a spectacular geyser of exploding tracers and fuel.

The scene was duly recorded by Spectre 15's cameras.

# FIFTEEN

# Bureaucrats

## PREY KOMNONG, CAMBODIA

The platoon listened to the diving aircraft and the explosions. They sounded close, even though the closest target was well over two miles away. They ducked when one of the jets circled overhead, but they kept moving slowly and steadily behind Hinh. The sound of the airplanes soon faded off in the distance and they breathed easier.

After an hour and a half, Hinh stopped the column and called Duan and Ba to the front for a conference. Hinh squatted at the edge of a tree line that looked onto a dark expanse of rice fields. He had proved himself an unerring guide during the harrowing night. He told them that the Prey Komnong base area was on the other side of the open field. They discussed where the security patrols would be and how to handle them. Duan listened carefully for airplanes and, hearing none, ordered Hinh to lead them across the paddy as quickly as possible.

Halfway across the rice fields they were challenged by a Vietcong patrol, but Hinh handled it smoothly and no one started shooting. At 5:00 A.M. the platoon was led into a narrow tunnel that opened into a cavernous underground bunker lit with small oil lamps. They placed their loads on the bunker floor, which was a rough-cut flat wooden platform built on coconut-log pilings driven into the mud just above the level of the ground-water table. The bunker was 100 yards wide and 300 yards long. It was full of every conceivable type of ordnance, neatly stacked by type.

The unexpected arrival of Increment 1008 caused a stir among the TG559 staff. Two supply officers at makeshift desks unceremoniously demanded Duan's route card. After a few moments of discussion both men began talking on field phones, seeking instructions on how to handle this unusual situation. Like all bureaucrats, they became visibly upset when a situation did not fit into the mold of their rules and procedures. Exceptions were unwelcome events.

Duan and Ba situated the men and checked them for leeches. In the light, they were a pathetic sight: skinny, bruised, bleeding, covered with mud. They had the haunted look of hunted animals.

Ky laid Trang's wet and stiff body on a stack of 130-mm artillery ammunition. He still talked quietly to his dead friend, carefully pulling leeches off the body. The others looked nervously at the scene, not knowing what to do or say. One of the supply officers noticed Trang and roughly yelled for Ky to get the wet body off of his precious ammunition. Duan gave the officer a withering look, and he sheepishly busied himself with some papers.

Duan went over and put his hand softly on Ky's shoulder. "I am sorry, Ky, but Trang is dead."

Ky looked at him a moment and said slowly, "I know. I didn't want him buried with leeches still on him. He hated leeches."

"I know. We all hate them. Let me help you get him into his poncho."

"We were so close to making it in together. We wanted to stay with you, Duan, and get in your unit, whatever it was. The flare could have hit me just as easy as it hit Trang. Why didn't it hit me?"

"I don't know Ky, but I have seen the same thing happen a hundred times. Two men stand together. One man dies and one lives. I have no answer."

They looked at each other soberly. Duan carefully picked up Trang and carried him to where several men had spread out his poncho. He lay the twisted body in the vinyl and then folded it over and tied the ends with thin strands of rope. Ky stood by and watched. His face was emotionless.

Minutes later a captain arrived in the bunker and perfunctorily shook hands with Ba and Duan. He questioned them on the irregularities of their route card. The last entry had been three days before, at the Phum Anchanh depot. The captain demanded a full explanation of where they had been all this time. He became irate when one of the supply officers reported that they had only twelve loads; six mortars and six ammunition bundles. The last entry on the route card from Phum Anchanh showed twenty loads.

Ba glanced at Duan. Duan's face was a mask of hostility.

Ba decided he had better handle this one. He began quietly to tell their story, starting with the B-52 raid. He lied steadily about where they had stayed and was careful not to implicate the people who had helped them along the way. He glossed over their meeting with Hinh.

The captain listened closely with a suspicious smirk.

"Why didn't you seek out a TG559 liaison team immediately after the B-52 raid?" he said in a high-pitched, sarcastic voice.

"They had all been killed by the bombs and the airplanes that came later. We were afraid of them. They had gotten many people killed by their stupidity, Captain," said Ba.

"We are not stupid and have taken precautions to preclude a recurrence of such an accident. Haven't you found the TG559 personnel helpful on your *truong chinh* south?" he whined.

"Yes sir. Some have been helpful. The ones in charge of the convoy were incompetent murderers," Ba responded evenly.

"Where did you say you stayed the first night after the raid?" asked the captain in his nasal voice.

"I didn't say, but we stayed in the jungle south of where the convoy was destroyed," Ba lied.

"What did you eat?"

"We had food in our packs from the Phum Anchanh depot."

"Why didn't you find a TG559 liaison team the next day?"

"We didn't know where they were."

"Who did you sell the ammunition to?"

"We didn't sell the ammunition. It was destroyed in the B-52 raid," Ba lied. They had lost some in the raid and had abandoned two of the missing loads to carry their wounded. One had been destroyed by the American spotter plane. Ba knew to keep accounting simple when dealing with TG559 bureaucrats.

"You are short five men. Where are they?"

"Killed in the raid."

"What did you do with the bodies?"

"We left them. We thought the American airplanes would come back. Later they did."

"Are you aware that TG559 has a strict policy that all bodies will be immediately buried and the graves marked for return to their families after our resounding victory over the Imperialists?" The captain put his hands on his hips and glared at Ba.

"Yes I am. We started with sixty men and our graves are spread out over six hundred miles. If we had stayed to bury the men killed by the B-52s, we would have been killed by the planes that came later, and someone would have to dig graves for us all."

"That is no excuse for disobeying TG559 orders," whined the captain. "Why did you bring this man's body with you and none of the rest?" he said, pointing to Trang.

Ba did not respond. He just looked steadily at his inquisitor. The captain glanced around at Duan and at the faces of the rest of the platoon. Their hatred and disgust were undisguised.

The captain then turned and began to question the platoon, seeking a confirmation or denial of Ba's story, which he did not believe. The first man he spoke to was one of the deaf porters who stared blankly at him, not understanding what had been said. In the awkward silence the captain reached out and grabbed his shirt. Quick as a snake Duan's hand grabbed his wrist in a powerful grip and yanked it away. He spun the captain around and looked deep into his eyes with a pleasant expression on his face.

"This man is deaf, captain, from the concussion of the bombs in the B-52 raid. He can't hear you. Should you choose to touch one of my men roughly again, I will have to report you to the Ninth Vietcong Division for violation of the longstanding order of the Revolution that officers may only physically punish soldiers who have committed offenses, have shown themselves to be cowards in the face of the enemy, or are slackards. This man is guilty of none of these things."

The captain glared at Duan, who continued to hold his wrist, staring him down. After a long silence Duan slowly slackened his grip. "You are right, captain. We are short some ammunition. Had you been with us instead of here in this beautiful and safe bunker, you would better understand why we don't have these valuable supplies." Duan spoke in a soothing and respectful tone. Then he launched into a detailed description of the B-52 raid, embellishing his story with characteristic style. When he had finished, the efficient captain stood spellbound like everyone else in the bunker. The sparkle came back to the men's eyes when Duan gestured to them and said proudly that they were among the very few who had lived to tell about a B-52 raid.

Just then a phone message confirmed that Increment 1008 had indeed been manifested on the ill-fated convoy. The captain, relieved to be out of the difficult position he had put himself in, issued orders for a detailed inventory of the cargo. After inspecting each item, he signed the papers balancing the all-important TG559 ledger of equipment consigned in the North and equipment received in the South.

The captain pretended not to notice as Duan pulled from the loads the weapons and ammunition he had meticulously scrounged over the past two months and passed them around to the men. He wanted no more problems from Duan and Ba, and he let it go. There was a small block at the bottom of his manifest form for the number of men who had made the journey. He carefully inked in the number thirty-five. The fact that twenty-seven men of the original platoon had not survived the trek was not critical. As the saying went, there were always more men, but war equipment was critical.

The porters left the hated loads sitting on the storage platforms, and no one looked back as they filed out of the bunker. Over the next week each man would feel weightless and light-headed at times, without the loads bearing down on them. The memory of the last two months would stay in their nightmares for the rest of their lives. The Old Man's Trail would be the defining event of their lives. Nothing could match the march south for sheer terror, hardships, and endurance. They were still fifteen years old, but they had been to the well and drunk deeply of what they were. Most had discovered that there was more strength and courage in them than they had ever imagined.

Ky brought up the rear, carrying Trang wrapped in the poncho. He had refused all offers of help with the body of his friend.

# SIXTEEN

# Responsibility

## NAKHON PHANOM, THAILAND

When General Kendal returned to the Surveillance Center, he found an embarrassed and apologetic chief of staff. The message that had been prepared earlier that night, citing Task Force Alpha's aggressive and innovative achievements in the interdiction war, had inadvertently been sent out and received by a dozen higher and adjacent headquarters. The subsequent losses made the message sound nothing short of foolish or stupid. Kendal quietly told the staff to cancel the message, which did little to lessen the appearance of an incompetent command.

It was now 5:00 A.M., and Kendal issued instructions for a memorial service that afternoon for the airmen who had perished. He also ordered a maximum effort that night into the Vietnamese southern Cambodian enclave. He left with his key staff members for the base Officers Club.

Task Force Alpha was a command that functioned at night and slept during the day. It was the mirror image of its adversary, TG559, where thousands of people struggled down the Old Man's Trail mostly at night. The base clubs opened for Happy Hour at 7:00 A.M. for pilots and crews returning from their night missions. The mood that morning was somber in the air-conditioned, beautifully appointed main lounge with its ten-yard-long polished mahogany bar. The general and his staff stopped by for several drinks and tried to raise the spirits of the dejected airmen. The pilots of the F-105s that had seen Fast Dog shot down by the missile told their story a hundred times, as did the survivors of Spectre 7 and Low Bird, who had been flown in for debriefing. It was a tense unwinding session with none of the usual laughing and joking. General Kendal called for quiet and told them all to get some rest, because they were going back to even the score that night. Then he toasted Fast Dog and the others who had died that night. There was a sober round of seconds to the toast, and most of the men began drifting off for breakfast.

Later, over steak and eggs and white wine in the General Officer's Mess, General Kendal would issue his orders for the night. He was disturbed when the sound of torrential rain on the metal roof forewarned the last surge of the monsoon. His airplanes would be grounded for another week. For the first time in memory, he flew into a rage when a courier brought him four "Personal for," top-secret messages from the Joints Chiefs of Staff; Commander-in-Chief, Pacific; Commander, U.S. Military Assistance Command, Vietnam; and Seventh Air Force—all specifically ordering him never to operate again in southern Cambodia unless specifically directed to do so. The message from the Commanding General, Seventh Air Force, his immediate superior, ended ominously. He was sending the Command Inspector General to Nakhon Phanom to conduct an inquiry into the events of the last week.

# SEVENTEEN

# Power

## KANTREUY PLANTATION, CAMBODIA

The cook noiselessly entered the commander's private bunker in the Kantreuy headquarters complex and spoke softly, saying that it was now 4:00 P.M. and time to get up. The COSVN commander swung his legs over the side of his hammock and accepted an American canteen cup of strong *cafe sua*. He thanked his cook and sat motionless for a few minutes, trying to shake the low-grade fever that had plagued him with migraine headaches for several weeks. Headaches always followed a malaria attack. He weakly accepted the two American aspirin the cook gave him. His bowels began to cramp painfully.

After a few minutes of silence he asked if there were any reports. The cook handed him a terse handwritten message from the TG559 commander. He sat with his head down and read the five sentences, then read the message again and raised his head to look at the cook, smiling, but still showing pain in his red eyes.

"Three American airplanes shot down last night. One of them with the new SA-7. The TG559 commander is taking pictures today for our propaganda campaign. The Americans won't bother us here in *Nam bo* for a while, even after the monsoon," he said. He paused, then added almost to himself, "They don't know how to wield power and are afraid of their press and public criticism. I think they are a very strange, but, unfortunately for them, predictable people. They drop tons of bombs and kill us by the thousands, then fold up their tent and go hide in their hammocks whenever someone accuses them of not playing fair or of not being good and just humanitarians. Peculiar behavior for such a brutal, aggressive, and powerful people."

"Yes sir," the cook agreed. "How many men did we lose last night?"

The commander looked at the message again. In the lower right-hand corner he read 72/45/30. He had not noticed the figures in his two previous readings.

"Seventy-two killed, forty-five seriously wounded, and thirty lightly wounded." He did not know it, but of the two company-size units involved in the action of the preceding night, only fifteen men had walked away unharmed.

"Not a bad trade-off for three American airplanes and a world propaganda victory. I think it was well worth it. *Muon doc lap phai do mau*—For freedom you have to spend your blood," he intoned like a prayer.

The cook repeated, *"Do mau, do mau, do mau*—Yes! Spend blood! Yes! Spend blood. Yes! Spend blood."

The commander asked for a message book and wrote a congratulatory message to the TG559 commander for the fine job he had done the previous night. In celebration of the victory he directed extra rations that night for the entire Ninth Vietcong Division, whose units had downed all three airplanes. He drafted a second message to the Central Unification Department, his immediate superiors in Hanoi, notifying them of his great success.

# EIGHTEEN

# Rewards

## PREY KOMNONG, CAMBODIA

After a big breakfast of rice, fish, and freshly baked bread, the platoon was moved, in the early morning rain, to a large underground billet bunker of the Ninth Vietcong Division, located a mile from the TG559 supply complex. The sprawling base appeared, even to a ground observer, like a typical jungle amid open rice fields. Its camouflage was perfect. The bunker was ten feet underground and had the standard rough-cut wooden floor built on coconut log pilings that rose just above the water table. The platoon moved through a series of connected chambers, each of which sheltered platoon- and company-size infantry units eating breakfast after a night of training or security operations. In each billet area someone recognized Duan, and the greetings from old comrades were profuse and genuine. The word spread that he was back.

As they arrived in the bunker chamber that would be their home, a man about Duan's age entered and grabbed him by the shoulder, spun him around, and embraced him in a bear hug. The men slapped each other on the back and talked excitedly. After a few moments Duan turned and escorted his friend through introductions to each man in the platoon. They respectfully bowed from the waist and shook his hand, cupping it in both of theirs. He was the commander of the 272d Vietcong Regiment.

When they got to Hinh, standing self-consciously with Hai and Thu, Duan told his old friend the whole truth of the past three days and the key parts that Hinh and the two women had played in their miraculous escape from the Americans and the fumbling clutches of TG559. The troops gathered around and listened, enthralled, as Duan wove his story of courage, stamina, and survival in the face of terrible odds. The crowd grew steadily and the appreciative comments were continuous as Duan held them spellbound with the images only a master storyteller can put in people's minds. The story was even better now, since he had had a chance to rehearse it on the TG559 supply bureaucrats two hours before. Never missing a chance to teach, Duan repeated his ultimate axioms for survival: Hide. Never shoot at airplanes.

After half an hour he concluded by telling of the bravery and discipline of his platoon throughout the whole ordeal. The veterans clapped enthusiastically, which embarrassed most of the young men. Duan's pride in them was their greatest reward.

The older men looked at the fifteen-year-old porters and saw themselves. They looked so young and haggard. But as the veterans knew, that was the way of the Revolution. The painful second birth from boy to man. The *I Ching*'s symbol of continual change: the fire in the lake.

Duan told the regimental commander of Hinh's desire to marry the pretty young woman shyly standing next to him. The commander smiled at them and addressed the crowd of troops.

"Those Brothers and Sisters of the regiment who do not know Duan surely have heard of him and his efforts for the Revolution. He and I fought our first battles together at Tu Le and Dien Bien Phu against the French, and in the South we were together for the great victory at Binh Gia in early 1965. It is a good omen that he has returned to our ranks at this time, and I have a special task for him." He paused and looked at Duan.

"Brother Hinh, who fought bravely at the Michelin Plantation battle, desires to marry this beautiful young woman." In spite of the fact that she was soaking wet and muddy, Hai was still pretty. At that moment she was showing considerable embarrassment at all the attention directed at her. There was a respectful round of applause from the troops.

Walking over to her he took her hands and said sternly, "Are you an American, a Cambodian, or a *my nguy?*" The ironic humor of the question never got a laugh. It was a question they all had to answer, and the punishment for lying was death.

"No, sir," Hai replied softly.

"Are you a supporter of the *my Thieu*—the American puppet president of South Vietnam?"

"No, sir. He is a *do cho de*," she said emphatically, which the troops greeted with a round of applause.

"Are you willing to join the NLF and fight for the freedom of our people?" he asked.

"Yes sir. I have been on a road-repair crew for three years and have already been working for the Revolution," she said.

"Good. Then you must know the promise of the party to you and your husband. We will support you and your husband. Should he be killed, we will pay for his funeral in your village. As his widow you would be taken care of by the grateful Lao Dong party. Should he be wounded seriously, we will help you and your family for the rest of your lives. As a revolutionary soldier's wife, you shall be entitled to all the necessities of life and in return you must share what you produce from the earth with the Revolution. You may choose to go home to your village and continue your valuable road-repair work, or you may stay here with your husband and the regiment. If you stay with the regiment, you will be trained for any one of many important jobs. How do you choose?"

"I will stay with the regiment and Hinh," she said without hesitation. Another round of spontaneous applause from the crowd.

"Good. You and Hinh are now married. As your commander my present to you is that you may use my private bunker today and tonight." They smiled shyly at each other. Privacy in a billet bunker complex was scarce. The commander's gift of his quarters was a lavish one.

Everyone pressed in to congratulate the couple.

The commander took Duan aside and asked, "How is this Lieutenant Ba who came with you? A good political officer or one of those slogan chanters?"

Duan responded promptly, "He was a slogan man. The Old Man's Trail cured him of slogans. They don't get you very far in the Truong Son Mountains." Both men smiled. The commander had been one of the ten who had survived with Duan on his first trip down the Old Man's Trail in 1959.

"Good. Then I will make him your political officer. You will take command of the First Battalion tonight." Duan was stunned. There was no system of rank in the Vietcong. Jobs went to whoever proved themselves. The highest rank Duan had ever held was sergeant major and that was only while in the north. When he was wounded he had been a company commander, the highest command usually allowed for non-party members.

"But I am not a party member. Battalion command only goes to party men," he protested.

"The situation has changed, Duan. Some of the old rules have to be cast aside. Our casualties have been too many for too long. Look at the troops we have left after Tet. They are boys. Many don't survive their first battle. The Americans have learned to find us because sometimes we are sloppy in our movement and camouflage, which is a matter of training. You are a master of cover and concealment. Even better than me," he said with a smile. "I don't have many real veterans left like you and you must teach them."

Duan looked long and soberly at his friend and said nothing else.

"Come now. I have something you must see," the commander said. He led Duan down a low-ceilinged tunnel. After several hundred yards they arrived at an underground hospital complete with two fully equipped operating rooms and wards with white sheets. Duan was amazed—this was a vast improvement over the primitive care he had received for his most recent wounds.

The commander spoke to a nurse who pointed toward a small bunker chamber serving as a ward. He motioned for Duan to follow as he led him to a cot where a small figure lay gazing at the ceiling through unseeing eyes. The commander kneeled and took the woman's hand.

"I have brought him as I said I would," he whispered to her. For a few moments she did not respond. Then she turned her head toward Duan.

The word escaped his lips as it always did, almost involuntarily. "Su? Su! How did you get here? What happened?" he moved to her side.

"Duan. Duan," she said, taking his hand. "I have missed you. My eyes have gone dark, and I think they will not come back to light. At least I can touch you, Duan," she said in her beautiful voice.

Both men knelt by the cot for a long time, each holding one of Su's small hands. They talked about many things and after a while she fell asleep. The commander took Duan by the arm and led him out into the connecting tunnel.

"How did she get here?" Duan asked.

"She requested transfer to the Ninth Vietcong Division right after your platoon passed through her way station. You know the rules. All volunteers for the NLF are immediately given their request. She was packed up in a couple of days and came down the trail by convoy, which is why she got here before you."

"What happened to her eyes? Why is she blind? When will she see again?"

"The best the doctors can judge, she was hit with some of the poison the Americans spray on the jungle. She remembers being on a trail by herself one day when a low-flying airplane dropped some foul-smelling, slick liquid directly on her. She says she threw up that night but felt better the next day and thought no more about it. Then everything turned hazy and gray one day on her journey here. She hasn't been able to see since then. None of the doctors have a cure, Duan. If she sees again the Immortals will have intervened." The commander shrugged.

Duan stood quietly for a long time. Finally he said, "The last thing she said to me on the trail two months ago was that she didn't think she would ever see me again. I thought maybe one of us would be killed. I didn't think of this."

"We leave for the Tay Ninh Forest in two days," his friend said finally. "We'll try to use the last of the monsoon for cover. I will assign her to your battalion. We have use for everyone, even the blind ones."

Both men were quiet. Each knew what the other was thinking. For how many more battles will our luck hold?

If they were ordered to Tay Ninh again, they would go and fight until they were killed or the Revolution won. Neither man had ever figured on surviving this war anyway, even though both had developed remarkable instincts that would make it hard for their enemies to do them in. Regardless of how good a soldier was, the risks were always great. The enemy was powerful and dangerous.

# NINETEEN

# "Spend Blood"

## KANTREUY PLANTATION, CAMBODIA

When the COSVN commander had finished drafting his message, he rose slowly from his hammock and unsteadily walked to the corner latrine and emptied his dysenteric bowels. The cook helped him back to his hammock and he carefully slid under the frayed issue blanket that provided little warmth in the dank bunker.

He looked into the eyes of his loyal comrade and cook and said weakly, "*Do mau.*"

The cook smiled his lopsided, snaggle-toothed, zealot's grin and said, "*Do mau.* That is all we have to spend, and each drop is worth a hundred airplanes. We must spend our blood to be free."

The commander smiled and drifted off into his tormented sleep.

# TWENTY

# Eulogies

## NAKHON PHANOM, THAILAND

A solemn group of men and women gathered at the U.S. Base Chapel at Nakhon Phanom to eulogize the death of their seven comrades. The chapel was packed as it always was for these events and many men cried unashamedly for their lost friends. General Kendal spoke personally for each dead man and then promised the mourners that America eventually would prevail over the powers of evil, oppression, and tyranny that opposed them. He promised that South Vietnam would be free.

To most present, their loss seemed a very high price to pay for such a remote-sounding objective. Most of the people at the memorial service were on their second or third tours. They had bombed and strafed the enemy with a vengeance for years and, somehow, he never seemed to give up. When the war seemed to be going overwhelmingly in their favor, suddenly a 140-pound Oriental soldier would stand up unexpectedly and shoot down an airplane. The doubts in the Americans' minds were mounting. The enemy loses 96 trucks in a night and tomorrow night there will be 2,000 more trucks in the jungle bouncing south at five miles an hour. Destroy another 96 trucks and the next night there will still be 2,000 trucks headed south.

Regardless of what they did, there were still 2,000 trucks on what appeared to be impassable roads in an uncharted jungle morass. It was disturbing. There seemed to be no rational answer. They bowed their heads and prayed as the chaplain concluded the service. Most of them had become religious in the course of their flying, but none could understand the enigma of a loving God in the midst of all this suffering. Nor could they understand how the enemy could take such a beating and still come back for more. It just didn't make sense. If they were evil godless Communists, what made them fight as they did?

Each of them inwardly included a prayer for themselves: a prayer that they would survive. At that point getting home was their most important goal.

## PREY KOMNONG, CAMBODIA

After nightfall, a guide led Duan's platoon out of the bunker complex to the Ninth Vietcong Division cemetery, hidden in the nearby jungle. Ky and two other men dug a grave with hoes in the wet soil while the others patiently waited in the rain. Ba had found a carpenter, and a rough wooden coffin lay next to the grave. Trang, their last casualty, would be the only one to get a proper burial. There were no coffins on the Old Man's Trail.

The men still looked haggard, but new uniforms, bush hats, and ponchos had taken away some of the tattered appearance they had had that morning. Each carried a rifle carefully protected under his poncho, muzzle pointing toward the ground.

They finished digging, and Ky and another man carefully lifted the coffin and eased it into the fresh grave, which already was beginning to fill with water. Duan spoke in a low voice.

"We have come a long way together, and I am pleased and proud of how well you have come through it. I am proud to have shared the good and the bad with men such as you. I wish Trang had made it too. We all know he was a friend and a good soldier. He helped each of us somewhere along the trail. He was strong and was always smiling." He paused.

"To live is to suffer. If a man follows the Way, he dies. If a man does not follow the Way, he dies. But if a man has the Way and dies, his soul will go to an abode of happiness. I believe Trang's soul has found an abode of happiness. We commend this fine man, our friend, to the Immortals."

There was a long pause. The only other sounds were rain and distant artillery along the border. Duan spoke again. "You have seen first-hand how dangerous and cruel the enemy is. If I have taught you anything, it is to be a shadow. Stay in the jungle, stay with the rain, hold to the night, to the uncomfortable places, and live.

"All of you will be assigned to my battalion. Listen to your commanders and learn your lessons quickly. You do not get second chances with the Americans. We will prevail. It is our land and the round-eyes have no place here. It doesn't matter how long it takes; we will win this. So save yourselves for the long fight. Save your blood. Survive. You must, because you have become my family."

He shook each man's hand, slapping him on the back and flashing his winning smile. He hugged them as a father would and told them he was proud. Each man stood taller as Duan spoke to him.

After they filled in Trang's grave and had formed up in a single column, Duan went to the front of the line and for the last time said to them, "*Tien len.*" In unison they responded, "*Tien len.*"

# About the Author

Tom Campbell served in the U.S. Marines for twenty-nine years, including two and a half tours in Vietnam. He retired from active duty in 1988.

He is now an award-winning lecturer in management and leadership in the College of Business Administration at the University of Texas at Austin. He is working on his second novel.

The **Naval Institute Press** is the book-publishing arm of the U.S. Naval Institute, a private, nonprofit society for sea service professionals and others who share an interest in naval and maritime affairs. Established in 1873 at the U.S. Naval Academy in Annapolis, Maryland, where its offices remain, today the Naval Institute has more than 100,000 members worldwide.

Members of the Naval Institute receive the influential monthly magazine *Proceedings* and discounts on fine nautical prints, ship and aircraft photos, and subscriptions to the bimonthly *Naval History* magazine. They also have access to the transcripts of the Institute's Oral History Program and get discounted admission to any of the Institute-sponsored seminars offered around the country.

The Naval Institute's book-publishing program, begun in 1898 with basic guides to naval practices, has broadened its scope in recent years to include books of more general interest. Now the Naval Institute Press publishes more than seventy titles each year, ranging from how-to books to boating and navigation to battle histories, biographies, ship and aircraft guides, and novels. Institute members receive discounts on the Press's nearly 400 books in print.

Full-time students are eligible for special half-price membership rates. Life memberships are also available.

For a free catalog describing Naval Institute Press books currently available, and for further information about U.S. Naval Institute membership, please write to:

Membership & Communications Department
U.S. Naval Institute
118 Maryland Avenue
Annapolis, Maryland 21402-5035

Or call, toll-free, (800) 233-USNI.